The Feast of Artemis

ANNE ZOUROUDI was born in England and has lived in the Greek islands. Her attachment to Greece remains strong, and the country is the inspiration for much of her writing. She now lives in the Derbyshire Peak District. She is the author of six *Mysteries of the Greek Detective*: *The Messenger of Athens* (shortlisted for the ITV3 Crime Thriller Award for Breakthrough Authors and longlisted for the Desmond Elliot Prize), *The Taint of Midas, The Doctor of Thessaly, The Lady of Sorrows, The Whispers of Nemesis* and *The Bull of Mithros*.

BY THE SAME AUTHOR

The Feast of Artemis

Anne Zouroudi

BLOOMSBURY

LONDON · NEW DELHI · NEW YORK · SYDNEY

First published in Great Britain 2013
This paperback edition published 2014

Copyright © 2013 by Anne Zouroudi

Map on page vii © 2013 by John Gilkes

The moral right of the author has been asserted

Bloomsbury Publishing Plc
50 Bedford Square
London
WC1B 3DP

www.bloomsbury.com

Bloomsbury Publishing, London, New Delhi, New York and Sydney

A CIP catalogue record for this book is available from the British Library

ISBN 978 1 4088 3753 5

10 9 8 7 6 5 4 3 2 1

Typeset by Hewer Text UK Ltd, Edinburgh
Printed and bound in Great Britain by CPI Group (UK) Ltd, Croydon CR0 4YY

MIX
Paper from
responsible sources
FSC® C020471

For Leo

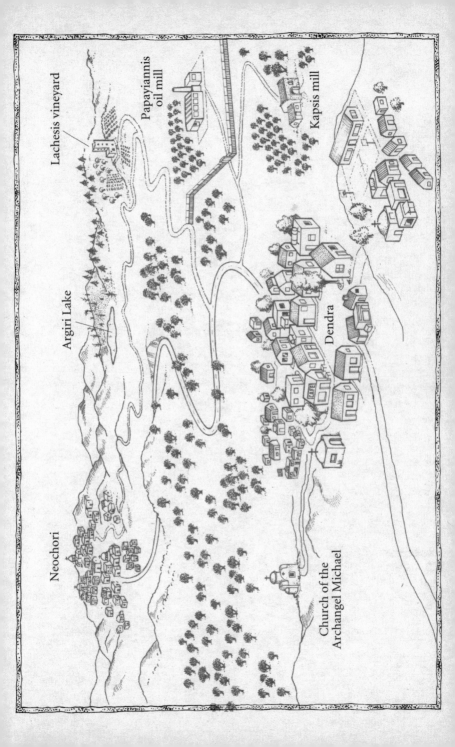

DRAMATIS PERSONAE

Hermes Diaktoros, the fat man	–	an investigator
Dino	–	Hermes's half-brother
Donatos Papayiannis	–	an olive farmer
Tasia Papayiannis	–	Donatos's wife
Sakis Papayiannis	–	Donatos's son
Amara Papayiannis	–	Sakis's wife
Marianna Kapsis	–	a rival olive farmer
Dmitris Kapsis	–	Marianna's step-grandson
Renzo Rapetti	–	an ice-cream seller
Lefteris Boukalas	–	a hotelier
Stavroula Boukalas	–	Lefteris's wife
Tomas	–	Stavroula's father
Katya	–	Stavroula's aunt
Meni Gavala	–	a vintner
Esmerelda Dimas	–	a newspaper editor
Spiros Zysis	–	an olive-oil wholesaler
Miltiadis Sloukas	–	a tailor
Dora	–	owner of a kebab shop, a widow
Xavier	–	Dora's son, a self-styled activist
Dr Fitanidis	–	a doctor at Neochori hospital
Arethusa	–	a waitress in Neochori
Takis Kapsis	–	a butcher

GLOSSARY OF GREEK LANGUAGE

amessos	–	immediately, at once
anthotyros	–	a goat or sheep's cheese, often eaten with honey and fruit
baklava	–	pastry made with chopped nuts and syrup
bourekakia	–	pastry-wrapped savouries
chairo poli	–	delighted to meet you (formal greeting)
doxa to Theo	–	thanks be to God
filé	–	friend
fraskomilo	–	mountain sage, often used to make tea
galaktoboureko	–	pastry filled with semolina custard
glyfoni	–	apple mint, also used for tea
graviera	–	a hard cheese used for grating
gyros	–	a kebab: grilled meat etc. wrapped in pita
kafebriko	–	a long-handled pot used for Greek coffee
kakomira	–	poor thing
kalé	–	popular and familiar form of address
kali mera (sas)	–	good morning, good day (polite/plural)
kali nichta	–	good night
kali spera	–	good evening

kalo mezimeri	–	good afternoon
kalos ton/tou/tous;		
kalos irthate	–	welcome
kamari mou	–	term of affection, lit. my pride, my son
kataifa	–	nut-filled pastry made with shredded dough
kefalotyri	–	hard sheep's milk cheese
keftedes	–	fried savouries of meat, vegetables, cheese or fish
kleftiko	–	Lit. 'stolen meat'. The origins of the dish lie with sheep-rustlers, who baked stolen animals in covered pits to prevent smoke giving away the thieves' location.
kokoras	–	cockerel
koproskila	–	vehement term of abuse
kori mou	–	my daughter
koritsia	–	girls
koukla/koukles	–	beauties, pretty girls (lit. dolls)
kyria (kyries)	–	Madam, Mrs (plural: ladies)
kyrie	–	Sir, Mr
malaka/es	–	common insult or term of abuse (singular/plural)
malista	–	certainly
manka	–	a not-quite gentleman or spiv
mikre	–	little one
mori!	–	exclamation of surprise
mou	–	my
panayia mou	–	by the Virgin
pappou	–	grandpa
pedia	–	people, everybody (lit. children)

periptero	–	kiosk selling cold drinks, newspapers, cigarettes etc.
poustis/es	–	slang term for homosexual (singular/plural)
salone	–	living room
santouri	–	stringed musical instrument made with mallets
skordalia	–	garlic sauce usually made with bread or mashed potatoes
souvlaki/a	–	skewers of grilled pork, lamb or chicken (singular/plural)
taramasalata	–	dip made from fish roe and olive oil
thea	–	aunt
theé mou	–	my God
theié	–	uncle, often used as a term of respect to an older man
toumba	–	children's game of tag
tzatziki	–	dip made from yogurt and garlic
yammas	–	cheers, good health
yassou/yassas	–	hello or goodbye (singular/plural or polite form)
yiayia	–	grandma
yie mou	–	my son

'Eat slowly; only men in rags
and gluttons old in sin
Mistake themselves for carpet-bags
And tumble victuals in.'

Sir Walter Raleigh,
'Instructions to His Son', 1632

One

The fire-pits lay across the hillside, graves of the unmourned beneath bare heaps of the dirt which had filled them. The pine planks acting as their markers bore rough-painted family names, and the menfolk were ready to play sextons, shovels close at hand for when the call came.

The Papayiannis men checked their watches, counting down the remaining minutes as they passed round the ouzo bottle, drinking to the win they were confident would be theirs, trading bawdy jokes and laughing lecherously and loud. To left and right the opposition waited, backs to their rivals and segregated in their clans.

Below them, the church's domes and arches straddled age-mellowed stone walls, where a bronze sundial was mounted on a marble plaque. Smart in the suit he had worn on his wedding day twenty-three years before, the mayor scrutinised the sundial, and when he judged the shadow of its arm to be touching noon, he gave a signal to the bellringer, who began a spirited tolling of the bell. The mayor ran to the courtyard gateway, and with his hands around his mouth to carry his voice, shouted up to the expectant men on the hillside, '*Pedia!* It's time!'

At all the pits, the men began to dig, throwing aside the dry topsoil, working fast to uncover what lay beneath.

But at the Papayiannis pit, the dry soil was only a shallow covering, quickly removed to reveal dark, damp earth beneath.

Sakis Papayiannis was first to notice the change. He held up his hand, and called the digging to a halt.

In surprise, his relatives pulled their shovels from the dirt.

'Are you crazy?' asked a cousin, in annoyance. 'We won't win by sitting on our arses.'

Sakis crouched down, and touched the newly exposed soil. Away to the right, the Kapsis men broke through the earth seal, and the fire-pit released trapped smoke and steam made mouth-watering with roast meat and herbs. They set their spades aside, and two of them pulled on leather gauntlets to dig with their hands. A boy ran out from amongst them, shouting as he reached the church, 'We're first! We're first!'

'That smells good,' said an elderly Papayiannis uncle, sniffing at a drift of Kapsis smoke. 'I heard Takis reckons he's sure of a win this year, and he's been working on his seasonings since Easter. I suppose it won't hurt that he's a butcher. He's bound to have the best animal to begin with.'

'Being a butcher didn't help him last year,' countered his great-nephew. 'And the judges are men of plain tastes. Good meat, well cooked, always does it.'

'What the hell's the problem?' demanded the cousin, who had drunk plenty of the ouzo and swayed slightly as he stood, as though the hill's gradient were throwing him off-balance. 'Let's dig, *malaka*. They're halfway down already, and we've hardly started.'

The other clans were finishing their spadework, and the air was full of tantalising smoke. Sakis placed his palm on the top of the fire-pit. The soil was cold. Putting his hand to his nose, he sniffed, and grimaced.

The mayor was coming up the hillside.

'Dig further,' said Sakis to his nephew, a strong lad in his Sunday-best denim jacket. The boy quickly shifted another half-metre of dirt, working up a sweat which broadcast his cheap cologne. The deeper he went, the darker and damper the soil.

The nephew stopped digging.

'Something stinks,' he said, pulling a face. 'Have the cats been at this?'

'Big cats, maybe,' said Sakis. He glowered towards the Kapsis clan. Now well in the lead, they were hauling hot stones from their pit, calling to each other to take care as they tossed them away into the long grass.

A lanky youth caught Sakis watching, and held up a bottle of beer in a mock toast.

'You slackers should get a move on!' he shouted, to laughter from those around him. 'The people want to eat today!'

The cousin took several unsteady steps in his direction.

'Dmitris Kapsis,' he said. 'That little prick wants teaching some respect. I'll soon sort him out.'

'Leave it. He isn't worth it,' said Sakis.

'He's right, though,' said the nephew. 'We're falling way behind.'

'Yes, for God's sake, Sakis, let's get on,' said the cousin. 'I've got a raging thirst, and there's nothing left to drink.'

'We're wasting our time,' said Sakis. 'There'll be nothing to eat from this pit. No *kleftiko* today.'

The men around him stared.

'What do you mean?' asked one. 'Why not?'

'Because it's cold,' said Sakis, bitterly. 'The pit's cold.'

The mayor reached the Kapsis's pit, and the Kapsis men offered him warm greetings.

3

'You've come at the right time,' one told him. 'We're just about ready to go.'

Their pit smoked and steamed like the entrance to hell. They raised a bier of chicken-wire from its wood-ash bed, and reverently laid the bundle it carried on the grass. With a hunting-knife, one of the Kapsis elders sliced through a charred, ash-dulled foil shroud, and with his fingers twitching away from the heat, peeled it back. Under the foil, he cut the nylon rope binding a brown-stained cotton sheet. The Kapsis men and the mayor all gathered round, and as the last covering was removed, they looked down on a roasted lamb, its skin glistening with its fats, flesh falling from its bones. The head was reduced to a skull with grimacing teeth, the footless shanks were scorched red; and though only the charred, twiggy remains of mountain oregano and thyme poked through the haphazard string stitching of the belly cavity, a fragrant steam affirmed that all the herbs' sweet essences had melded with the meat.

The Kapsis men were jubilant.

'It'll be hard to beat,' said one.

'Carve a slice, and let's try it,' urged another. 'Let the mayor have the first taste.'

But the majority shouted him down.

'It goes to the judges whole,' they said. 'Cut into it now, and we'll lose all the juices.'

'I'm happy to wait till the judging,' said the mayor. 'Congratulations, gentlemen. It's a triumph.'

The Kapsis lamb was carried down the hillside, whilst the mayor moved on from pit to pit. By the time he reached the Papayiannis men, they had dug down to the stones which covered their carcass. As the mayor approached, they fell silent.

'Gentlemen,' said the mayor, nodding to the group. He looked down into the cold pit. 'How's it going?'

'You see this?' asked Sakis. He picked up a handful of earth and held it out to the mayor.

The mayor was puzzled.

'What am I looking at?'

'Touch it,' said Sakis, and with reluctance, the mayor did so. 'It's cold. And wet. And you smell it.' He held the dirt to the mayor's nose. The mayor sniffed, and pulled a face. 'And look.'

Sakis reached down into the pit and with his bare hand pulled out a stone, which in the other pits would still be too hot to touch. He offered it to the mayor, who took it reluctantly. The stone was no warmer than blood-heat.

Sakis hauled out more stones, uncovering the Papayiannis lamb. He touched its wrappings, and shook his head.

'Let's get it out,' he said.

The men lifted out the lamb on its bier, and laid it on the excavated heap of dirt. In the pit bottom were more lukewarm stones, and under them, a grey mess of wet wood-ash. When the carcass was cut free of its bindings, the flesh was raw.

The mayor clapped Sakis on the shoulder.

'Your pit wasn't hot enough,' he said. 'Or the heat died too fast. It happens, sometimes.'

Sakis spread his arms, and beckoned his relatives closer.

'You see these men?' he asked the mayor, in a voice which, though reasonable, carried an undertone of anger at the affront. 'These men here, and I myself – we've been preparing *kleftiko* for generations. Our fire-pits burn hotter than Hades, and our pit didn't die, it was doused. Someone poured water on it, a lot of water. And worse than that.' He sniffed at his hand and offered it again to the mayor, who turned his face away. 'Somebody pissed on it.'

The mayor laughed, nervously.

'You don't know that,' he said. 'Cats, you know, if they smell the meat . . .'

'Are you suggesting,' asked Sakis, 'that I don't know the difference between cat piss and human piss? We've been sabotaged. This is an act of malice. And we all know where to look for the culprits.' He pointed towards the Kapsis's, where several men were filling in the pit, and the cousin spat in their direction. 'They should be disqualified.'

'How can I disqualify them?' asked the mayor. 'You don't know for certain that it was them.'

'But you concede there's been sabotage?'

The mayor hesitated.

'I have to say it does seem that way,' he said. 'But as to who it was . . .'

'We know who it was. And if you won't do anything, I will.'

'Please, Sakis,' said the mayor. 'Don't make trouble. Don't spoil the day. I know you as a reasonable man, and the time to settle scores isn't now.'

But Sakis yelled across to the Kapsis's.

'You cowardly bastards! Is that how men behave, pouring water on a fire in the night? Pissing on our family's food?'

The Kapsis clan jeered.

'No fire in your pit, and no fire in your balls!' they shouted back. 'Don't worry, we've got enough meat to spare for your women!'

They thrust their hips raunchily, and gestured at their genitalia in outrageous insults.

The taunted Papayiannis men watched uneasily, expecting Sakis to give the word to take them on.

But Sakis was striding away down the hillside.

'Where the hell are you going?' his cousin called after him.

'I'm going to tell the old man,' Sakis shouted over his shoulder. 'I'm going to tell Papa what those bastards have done.'

It was the day for honouring the Archangel Michael, and in the courtyard of the church, preparations for the festival were almost complete. Blue and white bunting fluttered between the trees; the soulful ring of *santouri* music played through tinny speakers rigged in the branches, and all around was the rich savour of food: apples baked with cinnamon, chicken braised with garlic, fried fish, grilled cheese and slow-simmered beef. Boys playing *toumba* ran in mad circles, ducking under laden tables where their mothers laid out bread and *baklava*; girls licked sweet cream from sticky cakes, and wiped chocolatey fingers on their party dresses. Beyond the courtyard gate, a gypsy hawker smoked in moody silence, a cloud of gaudy balloons bobbing over his head.

Sakis pushed through the crowd, ignoring anyone who spoke to him, making no apologies to those he jostled, until he reached the overhanging olive tree where the women of the family were gathered. His wife, Amara, was making space on the table for a pan of lemon potatoes; his mother and mother-in-law were debating where the *galaktoboureko* was best placed. Amongst the women, his father, Donatos, sat in his wheelchair, wearing his favourite fedora, his walking canes resting against the chair's frame. He was sharpening a long-bladed knife on a whetstone, concentrating on the rhythm of his strokes.

Amara saw Sakis approaching, and alerted the others, who all looked at him expectantly. The table for the Papayiannis *kleftiko* was ready, with a sheet of clear polythene covering a white cloth, and plates, napkins and forks all laid out; at the corner of the table was a silver trophy decorated with ribbons, inscribed for the previous year with the Papayiannis name.

Donatos drew the knife-blade lightly across his thumb-pad. A red line appeared on the skin. Satisfied, he leaned forward in his chair, and laid the knife alongside the trophy.

Across the courtyard, at the Kapsis tables, the first slices of roast meat had been carved. Through the gate, another clan's menfolk carried in their lamb, holding it over their heads to show off its quality. A cheer went up from their family.

'Here he is,' said Amara, brightly, as Sakis reached them. 'Here's the man of the moment!'

'How is it, son?' asked Donatos. The small act of leaning forward left him wheezing, and with his fast and shallow breathing, his ruddy face was growing more florid. 'Is it good?'

Sakis's mother, Tasia, wiped her hands on her apron.

'We're all ready for you,' she said. 'Where is it?'

But Amara saw the fury in Sakis's face.

'What's wrong?' she asked him. 'What's going on?'

'There's no *kleftiko*,' he said, angrily. 'Our pit was sabotaged.'

Behind him, his relatives shouted agreement and support. The drunken cousin forced himself forward, and started on his version of the tale, but the ouzo made him rambling and repetitive.

'Let me tell it,' Sakis insisted. At the neighbouring tables, the women fell into silence, listening as they were laying out their food. 'Those bastards . . .' He stabbed a finger towards the Kapsis's, where a loud toast was being drunk to begin the feast. '*Koproskila!* They doused our pit! And if that wasn't enough, they pissed all over it!'

Shocked, the women began to ask questions, raising their voices over each other to be heard. Donatos grabbed his

8

canes, and with his free hand, began to raise himself from his wheelchair.

'Donatos, sit down!' said Tasia. 'Get back in your chair, or you'll fall.'

'For Christ's sake, stop your nagging, woman!' said Donatos. 'I can manage perfectly well on my own two legs.' Out of the chair, he leaned heavily on his canes. 'Sakis, *yie mou*, let's go.'

'But where are you going?' asked Amara. 'Sakis, don't you go losing your temper!'

'Don't you let your father go looking for trouble, Sakis!' said Tasia. 'His heart's not strong enough to cope with any trouble!'

'There won't be any trouble,' said Donatos. 'But this has gone on too long. I'm handing this over to the law. We're going to find a policeman.'

Donatos walked painfully with his canes, halting every few steps to catch his breath, Sakis following close behind, both men giving only curt responses to those who offered greetings. Beyond the courtyard gate, outside the church precincts where they were permitted to smoke, a group of men was gathered, watching people make their way up to the festival from the town. The narrow road below was lined with cars, trucks and vans. Amongst them was a police car.

Donatos was badly out of breath. Against a wall was a broken-backed bench, where three plump girls in frothy dresses dipped into bags of candy floss.

Donatos stopped in front of them, and raised one of his canes.

'Shoo, pretty ones,' he said. 'Shoo, and let an old man sit down.'

Silently, the girls slipped down from the bench, and sloped scowling away. Donatos sat down heavily, closed his eyes and leaned forward almost on to his thighs, as if trying to bring oxygen to his head. For a few moments, he was still. Then he sat back, and looked up at Sakis, who was watching his father with concern.

'Are you still here?' asked Donatos. 'Go and tell them to come up here. Tell them I want to speak to them.'

'I'll do my best,' said Sakis. 'But what if they won't come? Maybe it would be better if we went to them.'

'They'll come. Just tell them who I am,' said his father.

Sakis walked away, towards the police car. Donatos pulled a waxed bag from his pocket. He propped his canes against his knee, and peered into the bag, at several golden pieces of almond praline – whole almonds encased in brittle caramel. He searched for a piece the right size, but not finding one, he broke a large piece in half, and put one of the halves in his mouth. He sucked and savoured the hard sweetness, then crunched it between his teeth, breaking into the nutty smoothness of the almonds as he chewed. And very briefly, his face relaxed into a smile.

The police officer at the wheel of the car was chewing gum, his jaw moving like a goat's, his tongue clicking lightly with every clamping of his teeth. His colleague – who was barely more than a boy – was dipping into a large bag of Cheetos. As Sakis approached, the driver watched him in the side-view mirror.

'*Yassas*,' said Sakis, when he reached the driver's open window.

The driver wished him the same; when he spoke, the glob of gum showed in his mouth. He had recently been to the barber's; the line of his short haircut was immaculate, the nape of his neck shaved smooth.

'Can I trouble you to come and talk to my father?' asked Sakis.

'He'll have to come to us,' said the driver. 'We're not allowed to leave the vehicle, in case of an emergency. We have to stay close to the radio.'

'But he's too infirm to come down here. He wants to make a complaint. We both want to make a complaint.'

'He'll be leaving the church eventually, so why not now?' asked the driver. 'Or is he planning to stay up there all night?'

'If he comes down, he won't easily get back up again,' said Sakis. 'We used a wheelchair to get him up there, and it took the best part of half an hour. My father is Donatos Papayiannis. His cousin was one of your chief inspectors, for many years.'

The policemen looked at each other, and pulled faces to confirm Donatos's name meant nothing. The younger man reached into the bag for another Cheeto. He put it in his mouth, and sucked staining orange powder from his fingers.

'I don't know him,' said the driver. 'What's your complaint?'

'Sabotage,' said Sakis. 'We had a pit, a *kleftiko* pit, and someone doused it.'

The driver's eyebrows lifted a touch. His colleague smirked and looked away, as if something outside the car had become suddenly interesting.

'How did they sabotage it?' asked the driver, tightening his jaw to stop a smile breaking through.

'With water,' said Sakis. 'And they urinated on it.'

The driver's eyebrows moved higher. His colleague snickered, and tried to disguise it as a cough.

'I have to say,' said the driver, 'that pouring water isn't a criminal offence. Did it cause any damage?'

'Of course it did!' said Sakis. 'It doused the fire-pit! Instead of roast lamb, I've got a raw carcass!'

'It's still a carcass, though,' said the driver. 'Relight your fire, and there's no problem, surely?'

'With their piss on it?'

The driver looked uncomfortable.

'I know who did it,' said Sakis. 'They're up there in the church, now.'

'Did you see them?'

'No.'

'Do you have any witnesses?'

'No.'

The driver sat up in his seat.

'Tell you what I'd do, in your shoes,' he said. 'If you think you know who did it, go and have a quiet word. But it sounds like a prank to me. I'd try and see the funny side, if I were you. There's always next year.'

Sakis fixed the officer with a glare.

'Are you new here?' he asked. 'New in Dendra?'

'I've been here a couple of months,' said the driver. 'What's that to do with anything?'

'Never mind,' said Sakis, walking away. 'Forget I mentioned it. Like you said, I'd do better to sort it out myself.'

Two

In ages past, the ancient citadel was a formidable defence against enemies from the sea. The outer walls of great stone blocks had survived intact, and in many places had kept their jagged battlements; but the watchtowers were roofless and disintegrating, and little was left of the buildings where soldiers had eaten and slept but their outlines in rubble, with weeds and grasses growing where there had once been floors.

The ascent to the citadel was steep, and missing cobbles and loose gravel made the path hazardous, but the man approaching the stronghold moved with confidence, and at a good pace for one considerably overweight. Passing through an arched gateway, he wandered for a while amongst the traces of old rooms. Finding an open well, he tossed in a coin, counting the seconds of its fall to measure the depth, but the coin's chink as it bounced off the shaft's rocky protrusions only faded away, and the sound of its hitting bottom was too distant to be heard.

The ruins seemed desolate, and lonely, as if those who had stood guard in the watchtowers and challenged strangers at the gates were still missed. The fat man climbed up to the wall-walk behind the ramparts, and gazed out over the land the citadel had once protected. The countryside was becoming green with the autumn rain; acres of silver-leaved olive trees covered gently sloping hills. Some way off lay a town, and round about were smallholdings and farms, all connected by a sparse network of roads. To the north, there were high mountains, and to the south, in the distance, the sea.

The wind, high up, was strong, its gusts bending the long grasses and tousling the fat man's greying curls, which were overdue the attention of a barber. His owlish glasses gave him an air of academia; under his raincoat, his bark-brown suit was subtly sheened, and expertly tailored to flatter his generous stomach. His pale green polo shirt had a crocodile on the chest, and on his feet he wore white shoes, old-fashioned canvas shoes of the type once used for tennis; in his hand was a sportsman's hold-all in black leather, painted in gold with the emblem of a rising sun.

Overhead, a circling eagle cried. The fat man raised his coat collar against the wind, and left the ramparts by a stairway of rough steps, where the mortar between the stones had long ago been washed away. The steps led to a once substantial building; the lines of its foundations were distinct, and a single cornerstone was still in place, a large block left behind when the walling stone had been pilfered for newer buildings. Towards this ruin's eastern wall, almost buried and lost to the dirt and weeds, was an altar.

The fat man crouched, and felt the faint grooves which were all that remained of the altar-front inscriptions. He traced a 'D', and an 'I', a 'Y' and a final 'S' – enough to identify the name of Dionysus, ancient god of the vines – and, seeming pleased with this discovery, he patted the stones, and rising to his feet, returned to the ramparts.

As he leaned on the battlements, he saw a plume of smoke rise behind the town; minutes later, a second plume appeared,

14

followed by a third, and a fourth. The fat man watched until the smoke dispersed, carried away by the wind. Then he left his post on the ramparts, and made his way back down the path to the road far below.

In the car park below the citadel was a single vehicle – a vintage sports car with a stretched bonnet and bold tail-fins, and the grime of the road covering its white paint. The fat man placed his hold-all in the passenger footwell and slipped in behind the wheel, where the seat was set well back to accommodate his bulk. When he turned the ignition, the engine gave a roar, and blew an oily black cloud from the exhaust; but the fat man seemed unperturbed, and resting his arm on the central console, he put the car into gear.

He headed in the direction of the smoke he had seen from the ramparts, following the road in its broad sweep towards the coast. On the radio, reception was poor, and the rich voice of Notis Sfakianakis faded in and out with the curves in the road. There was little traffic: a few freight trucks, a tractor and a number of cars spattered with rural mud, which though battered and scratched, tore past the fat man, who motored at a steady pace, admiring the views. Within a few kilometres, a sign showed an approaching junction and a road joining from the left; and since that was the direction of the smoke, the fat man flicked on his indicator, and – even though there was no other traffic in sight – moved cautiously to the centre of the road to execute a careful turn.

The road he found himself on was less straightforward in its intentions than the highway he had left, first following the path of a river, then winding in looping bends. He passed a run-down smallholding, where a mange-tormented dog began a frenzied barking, and thin sheep foraged around the tree roots in a lemon orchard. A roadside booth advertised oranges, though there were neither oranges, nor salesman; but a little further on was another makeshift stall, a table and a shabby kitchen dresser sheltered with a tarpaulin. Here, under a sign reading 'Local Produce', sat two men, a bottle of red wine on the ground between them, each with a glass in his hand. One seemed obviously a farmer, dressed in a flannel shirt and jeans and with a weather-leathered face; but the other made him an unlikely companion, having the look of an ageing hippy.

The fat man cast an eye over the pair and allowed himself a smile; the two seemed set there for the duration. But as he motored by, the hippy leaped to his feet, and glass still in hand, chased after the fat man a few paces, then stood in the road, waving his free hand in the air.

'Stop!'

The fat man heard the shout, and glanced in his rear-view mirror. Seeing the hippy there waving, he slammed on his brakes; and as the hippy began to run slowly towards the car, the fat man reversed in his direction.

He stopped alongside the hippy, who was somewhat glazed and smiling. His yellow T-shirt was splashed with wine spilled as he ran; below his tan cord trousers, his sandalled feet were dusty, and his toenails much too long. His neglected beard grew to his chest, his hair down to his shoulders though his high forehead was bald. Beneath unkempt eyebrows, his eyes were very blue. The smell of alcohol seeped through his pores and was on his breath; the flaking skin on his dry lips was black from the wine.

He grinned, showing his wine-stained teeth, and swaying slightly, held up his glass in a salute.

'*Yassou*, Dino,' said the fat man.

'I thought it was you,' said Dino. 'How's life been treating you, brother?'

*   *   *

In the cramped space behind the Kapsis family's tables, the women were uncovering more food.

'What have you brought, *kalé*?' one asked her sister.

'I made my aubergine pilaf.' She lifted the cloth from an heirloom *tapsi* – a vast brass-handled copper pan, much dented from knocks on stone ovens – to show a mound of rice flavoured with cloves and bay, mixed with aubergines, almonds and currants. 'And a loaf of my cheese bread.' She unrolled the loaf from a white napkin, and laid the bread towards the front of the table where it could be admired. Scents of yeast, warm feta and oregano rose from its crust. 'What about you?'

'I brought sausages with green beans. They're Takis's best.' The first sister pointed to a cast-iron pan. The sausages were pork, minced with the pig's liver and its kidneys, well seasoned with paprika and parsley, stewed with the beans in a piquant tomato sauce. 'And I made *revani*, Mama's recipe.' On a blue plate, her semolina cake sat in a pool of its own cinnamon-spiced syrup. A slice was missing from the end. 'I thought I should try it, in case I hadn't used enough sugar, but I worried for nothing.' She turned to a pretty girl busy beside them. 'Where's Marianna?' she asked. 'Where's your aunt?'

The girl pointed to a corner of the courtyard, where several wine barrels had been mounted on trestles, and a gaggle of grandmothers bickered over an arrangement of carafes and cups. Close by, a tall and ample woman talked with another much more petite, until the petite woman excused herself, and bent to make adjustments to the wine taps. The tall woman began to make her way towards the Kapsis tables, faltering in patent heels.

'Here she comes,' said the pretty girl.

'About time,' muttered one sister to the other.

From across the courtyard, Amara Papayiannis watched Takis Kapsis carve the *kleftiko*, sweating from the heat of the roast and the alcohol he had drunk. The clan's women were gathered round him, holding out platters for him to fill.

'Look at them,' said Amara. 'Carrying on as if nothing happened. I'm going to tell them what I think.'

'Leave it, *kalé*,' said her mother. 'The men will sort it out.'

'What will they do?' asked Amara. 'Bleating to the police will help nothing.'

'It's not for us to take it on ourselves. We've plenty of food anyway, without the lamb.'

'You'd let them get away with it, but I won't. Enough is enough, Mama. Sakis is so upset, and this kind of stress is bad for Donatos's heart. Sometimes we have to stand up for our self-respect. For our family. What does the bible say? An eye for an eye, and a life for a life.'

'That's not what Christ said, though, is it?' Her mother made a triple cross over her heart. 'We should turn the other cheek, that's what he'd say. Look, there's Papa Kostas. You can ask him. He'll tell you what's right. Papa! Papa!'

She picked up a dish of baked figs, and held it up whilst beckoning to the priest, who was moving from table to table, accepting tastes and morsels from the housewives of his congregation.

'*Kyries*, *kali mera sas*,' he said. For his age, he was a good-looking man. Amara's mother went a little pink.

'I was wondering if you'd try one of these,' she said, and offered him the plate.

The priest's hand hovered over the honeyed figs, until he chose the plumpest. He bit into it, and closed his eyes in pleasure. Amara's mother waited for his verdict.

'Marvellous,' said the priest, smiling broadly.

'I wasn't sure,' said Amara's mother. 'I used pistachios with the apricots in the stuffing, and I wasn't sure it would work. Usually I use walnuts, but I thought this year I'd be more daring.'

'Sometimes it pays to be daring,' said the priest, and gave her a wink. 'These are a delight, a triumph!'

'Have another,' she said. 'Please.'

He hesitated only for a moment.

'They really are very good,' he said, and bit into the soft flesh.

'Whilst you're here, Papa,' said Amara's mother, 'can you advise my daughter? She has a question she'd like to ask you, haven't you, Amara?'

She looked round for Amara, but Amara wasn't there.

Marianna was a little out of breath; the tray she was carrying was heavy. Two small girls followed behind, both struggling with wicker baskets which knocked their shins.

'*Koritsia, koritsia*,' she said. 'I'm late, I'm late. Have you been coping without me?'

'We've coped,' said one of the sisters, shortly. She looked Marianna up and down. The sister's hair was grey, and cut matronly short; she and Marianna were the same age, but Marianna's curled hair was bleached a nicotine blonde. The sister was too modest to think of make-up, but Marianna wore coral lipstick, with rouged cheekbones and peachy powder on her nose. 'Are those more new shoes? I'd never be able to walk in anything like that.'

'We're nearly ready, *Thea*,' said her niece.

Marianna cast her eyes over the table.

'Evangelia, don't put that there,' she said, pointing to a courgette pie, glazed and cut into perfect diamonds. 'Move it to the back, then I can put my tarts down here at the front.'

'What have you brought, Marianna?' asked one of the sisters.

'Saffron cheese tarts,' she said, and lowered her tray on to the edge of the table. The tarts were of crimped golden pastry, filled with yellow custard spotted brown where the oven's heat had caught the tops. 'And my two little angels here . . . Put the baskets down, *koukles*, there near Evangelitsa.'

The niece reached down into the baskets and began to lift out jars: pickled sticks of celery, sour-cherry spoon-sweets, little black sea-snails in brine. In the second basket were bottles of olive oil, and long loaves of fresh bread.

'Slice the bread, Evangelia,' said Marianna, 'and pour some oil into those dishes, those small glass ones. We'll give everyone a taste of Kapsis oil today, and let the people judge who makes the best in Dendra.'

She was rearranging the saffron tarts on the tray, making sure the most perfect were towards the front, when Amara reached the Kapsis tables, and tapped Marianna on the back. Marianna turned round.

'Amara,' she said, coldly. 'What can I do for you?'

'Oh, I think you've done plenty for us already,' said Amara. The colour in her cheeks was as high as Marianna's, though Amara was wearing no rouge. 'So I've come to repay the compliment.'

'I've no idea what you're talking about,' said Marianna. The sisters and Evangelia were staring at Amara with the same coldness as Marianna. 'If you don't mind, we're busy.'

'The thing is with you Kapsis's, you're so underhand. Devious as snakes. And as for pissing on good food! You're no better than a bunch of barbarians!'

'I beg your pardon!' Marianna objected loudly.

'How dare you!' exclaimed one of the sisters. 'Takis! There's trouble here!'

'Oh, there's no trouble you haven't all earned,' said Amara. 'Like I said, I'm just here to return the compliment.'

She scanned the dishes on the table, like a diner making her choice. The dainty saffron tarts caught her eye; and tossing back her head, she spat over them with gusto, contaminating them all with a spray of spittle.

'*Mori!*' exclaimed the sister. 'The woman's gone mad! Takis! Come quick!'

Marianna, in shock, stood with her hands to her face, whilst Amara summoned more spittle into her mouth, and delivered another spray over the courgette pie. Then, as a parting shot, she spat with all her might into the aubergine pilaf. One of the sisters tried to grab her by the hair, the other by her dress; but Amara was too quick for them, and disappeared into the growing crowd.

The fat man parked alongside a red motorbike resting on its stand. The farmer's old bicycle was propped against the dresser, whose shelves were filled with odd-sized jars of honey and fruit preserves, and bags of mountain herbs. The table display was of wine, in anything which would hold liquid – green and clear glass bottles, cooking-oil containers, a rubber-stoppered demijohn or two – and there were several small bottles of *tsipouro,* crude home-distilled spirit.

The fat man lifted a jar of honey from the shelf, and held it up to examine its clarity. His expression as he returned it to its place suggested approval. Dino was already back in his chair, and had refilled his glass. The farmer rose from his own fraying cane-bottomed chair and hauled an orange crate from under the table. Then, he faced a dilemma, wondering whether to offer the fat man the orange crate, or whether to be more polite and offer his own seat.

'Better give him your chair,' said Dino to the farmer, and he took a long slug of wine. 'I don't think that orange box will take his weight. You've put on a few kilos, Hermes.'

The fat man patted his stomach as he sat down on the farmer's chair.

'Life is good,' he said, in the impeccable Greek of TV newscasters, enunciating each word perfectly. 'And I indulge myself too much. But you've lost more since I saw you. Are you eating at all? Or are you relying entirely on the fruit of the vine for your sustenance?'

'Ah, now,' said Dino. He tilted his glass and held it up to the sun, so the light through the wine showed the richness of its colours, sanguine in its shallows, deepest purple in its depths. 'When it's nectar of this quality, what else do we need? But I'm forgetting my manners.' He waved a casual hand towards the farmer, showing on his fingers a pair of rings in twisted silver. 'Meet my new friend, Yiorgo.'

'Yianni,' corrected the farmer.

'Forgive me,' said Dino. 'I'm not good with names. This is my big brother, Hermes.'

'Half-brother,' corrected the fat man. 'Same father, different mother.'

'*Kalos irthate*,' said the farmer. 'But you two don't look like brothers. You don't sound like brothers, either.'

'I shall take that as a compliment,' said the fat man.

'The paths of our lives have been diverse,' said Dino, 'and the company we keep is very different. I think you wouldn't contradict me in that assessment, would you, Hermes?'

'I would be loathe to contradict you in anything.'

The farmer handed the fat man a tumbler, and since Dino had almost finished the bottle tucked under his chair, opened more wine and began to fill the fat man's glass. When the tumbler was half-full, the fat man stopped him.

'Only a taste for me,' he said.

Dino shook his head in mock despair.

'Always so puritanical!' he said. 'It's a beautiful day, and what can there possibly be out there that can't wait? Relax for once, Hermes, and live a little!'

'I do my share of living,' said the fat man, mildly. 'But I have responsibilities, and as you well know, unfortunately there are always matters that won't wait.'

'Responsibilities wear a man out,' said Dino. 'Take a leaf out of my book, and have nothing to do with them. Have you seen our parent recently? I've been thinking about paying the old goat a visit.'

'Maybe you should,' said the fat man. 'He was asking about you, last time I saw him.'

'And what did you tell him?'

'The truth. That I hadn't seen you in a long while.'

Dino threw back his head and laughed, a laugh made long and loud by intoxication, and with a burbling undercurrent which turned the laugh into a tarry smoker's cough.

'Always the diplomat, eh, brother?' he said, when he had recovered from his coughing. 'So you didn't divulge the shady circumstances in which you found me? Maybe that's just as well. But come on, at least give this wine a fair trial. This gentleman here is a master of his art, and he makes a wine to make you sing.'

The fat man held up his glass to the farmer.

'*Yammas*,' he said. The farmer, seated uncomfortably on the orange crate, returned his toast, and the fat man tasted the wine.

'So what do you think, brother?' asked Dino. 'I'd say a mildly vegetal nose, with a pleasant earthiness, and some supple and distinctly easy flavours of red and blue fruit.' He tasted the wine again, drawing it noisily over his tongue.

'Delicious, if somewhat light by the standards of this region. A tangy finish, it's clean, it's crisp, and as perfect a young wine for everyday drinking as you'll find.'

'I agree it's good,' said the fat man. 'What grape is this? If I were guessing, I'd say *Agiorghitiko*.'

'Yes,' said the farmer. 'But I blend it with a little *Korinthiaki*. Not too much, just enough.'

Dino drained his glass.

'And beautifully blended it is,' he said. 'A drop more of this, and then we might try the *tsipouro*. Yiorgo, what do you say?'

'I expect he'd say, if he weren't too polite, that he'd like to see the colour of your money,' said the fat man. 'Another hour or two of your company, and he'll have nothing left to sell.'

Dino grinned.

'You're right,' he said. 'But I'm afraid I find myself short of cash. Tell you what, you put some money on the table, and we'll make a night of it. It'd be good to catch up, find out where you've been, who you've seen.'

The fat man looked around.

'Are you alone? Where's that friend of yours?'

'He's laid up,' said Dino. 'He suffers with the gout, been suffering for years. He's not one for being on the road, these days. He'd rather grow vegetable marrows. But it's an ill wind. He was getting heavier by the day, and it was costing me in petrol. I travel lighter now. What do you think to my wheels? Seventy-three horse-power! A traveller's bike, perfect for my free spirit. There's nothing like the feel of the wind in your hair, heading down the road with no particular place to be. I'll give you a ride, if you like. She and I have done a few miles together, since you and I last met.'

'If you've been very far on something so powerful, it's a miracle you're still with us,' said the fat man. 'I don't suppose you wear a helmet?'

'Helmets are for *poustes*.'

'Helmets, in my experience, are for those who wish to avoid disfigurement, brain injuries and death. No doubt you'll condemn my view as over-cautious. But I've seen too many avoidable tragedies brought about by those machines.'

He became reflective, until Dino nudged him.

'Drink your drink, big brother! A toast to those whose lives are short! What a piece of luck to see you! I miss you, you know.' He draped his arm around the fat man's shoulders. 'Where are you heading, anyway?'

'I have a place not far from here in my sights,' said the fat man, drinking more of his wine. Dino withdrew his arm, and the fat man stretched out his legs, and flexed his feet in their white shoes. 'I was up on the hills, and I saw the smoke of several fires. Do you know what it might have been, Yianni?'

'Dendra, no doubt,' said the farmer. 'It's the saint's day of the Archangel Michael, and the town of Dendra holds a feast today. Every year they have a competition to see who can make the best *kleftiko*. It's hotly fought, I'll tell you. That'll be what you saw: the smoke from them opening the fire-pits.'

Dino's eyes shone.

'A feast!' he said. 'Let's go!'

'Archangel Michael, of course,' said the fat man. 'I had forgotten. Did you know his festival replaced the ancient feast of Pyanepsia, in honour of the goddess Artemis? They made her offerings of fruit and pulses, and carried olive branches covered in honey and oil. It will be interesting to see what remnants of the old feast remain.'

'Still the walking encyclopaedia!' said Dino, slapping him on the back so the fat man's wine slopped dangerously close to the rim of his glass. 'Come on, let's go! There'll be wine, women and song! I'll race you! How far is it, Yiorgo?'

'Yianni,' said the farmer. 'Not far. Ten kilometres along this road, maybe a dozen.'

Dino was already out of his chair, staggering as he stood.

'You can join me,' said the fat man, 'but I shall do the driving. I wouldn't want to explain to Papa, if I let anything happen to you.' Finding his wallet, he gave the farmer several notes. 'Here's payment for what he's drunk, and a little extra for taking care of his mount. I'll bring him back to pick it up tomorrow.'

The fat man's car interior smelled of leather, and faintly of wax polish. Dino ran his hand over the dashboard.

'Nice wheels,' he said. 'Where did you get this?'

'This is a rarity,' said the fat man, looking over his shoulder before he pulled out into the road. 'It was produced by a racing driver, Antonis Tzen, a genius thwarted by protectionism and bureaucracy. Only ten were ever made.'

'Won't it go any faster?'

'Better to take our time,' said the fat man. 'The roads are full of careless fools like you.'

The farmer had directed them to Dendra's southern side where the church of Agios Michaelis was located, but every parking space was taken and every side street was lined with cars. The fat man drove instead towards the town's centre, and parked in a quiet square he found by squeezing the Tzen down a lane almost too narrow.

The square was bordered by archaic buildings picturesque in their decay. The three-storey houses were habitable on only one or two floors; above that, the doors to crumbling balconies were sealed with nailed-on crosses, and the stones and timbers of the houses' construction showed grey where the perishing stucco had fallen away. A few small retailers – a watch-seller's, a bridal boutique, a lingerie shop for the mature woman – were closed for the feast day, their window displays unlit and unalluring. There was a chapel, where a shaggy mongrel slept on the steps; alongside the chapel, a long dry fountain was set into a wall, its brass spouts in the shape of dolphins' heads, its stonework carved with Arabic script and palm leaves.

As the fat man took his hold-all from the boot and locked the car, Dino wandered over to the dog and stroked its head. The dog, sleepy and placid, rolled on to its back, and Dino rubbed its belly.

The fat man was studying the fountain. Dino pressed his nose against the glass of the lingerie shop, and called to the fat man to laugh with him at the sizeable girdles and generous brassieres.

'Look at this!' he called, pointing to a flesh-coloured corset. 'Would you tussle with a woman wearing that?'

But the fat man seemed absorbed in the fountain.

'This is charming,' he said, as Dino joined him, bringing with him the pungent smoke of the fat French cigarette he had just lit, a dark tobacco with no filter. 'It's Ottoman, of course. No doubt there was a mosque somewhere near here. They built the fountains near their mosques for ritual washing.'

'It's a monstrosity,' said Dino, glancing at the fountain. 'What's more, it's been here hundreds of years, and it'll be here when we get back. Which isn't true of the feast. That's today only.' He held out his pack of cigarettes to the fat man. 'You want one of these?'

The fat man glanced at the packet.

'Thank you, no,' he said. 'You should smoke Greek cigarettes, and help keep our farmers in business.'

'If our farmers want to stay in business, they should grow better tobacco,' said Dino. 'Are you still smoking those quaint things you used to like?'

The fat man smiled, and reaching into his pocket, took out a pack of his own cigarettes – an old-fashioned box whose lift-up lid bore the head and naked shoulders of a 1940s starlet, her softly permed platinum hair curling around a coy smile. Beneath the maker's name ran a slogan in an antique hand: *The cigarette for the man who knows a real smoke.*

'You mean these?'

He chose one from the box, and lit it with a slim, gold lighter.

'I'm surprised you can still find them,' said Dino. 'I thought they went out of business years ago.'

'No, they're still in business,' said the fat man. 'I pay the factory a visit, from time to time, whenever I'm nearby.'

'You pay them a visit?' Dino laughed. 'That's what I love about you, brother. The world keeps changing, but you just keep on being you.' He sniffed the air, which carried the smokiness of grilling meat. 'I smell food, and I'm starving. Let's go whilst there's still food to be had!'

Along the tree-lined avenue and through the streets, the people were promenading to the feast. The men were shaven and smart in suits or Sunday jackets, shoes polished and fingernails scrubbed and clipped, the older women were respectably matronly in shift dresses and good coats. The young girls were parading their outrageous finery – short skirts, stilettos and cleavage, bordello make-up, paste jewellery and lush hair – and at the junctions, stern policemen eyed them from behind dark glasses as they halted traffic to let the crowds pass.

Traditional music from the PA system set a buoyant mood, and from time to time Dino broke into a dance, skipping a few cross-steps of a *syrtos*, circling and slapping his heel in a *zembekiko*. His casual appearance made him conspicuous, and he made himself more so by clutching at the hands of passing girls, paying fawning compliments to shapely beauties in high heels.

'Take care,' said the fat man, as another girl snatched away the fingers Dino had tried to kiss. 'You'll regret your disrespect when one of them slaps your face.'

'They're the ones I like,' said Dino. 'The fiery ones.'

'But fiery girls often have fiery relatives in the wings. Don't make trouble here, Dino. I haven't come here to bring trouble.'

They found the feast a kilometre away, on a hillside with a view over the town. The church of the Archangel Michael was an architect's dismay, a mismatched confusion of domes, archways and stairs, awkwardly alloyed with outhouses and storerooms unused since its days as a monastery. The last monk had been laid in his courtyard tomb over fifty years before; today he was sharing his burial ground with a crowd.

The fat man led Dino between the banqueting tables. Wherever there was a place to sit, people were eating. As they came close to the wine barrels, Dino caught the fat man's arm.

'Here we are, brother,' he said. 'I'll go and get us a drink.'

The fat man looked over to where the grandmothers were handing out carafes; too busy to drink themselves, they seemed the only ones at the gathering entirely sober. Papa Kostas had found a chair beside them, and, ruddy-faced, raised his glass to everyone who came near. The petite woman who had been talking to Marianna Kapsis was filling the carafes, taking care not to lose any wine through the dribbling barrel taps.

'It will be impossible to find seats in here,' said the fat man. 'Find us a place outside, and I'll bring you a plate.'

The fat man took a while to review what was on offer: full-bodied stews with pasta and potatoes; buttery-crusted pies of feta, greens and dill; pan-fried *keftedes* of octopus, cheese and beef; crisp *bourekakia* of shrimps, and baked peppers brimming with rice. But most tempting of all was the *kleftiko*. The heads from seven of the carcasses were gone, handed out as favours to officials; the meat – which fell from the bones and left them clean – was being sliced and plated by men in women's aprons, whilst others handed out bread baked in olive-wood ovens, and *tzatziki* so spiced with garlic, it burned the tongue.

The fat man hooked his hold-all over his shoulder, and accepted two portions of *kleftiko* from men who seemed particularly cheerful, and were showing off a winners' shield. Holding the plates up high, out of the range of careless elbows, he set off around the courtyard perimeter towards the gate.

Halfway there, he paused. An eighth lamb was laid out, in a bizarre display. The flesh was barely touched by heat – enough only to discolour it to an unappetising grey – and yet it too seemed to have won an award. Bemused, the fat man leaned over to read the shield's engraving, and in doing so caught something unpleasant in the smell coming off the beast: blood, smoke and oregano combined with a sharp, ammoniac tang.

The award had been won in the previous year. He might have asked for an explanation, if there had been anyone to ask, but the Papayiannis tables were deserted.

Dino had found a pair of rocks which made reasonably comfortable seats. He poured large measures of wine, and raised his glass to the fat man before he drank. The fat man chose a piece of crisp-skinned lamb, and ate it with a generous smear of *tzatziki*.

'This is truly excellent,' he said, taking a bite of bread.

They ate, and drank, and discussed the best method of preparing *kleftiko*, and disagreed over whether it needed any seasoning other than salt. They argued over whether dill or mint was a better flavouring for *tzatziki*, and whether olive or apple wood was best for baking bread.

When Dino went to fetch more wine, he was gone for some time.

'I was talking to the lady in charge of the barrels,' he said, settling himself back on his rock. 'She seemed to know a fair bit about wine. A nice-looking woman, too, but too old for me. You should have a look for yourself. I found out her name for you – they call her Meni – and I'm telling you, she's just your type. Go on, have a look for yourself, see if you can catch her eye.'

But when the fat man returned to the courtyard to refill their plates, he avoided the press of people around the wine barrels. He chose potatoes *lemonato*, a few snails in vinegar, spiced beef flavoured with Metaxa and red mullet grilled over coals. When that was gone, he went to find dessert, and brought back honey cakes with sweet cream and a syrupy walnut *baklava*. Dino went again for wine, but the barrels were running dry, and he came back with the carafe only half-full.

'That's all there is,' he said. 'They're clearing the tables for dancing.'

'I don't dance,' said the fat man. 'As you know.'

'Ah, come on, brother!' Dino punched him in the arm. 'It'll be fun.'

'Not for me.' The fat man rubbed his swelling stomach. 'There's no dancing inside me this evening.'

In the town down below, a fresh column of smoke was rising into the dusk. A young boy ran by, heading downhill.

'Eh, *mikre*!' Dino called after him. 'Where are you running to?'

'Down to the square!' shouted the youngster, over his shoulder. 'I'm going to leap the bonfire!'

'Leap the bonfire!' Dino was slouching on his rock, but at the boy's words, he sat up straight. 'That sounds like something I should try. I'll show them how it's done.'

'Don't be ridiculous,' said the fat man. 'You're half-drunk, and far too old for such stunts.'

But Dino stood, and hands on hips, grinned down at him.

'You think so? I shall take that as a challenge!'

He set off after the boy. Slowly, wincing at his overfull stomach, the fat man gathered up the detritus of their feast, and when he had disposed of it properly, reluctantly followed his half-brother down the hill.

Democracy Square had been the project of prosperous citizens, three generations before. Paved in tawny marbles, there were dignified, ochre mansions on all four sides, with ornate balconies on every storey and pretty French windows painted coral and white; the largest building had become a folk museum, another was the National Bank, whilst the others served as restaurants and *kafenions*.

At the heart of the square, a fire burned. From time to time, its bow-legged and toothless guardian fed it olive branches, or poked it with a rake to let the fuel burn through. Around him, boys and youths shouted taunts and dares, shoving each other towards the heat, whooping and jeering as they waited for the flames to die back.

The prospect of the spectacle was drawing people from the church, and the *kafenion* tables were all taken, but Dino had found space at the Odyssey *ouzeri*, a cheap place favoured by traditionalists and old men. His order for wine had already been brought out. As the fat man sat down, Dino filled his glass.

A matron in widow's black approached the fire, and threw in the dried remains of a May Day wreath. The dead flowers flared briefly in the flames, and were gone.

'Why do they do that?' asked Dino. He sniffed his wine, and pulled a face.

'More commonly, the wreaths are burned at midsummer,' said the fat man. 'I assume the ceremony here is a hangover from first-sowing celebrations related to Artemis, and the replacing of the last year's offerings in the temples.'

An old man with a leather bag slung over his paunch was moving between the tables, carrying a staff filled with lottery tickets.

'*Kali spera sas*,' he said to Dino and the fat man. 'Lottery?'

'What do you think, brother?' asked Dino. 'Are you feeling lucky?'

'Perhaps,' said the fat man. 'How about you?'

'I never gamble,' said Dino.

The fat man's eyebrows lifted.

'You say you're going to jump that fire, and you don't regard that as a gamble? Here, friend, I'll take one.'

'You should, *kyrie*, you should,' said the lottery seller, who stank of ouzo's aniseed, and sweat. 'Top prize this week is twenty million.'

He held out the staff of tickets, and the fat man chose one, apparently at random.

'It's no gamble,' said Dino, staring at the fire. 'Anybody's grandmother could get over that.'

The fat man paid for his ticket, and studied the numbers. As the lottery seller gave him his change, he offered him the ticket back.

'A gift for you,' he said.

The lottery seller was confused.

'That's your ticket,' he said. 'I just sold it to you.'

'And I'm making a gift of it, to you. Please, take it. Perhaps you'll be lucky.'

The lottery seller looked doubtful.

'I'm not a lucky man,' he said. 'Bad luck has ridden me for years.'

'The offer's there,' said the fat man. 'Take it or leave it, friend.'

'I'll take it, thank you,' said the lottery seller, folding the ticket and slipping it into his shirt pocket. 'If I win, I'll buy you a drink.'

'I'll look forward to it,' said the fat man.

As the lottery seller wandered away, Dino was still studying the blaze.

'I don't know about anybody's grandmother,' said the fat man, 'but to me, those fit young men don't seem as confident as you.'

'Then it's time they had a bit of a prod,' said Dino, and he drained his glass and headed towards the fire.

The fat man took a sip of his wine; it was sour, and musty, and so lacking in body it might have been watered down. The patron brought out a dish of salted peanuts, which the fat man, being not at all hungry, at first ignored; but being fond of peanuts, before long he took a few, and popped them one by one into his mouth.

Dino was talking to the boys, trying to persuade them to jump; he was pointing to the bonfire, then measuring his estimation of the flames' height against his body. He marked a point on his upper thigh; a young man disagreed with him, touching the side of his hand to mid-chest.

Dino laughed, kicked off his sandals, and walked away from the fire, until suddenly, with a cry that was almost a

34

roar, he ran at the blaze. Heads turned to watch. Dino's speed was surprising, and the fire's guardian, seeing him coming, grabbed the shoulder of a boy in Dino's path and pulled him out of the way. For a few moments, the only sound was Dino's bare feet slapping on marble; then, as he reached the fire, he shouted again, and leaped. His feet passed through the flames, and he landed heavily on the other side, staggering to keep his balance.

He grinned, and theatrically bowed. There was a ripple of applause, and a single cry of 'Bravo!'

As he sat back down in his chair, Dino clapped the fat man on the back.

'So what do you think, Hermes?' he asked, still grinning, pouring himself more wine. 'Your turn next!'

'You've had far too much to drink,' said the fat man. 'And I prefer to keep my dignity intact.'

Led by Dino's example, the fire-leaping had properly begun, though the guardian was protesting that the blaze was still too high. Alongside the woodsmoke was the smell of burning fabrics – the singeing of trouser hems, and the scorching of shoes.

Dino watched in amusement, and drank his wine. The fat man, feeling weary, let his eyes close.

'No!'

Gasps came from several quarters, and the fat man opened his eyes. A shriek of intense pain rang out, piercing and distressing as an animal in a trap. The fire's guardian had thrown aside his rake, and seemed inexplicably to be stretching his hands into the flames; but other hands were reaching out to him from within the blaze, and the guardian seized them, and with an energy far beyond the capabilities of a man his size and age, pulled a figure from the fire and to its feet.

35

It was a youth, and he was burning. Flames had hold of his jacket sleeve and his hair, and one leg of his jeans was blackened and smoking; yet paralysed by shock, he seemed incapable of any action to help himself, only shouting, over and over, 'Put it out! Put it out!'

The guardian's hands were raw and blistered, but he began to pat the youth's hair, and succeeded in putting out the flames there. A waiter snatched the cloth from one of his tables, and as plates and tumbled glasses smashed, ran to the youth, wrapped him in white linen and knocked him down, rolling him to douse the fire until others rushed up with bottles of water, and poured them over the covered figure.

Women were shrieking and crying. The children had all become quiet.

'Is there a doctor anywhere?' shouted the waiter, crouching by the youth's covered head, adjusting the cloth to give him air. 'A nurse? *Theé mou*, isn't there anybody?'

'They've called for an ambulance,' someone told him.

Minutes went by. The fuel of the bonfire lay scattered and glowing, its smoke blending with the smell of the youth's burned clothes and hair. Ashen-faced people pressed around the boy, anxious to help, but ignorant of what to do. The youth himself was troublingly still.

An ambulance arrived, sirens blaring, blue lights strobing off the ochre walls. The paramedics worked quickly, and took the boy away.

A doctor was finally fetched to the guardian, who sat at a *kafenion* table with his burned hands resting on his knees, unable to drink the whisky he'd been brought. As his injuries were salved and bandaged, he refused the doctor's offer of painkillers.

'I never felt it,' he said. 'I never felt a thing.'

'You'll feel it, soon enough,' said the doctor, and he left a bottle of tablets beside the whisky.

'*Panayia mou*,' said Dino, deathly pale. 'How did he miss his footing? Do you think he'll be all right?'

'A terrible misfortune,' agreed the fat man. 'As dreadful an accident as I have seen.'

The patron stood behind them, solemn-faced, with a tray tucked under his arm.

'Accident my backside,' he said. 'A Kapsis youth, and a Papayiannis there to make trouble? There's history there, and bad feeling which goes way back. Anyone in Dendra'll tell you, that boy didn't miss his footing. Take it from me, that was no accident at all.'

Three

The sobered people drained their glasses and signalled for their bills, and the waiters broke off their recounting of the drama to take customers' payments, before hurrying back to the conversations they had left. The crowds drifted away, and before long, the square was all but empty.

The fat man paid for the wine, and was ready to leave.

'Stay!' insisted Dino. 'The night is young! Let's have another carafe.'

The fat man shook his head.

'Not for me,' he said. 'I've had far too much already. I shall find myself a bed for the night, and hope the price of your company won't be a sore head in the morning. Why don't you come with me?'

'No thanks,' said Dino. 'This is a festival, and festivals don't end until I've seen the dawn.'

'It will be difficult to go on with the festival by yourself. Plainly, the majority has called a halt to the celebrations, out of respect for that young man's misfortune.'

'Damn the majority,' said Dino. 'That young man's misfortune – terrible though it is – is only proof that my life's philosophy's right. We must seize the day, brother, and seize the night too! Patron! Bring me another carafe!'

'As you wish,' said the fat man. '*Kali nichta*, then.'

His gait as he crossed the square was somewhat unsteady. Dino called after him.

'Hey, Hermes! Where will I find you?'

'It's a small town,' said the fat man, without looking back. 'No doubt you'll manage to track me down.'

He found himself on a quiet cobbled lane, looking up at the brightly lit Hotel Byron – a *pension* formed from three antiquated buildings, with its entrance at the top of a long stairway. He made heavy weather of the steps, swaying backwards and forwards alarmingly until he found a handrail, then climbing much slower than his usual pace. When he asked for a room, he forgot to ask its price, and set off up the internal staircase, key in hand, with no memory at all of the owner's instructions on how to find his bed. As he stood swaying on the first-floor landing, a glance at his key-fob reminded him he was in Room 11, though he had no idea whether that would be on the first or second floor. Unable to remember, he stumbled searching along the first-floor corridors. Room 11 wasn't there.

When he returned to the head of the stairs, the owner was waiting.

'The very person,' said the fat man. 'Could you perhaps remind me where I need to go?'

'Been at the feast, have you?' asked the owner.

'I have.'

'That feast is responsible for a lot of amnesia. Next floor up, second on the left.'

The fat man thanked him, and by repeating 'second on the left' over and over, found his room, though the lock was reluctant to take the key, and he spent several minutes persuading one into the other. Finally inside the room, he tossed his raincoat on to a chair and lay down fully clothed on the bed, thinking he would close his eyes just for a few minutes.

He was woken by sparrows squabbling in the branches of a lemon tree growing so close to his window, he might reach through and pick its fruit. Beside his bed, the lamp still blazed. Somewhere below, dogs whined.

The fat man assessed his condition. Having slept without blankets, he was cold. His mouth was dry, and the surface of his tongue felt brittle. Swollen veins at his temples pulsed with headache, and his bloodshot eyes were sore.

His watch showed a little before six. Swallowing nausea, he got up from the bed, turned off the lamp, and looked out of the window on to dog kennels and a run where three hunting dogs – liver-and-white pointers – waited at the gate. With pauses to rest, he undressed slowly, placing his shoes side by side under the dressing-table, hanging up his raincoat and his crumpled suit, folding his polo shirt over the chair-back. In the bathroom, he drank a glass of water, but as it hit his stomach, the nausea grew dangerously worse.

He ran a fresh half-glass of water, sat down on the bed with his hold-all beside him, and searched it until he found a tin which had once contained strong peppermints. Inside, where the scent of peppermint oil still lingered, were folded papers of medicinal powders, finely ground and speckled with blue and grey. He tipped the contents of a wrap into the water. Lacking a spoon, he swirled the powder in the glass with his finger, and whilst the powder was still held in the water's whirlpool, drank it down in a couple of swallows, grimacing at the foulness of the taste.

Until he was certain the mixture would stay down he stayed very still; and when he was as sure as he could be, he turned his pillows so the cool side was uppermost and lay down, pulled a sheet and blanket over himself, and slept.

He woke again a little before ten. The headache and the nausea were almost gone.

Standing at the end of the bed, he prepared to do his morning stretches and toe-touches, but when he bent towards his feet, he was unsettled to find he couldn't see them. Frowning, he faced the wardrobe mirror, and convinced himself that, though his belly was undoubtedly generous in its proportions, there had been no significant increase in its size; but disheartened by the disappearance of his feet, he allowed himself to forgo his exercises for that morning, and stepped into the shower.

The water was hot, and he stayed under its jets for a long time, until he felt the remnants of his hangover were washed away. He dried himself, and tried to wrap a towel around his waist, but the towel seemed to be too short to stay in place. He soaped his face with a badger-hair brush, and shaved with a silver-handled razor, then splashed on a few drops of cologne – a recent gift from an old friend, a blend of bergamot, white cedar and oak moss, and underlying all, the heady, sweet *crème brûlée* of *immortelle*. He ran a fingerful of pomade through his damp curls, and cleaned his teeth with powder flavoured with wintergreen and cloves, then ran the tip of a steel file behind his fingernails and polished each one with a chamois buffer.

In his hold-all, he found a mauve polo shirt with a crocodile embroidered on the chest and pulled on a pair of pewter linen trousers too lightweight for the season, though he struggled with the buttons and found the waistband somewhat tight.

The suit he had accidentally slept in was creased almost beyond redemption. He folded the jacket with its satin lining to the outside and draped the trousers over his arm, and took both with him on his search for breakfast.

The hotel's interior walls had the distorted lines of old plaster, and were painted a bold yolk-yellow. A miscellany of original artworks hung along the corridors and on the staircase: milky watercolour seascapes and splashy cubist daubs; portraits of ladies in silk, and long-vanished rural landscapes; a mildewed street map of Rome dated 1850. The door to each room was different – a rose-painted porcelain knob to open one, an elegant brass handle for its neighbour. On mismatched side tables there were vases of flowers and a number of curios: baby shoes in intricate, fragile lace; a black-haired monkey's paw with the amputated wristbone encased in silver; five military medals arranged on blue velvet.

The fat man examined everything on display, and his progress downstairs was slow. When eventually he reached the hotel's reception, there was no one behind the desk, though the restorative smell of coffee was in the air. Through the open front door, sunlight brightened the steps and a garden terrace.

He stepped up to the desk, and brought his hand down on the brass bell provided to ring for service.

The proprietor came from the dining room. A short man dressed in an unflattering hooped T-shirt and home-knitted cardigan, he was clean-shaven except for a flamboyant moustache somewhat blacker than his silvered hair. Seeing the fat man, his smile broadened.

'*Kali mera sas, kali mera!*' he said. 'How are you feeling this morning?'

'*Kali mera*,' said the fat man. 'I'm better than I had a right to expect. I'm afraid when I arrived here last night, I was somewhat the worse for wine. I met up with my brother, who is notorious for leading his companions down pathways better avoided. Happily I carry with me an excellent hang-over cure my aunt makes for my uncle. She never tells what's in it, but I detect wormwood – certainly there's something in it that's horribly bitter. Her claim would no doubt be that wormwood settles the stomach, but it might as easily be in there to punish my uncle's and my excesses, since my aunt is a woman who doesn't drink. And this morning, I fully under-stand her teetotalism. It's thanks to her you see me undeserv-edly fresh and prepared to face the day, and ready for breakfast, if there's any available. Will you forgive me, though, if I tell you I've forgotten your name?'

The proprietor laughed.

'You didn't ask it,' he said. 'No offence, friend, but you could hardly remember your own name last night, never mind anyone else's. Lefteris Boukalas. Welcome to the Hotel Byron, in case you can't remember me welcoming you last night.'

'Thank you. Before I eat, I must confess – rather shamefac-edly – to a sin I have never before committed. I fell asleep in my clothes, and now my suit is very much the worse for wear. I wonder if you could arrange to have it pressed?'

'Gladly. My wife will see to. I'll have her hang it in your room when it's done.' Lefteris took the suit, and laid it over the back of the chair behind the reception desk. 'I think it's warm enough to sit out on the terrace, if you'd like. Or would you prefer the dining room?'

'I think the dining room,' said the fat man. 'Even though I feel recovered, I'd like to delay full daylight as long as possible.'

The dining room was of the nineteenth century, with latticed windows set deep in substantial walls. The furni-ture was from the period, but each piece was unique; the tables were varied sizes and shapes, and the elegant dark wood chairs were of several designs, with all their seats upholstered in different fabrics. There were more paintings on the walls, and in a glass-fronted alcove, a leather-bound collection of the works of Byron, in German Gothic print, with one volume open at the second canto of *Childe Harold*. An ornate French clock, its porcelain face painted with a dancing couple, ticked quietly in a corner; on a window sill was a vintage typewriter, with the Greek alphabet marked on its round keys. The tables were covered in peach-coloured cloths, and laid with crockery in pastel porcelains. At one end of the bar was a Russian tea urn, and under the shelves of spirits, an ambitiously sized stainless-steel coffee maker.

Lefteris invited the fat man to sit at a window table.

'Coffee?' he asked. 'Greek, French, Nescafé, a *frappé*?'

'Thank you, Greek, no sugar,' said the fat man, taking a chair. 'Would you make it a double?'

'*Malista*. And shall I squeeze you some orange juice? We've a couple of trees out back, and the fruit's wonderfully sweet.'

'Yes, please.'

'Croissants, rolls, yogurt, almond cake?'

The fat man recalled all he had eaten at the feast, and was about to decline.

'Everything's baked fresh this morning,' said Lefteris.

'In that case,' said the fat man, 'a little of everything.'

The juicer was loud, and the fat man sat in silence until Lefteris brought over a glass filled with pulp-thickened juice.

'So where're you from?' asked Lefteris, as he went back behind the bar.

'Athens,' said the fat man. 'Though I'm rarely there. I travel a great deal.'

'I could tell by your accent you're not from round here. You travelling with your brother?'

'Half-brother. He comes from further north. We ran into each other yesterday. We haven't seen each other in quite some time.'

Lefteris spooned coffee into a *kafebriko*.

'Where's he staying? I've rooms here, if he wants one. Will you be staying long yourself?'

The fat man frowned.

'Now you mention it, I have no idea where he's staying,' he said. 'It's quite possible he hasn't slept at all, and he might only now be thinking about finding himself a bed. My concern with him always is that he so easily gets himself into trouble. His love of the bottle carries him away, and sometimes it's hard not to get carried away with him. As I did last night. Maybe he found a room at another *pension*. I shall go and find him in a while. He won't leave town without me. He has no transport of his own, and he isn't one for buses. Can I ask you, by the way – that poor young man who got burned last night, what news of him?'

Lefteris lit a gas-burner, and put the *kafebriko* on the heat.

'You heard about that, did you?'

'Worse than that. I saw it. At least, I saw the aftermath of his fall.'

'Fall?' Lefteris's eyebrows lifted. 'You reckon he fell?'

'How could it be otherwise? A dreadful accident, surely?'

'If the boy's name wasn't Kapsis, you would think so,' said Lefteris, as he assembled the fat man's breakfast.

'What do you mean?'

Lefteris didn't immediately reply. He waited for the pot to boil, and poured the coffee into a cup, filled a glass with iced water and carried both to the fat man's table; then he brought him his food, and fetched a basket filled with pots of preserves –

45

peach and fig jams, and marmalade – each with a dainty spoon for serving.

'All my own work,' said Lefteris, with some pride. 'From the growing to the boiling and the bottling. I recommend the peach especially. I add a few pods of cardamom to bring out the flavour of the fruit.'

'That's a combination I haven't tried,' said the fat man, 'so peach it will be. Will you join me whilst I eat? I'm curious to hear more about last night.'

Lefteris pulled out a chair and sat down. The fat man spooned peach jam on to his plate, cut a piece off a crisp and flaky croissant, smeared it with jam and popped it in his mouth.

'Delicious,' he said. 'As you say, the cardamom really lifts the flavour. So tell me about the Kapsis boy. First of all, how is he?'

Lefteris shook his head.

'Not good,' he said.

'That doesn't surprise me.' The fat man looked sombre. 'I'm afraid he was badly burned before the flames were put out.'

'The family are at the hospital, of course, and I hear the staff are taking the best care of the boy. They've got him isolated and sedated. It'll be a great shame if he's scarred. Dmitris is a good-looking boy.'

'How old is he?'

Lefteris shrugged.

'Fifteen, sixteen. A high-school pupil.'

'Why do you say this accident was no accident?'

'A long-standing disagreement about olives. Dendra, as you may have noticed, is at the heart of olive country. Most families have a few trees, and some have gone a step further, and made a business out of it. The Kapsis family, for one. And the Papayiannis clan, for another. They have adjoining orchards, and over the years, they've both of them managed to acquire themselves a fair piece of land. And they rubbed along quite well together, for many years. Did you try the *kleftiko* last night, by the way?'

'I did,' said the fat man, and patted his stomach. 'I ate rather more than I should have.'

'It was the Kapsis clan who took this year's prize. And probably well deserved, except they had no competition from last year's winners.'

'Who were . . .?'

'The Papayiannis's.'

'Did the Papayiannis's not wish to retain the honour?'

'Certainly they did, and they might have done so, had their pit not been sabotaged.'

'Sabotaged? How?'

'The pits, as you'll know, are left for many hours, usually overnight. The finish time of the competition is fixed, but the entrants are allowed to roast their meat for as long as they think best. Papayiannis's favour the longest possible cooking, so they start their roast the night before. But once they left their pit, someone doused it.'

The fat man looked at him.

'The uncooked lamb I saw. That was theirs.'

'No doubt. No doubt either, in truth, of who the culprits were, but how could you prove it? So the general view is that the accident that befell poor Dmitris was revenge for the sabotage of the Papayiannis *kleftiko*.'

'One act malicious, the other vicious. How can it have come to that?'

'I suspect Dmitris wasn't expected to be so badly hurt – just a stick between his ankles as he jumped, and down he'd go. Ill considered, at best. The act of a youngster, in my view, who wouldn't properly have thought of the possible consequences.

But the feud between those families is long-standing, and the blood between them is bad.'

The fat man had finished his yogurt, and cut himself a triangle of almond cake.

'And what's behind all that bad blood?'

'A boundary dispute. In the old days, there were no fences. Walls fell down, or were taken away to make other walls, and no one cared. People relied on memory. They knew where their land ended, and their neighbours' began. Maybe there were misrememberings and mistakes, from time to time. But between those two families, a misremembering was made worse by an offence. A young girl was jilted by a lad who decided hours before the wedding that his heart lay elsewhere. It's a common enough story, but the groundwork was laid for bad feeling.'

'How long ago was this?'

Lefteris shrugged again.

'Twenty, thirty years ago. Maybe more. They went to war then over the land issue. Fences went up, and were torn down, and moved here, there and everywhere. Childish, it sounds, and it was. But then a couple of years ago, there was a big change. Old man Papayiannis – who's as shrewd a businessman as you'll meet – decided to embrace the future. He'd read that he could get better oil yields by investing in new equipment, and that's what he did. He raised the money by putting all his eggs in one basket, selling off the family fruit orchards to specialise only in olives. He built a new mill for his new equipment, and that cost him more than he could afford. But he was right. He did get better yields, significantly so, and folks said the oil he was producing was better quality, too. People who'd paid Kapsis's to crush their olives at their mill, deserted that ship and went for the new method. Kapsis's, meantime, did nothing but bad-mouth Papayiannis's, and talk about how the old ways are the best, and how purity and quality and taste could only be produced using two grinding stones and a donkey. Which may or may not be true.'

'And what's your view? Who produces the better oil?'

Lefteris laughed.

'You won't draw me on that,' he said. 'You must judge for yourself. Try both, and you tell me.'

'I will,' said the fat man. 'But how did it escalate into last night's tragedy?'

'Very simply. Every little thing that happened – a dead goat, a broken-down tractor, a cracked pane of glass – each blamed on the other. There're no accidents on either side, any more, no acts of God. Everything amiss, everything bad that happens, is blamed on the opposing clan. And some of those things might rightly be put down to malice. The *kleftiko*, most certainly. Dimitris's accident, probably. And I'll tell you what – it's time all their heads were knocked together, and the business was sorted, once and for all, because that boy is paying the price for all their nonsense.'

'The gods visit the sins of the fathers upon the children, as Euripides says. I agree in this case it seems unjust.' The fat man finished the almond cake, and drank the last of his juice. 'You asked me how long I will be staying. It was my intention to leave today, to return my brother to where I found him and be on my way. But I find myself both intrigued by the depth of this feud, and concerned for those involved in it. With the boy so badly injured, it seems impossible that there won't be an attempt at revenge.'

'I agree,' said Lefteris. 'The Kapsis's will never let this lie.'

'You may be surprised. People can be reasoned with, given the right incentives. So I shall stay at least another night, and visit these two olive growers to make my own judgement on their oils. It's as good a place as I can think of to begin.'

'And will your brother be wanting a room?'

'I hope not,' said the fat man, 'for your sake.'

Four

Having no memory of the route he'd taken to the hotel, the fat man was uncertain he would be able to find his car, and as he followed Lefteris's directions back to Democracy Square, none of the landmarks the proprietor had mentioned were familiar. The fat man's only recollections were of ill-lit alleyways and treacherous cobbles, but Lefteris's route was all on broad and level pathways.

The mood in the square seemed blue, and morning-after torpor subdued the waiters' back-chat as they carried coffee to a scattering of customers. A municipal truck rumbled slowly round in a swirl of circular brushes, whilst the driver's colleague emptied rubbish into a reeking oil drum strapped to a pushcart. The ashes of last night's fire had already been swept away; no marks were left on the marble but the damp whorls of the street cleaner's bristles, fading in the warmth of the sun.

At the Odyssey *ouzeri*, a man with the wearied, drooping features of a perpetual drinker was steeling himself for the day's first brandy. The patron sat at one of his own tables, cleaning his fingernails with the tine of a fork.

'*Kali mera sas*,' said the fat man. 'Do you remember me? I was here last night with a companion.'

The patron looked him up and down, taking in his unseasonal trousers and his white shoes, so discordant with the classic styling of his raincoat.

'Scruffy-looking fellow, on the skinny side?' he asked.

'That would be him.'

'Friend of yours, is he?'

'A relative.'

'I remember him, all right,' said the patron. 'He found himself some companions and drank until after three. Very free with his hospitality, he was. All the drinks were on him. Then he sent me inside for one last round, and by the time I brought out the tray, he'd disappeared. A very generous man, at my expense. If you're a relative, maybe you could settle up on his behalf?'

The fat man frowned.

'Where did he go?' he asked.

'I've no idea,' said the patron. 'Probably found himself some bench to sleep it off. I've got the constabulary on the lookout, and they'll no doubt find him, by and by. But if you'd like to take care of it now, I'll let them know the problem's fixed.'

But the fat man shook his head.

'I won't pay his debts, but I give you my word I'll make sure he does. If he reappears – though knowing him, he won't be rising early – maybe you could ask him to come and find me at the Hotel Byron? Please tell him Hermes was asking for him, and that's where I'll be.'

The fat man walked the full length of the square, and left it by a street he judged would lead him to his car. Few people were about. Though shops closed for yesterday's feast were open for business, their staff were largely idle, and on the main thoroughfare glimpsed between buildings, traffic was light. Finding a lane he thought he recognised, he followed it to its junction with another he was less sure of; but its end brought him back to the small square where he and Dino had parked.

There were balled-up *gyros* wrappers in the fountain bowl, and an empty beer bottle balanced on a dolphin's brass head. On the Tzen's boot, someone had finger-written *Clean Me* in the dirt. The watch-seller's, the bridal boutique and the lingerie shop were all open, though display lights made them no more inviting than they had been yesterday; and across the square, the shutters had been raised on a premises the fat man had not previously noticed. Under a navy and white striped awning there were tables and chairs arranged along its frontage, where the owner stood on a stepladder, watering hanging baskets filled with trailing geraniums. Pots of flourishing lavender were placed either side of the door, and a carefully painted sand-wich-board advertised handmade Italian ice cream.

The fat man wandered over to the *gelateria*. A card listing ice-cream flavours was taped inside the window, alongside several yellowing newspaper cuttings – reviews, and photo-graphs of the man on the stepladder shaking hands with camera-savvy dignitaries. The fat man read one of the captions: 'Lorenzo Rapetti receives his award from Yiannis Kanellopoulos, Minister for Culture and Tourism'. Propped against the glass was a signed, glossy photograph in a frame, a head and shoulders shot of a famous film star, though the picture wasn't recent; the film star had long ago lost his looks to smokers' wrinkles and a paunch.

The owner climbed down the stepladder. His apron was spotlessly white and well starched; he carried scents of laun-dry, and the smell of bleach. He wore a St Christopher medal-lion round his neck, and red socks and tassled loafers on his feet.

'I was admiring your display,' said the fat man. 'The praise for your ice cream is impressive. May I introduce myself? Hermes Diaktoros, of Athens.'

'Thank you. They call me Renzo. And you should try my ice cream for yourself. I think you won't be disappointed.'

'Where are you from?' asked the fat man, hearing the accent in Renzo's speech. 'I suspect you're not a native of Dendra.'

'I come from a little town near Genoa, a beautiful place where my family has lived for four generations. That's where I have roots. All my family are ice-cream makers, so in that area, it's hard for me to make a living. I came here because there's no competition to speak of. Only me.'

The fat man glanced at the long list of Renzo's flavours.

'Unfortunately, it isn't long since I finished breakfast,' he said. 'But even so, I do think I'd like a little taste.'

Renzo put down his watering can.

'Please, come inside.'

A glass-covered counter stretched across the back of the shop. By the cash register were towers of cones and boxes of sprinkles – rainbow and chocolate sugar strands, white and milk chocolate chips, chopped toasted hazelnuts and green pistachios – and bottles of syrups – raspberry, chocolate and butterscotch. There were tubs in three sizes and two sizes of spoons, and for those taking their order home, cake boxes waited for assembly, with curling ribbon to tie them with coloured bows.

Renzo was washing his hands. The fat man looked down through the glass, on to the myriad flavours in the freezer below: the palest of creamy vanillas and dark, cocoa-rich chocolate; the natural green of pistachio and the brighter green of mint; the subtle yellow of banana, the strawberry's soft pink and the fresh tints of sorbets in lemon, orange and watermelon.

Renzo dried his hands on a clean towel, and spread his arms over the freezer.

'Welcome to my empire,' he said. 'All my flavourings are natural, and everything you see is made in my kitchen here.'

'It all looks fabulous,' said the fat man. 'And to do it justice, I should come back when my appetite is better. But I could manage a little now, I'm sure.' He lingered over the coffees and caramels, and the three-striped Neapolitan. 'Perhaps a half-scoop of two flavours. What's this one here?'

'Turkish delight. A rosewater-flavoured ice cream with a dark chocolate swirl.'

'I shall try a little of that. And a little strawberry too, because it's my favourite.'

Renzo took a steel scoop from a basin and a small tub from the stack, and expertly dispensed the ice cream, planted a spoon in the Turkish delight, wrapped the tub in a navy and white striped napkin and handed it to the fat man. The fat man laid his money on the counter.

'Please,' said Renzo, 'take a seat, and enjoy it.'

The tables and chairs outside were ornate wrought iron painted white. Under one of the tables, a tan and black terrier was curled asleep, a red leather diamanté collar around its neck. As the fat man took a seat, the dog first raised an eyelid, then lifted its head and sniffed mistrustfully in his direction before struggling to its feet, and slinking away to lie under another table.

'You've done the impossible, and chased my dog away,' said Renzo. 'Usually he won't give up that table except for rain, or dinner. That's his place, and there he stays. He's an old man, and he sees no reason to defer to anyone, not even me.'

A small boy entered the square, preoccupied with the bottle cap he was playing with, but noticing the terrier shifting to get comfortable in its new spot, he narrowed his eyes to take aim, and launched the bottle cap at the dog. The cap fell short, but still the dog cowered and flattened its ears. Indifferent, the boy skipped away.

'What an unpleasant child,' said the fat man.

Renzo crouched next to the terrier, and to soothe it, stroked its head with the side of his finger.

'Those kids are no better than animals,' he said, 'and some of them are worse. They think I have peculiar foreign habits. Keeping a woman's dog is bad enough, but to keep it as nothing but a companion is beyond their understanding. In his youth, he would have given as good as he got, and nipped that lad's ankles. But that's far beyond him now, as you can see.' He rose, and sighed, and bent to retrieve the bottle cap from where it had landed. 'They care for nothing. Look, see what they do?' He pointed to the rubbish left in the fountain. 'What will they grow up to be, when they learn no respect for anything? It will be me who cleans it up, in the end. No one else will do it, only me.'

'Sadly, you cannot control those around you,' said the fat man. 'But if you are doing your best, isn't that enough?'

'I suppose you're right. And I do do my best. But, sometimes . . . So, tell me. What do you think?'

The fat man let a spoonful of strawberry ice cream melt in his mouth, and found it sublime – creamy, but enlivened by the tang of ripe fruit.

'Wonderful!' he said. 'Really, this is something special!'

Renzo smiled.

'I boost the taste with wild strawberries. I manage to find a few, in the season. And I add just a very few mint leaves, to bring out their true flavour.' Intrigued, the fat man tried the strawberry again, and there, very subtly, was a touch of mint. 'And I use no vanilla in the base. I use an unflavoured cream base, as I do when I make the lemon. Vanilla does nothing for either fruit.'

The fat man tried the Turkish delight, discovering a rosy sweetness and dark tendrils of demi-sweet chocolate.

'You present me with a dilemma, Renzo. I don't know which to enjoy first, and which to save till last. Your prizes are well deserved.'

Renzo shook his head.

'When I won those prizes, my ice cream was really something, in a class above what you're tasting now, and as it was meant to be. But things change. Nothing in life should be taken for granted.'

As the fat man finished his ice cream, a woman entered the square with a wicker basket on her arm. Her pace was steady, but when Renzo called out *Kali mera*, she walked faster, giving him no more than a silent nod. As she reached the square's far side, coming towards her was a man, carrying over his shoulder a long, wrapped parcel which seemed heavy enough to weigh him down. The woman greeted him affably, and offered some comment on the weather, and the man answered her politely.

As the man grew close to the *gelateria*, Renzo again called out.

'Hey, Miltiadis, how's it going? *Vre*, come and have a coffee. It's on me!'

The man lowered his head, and looked away.

'Another time,' he said, and went on by.

The fat man was watching Renzo. Catching his eye, Renzo gave a shrug.

'You see I'm a popular man,' he said. 'I try, and I'm rebuffed.'

'What was he carrying?' asked the fat man.

'Cloth,' said Renzo. 'He has a tailor's shop, in the next street down.'

The fat man pulled at his waistband, which was digging into the folds of his stomach.

'I'm afraid I need the services of a tailor,' he said, ruefully. 'I shall pay him a visit, later on. Renzo, I thank you for the pleasure you have given me with your wonderful ice cream. No doubt I shall see you again, before I leave.'

Five

The fat man drove carefully down the narrow alley away from the square, and following Lefteris's directions, turned right on to Dendra's main thoroughfare to make his way towards the olive groves at the town's perimeter. By a chapel which predated the buildings of the outskirts by several centuries, he took the left fork towards open country. To east and west, the land lay in drifts of low hills and shallow valleys. The new growths of grasses and clovers invoked by autumn rains gave the illusion of fertility; but rocks and stones were everywhere in the fields, and limestone outcrops made barren islands in meadows stippled with white crocuses and rosy-purple colchicum.

In the groves, the silvery-leaved olive trees grew in orderly rows, the vast black nets for gathering their fruit in rolls around their roots or spread across the ground ready for the harvest. Many of the trees were uniform in age, but all were diverse in their anatomies; the passing centuries had contorted each one uniquely, twisting only the branches in some, distorting others with huge swellings from the roots, or opening fissures and holes where daylight shone through and a man might without difficulty pass his fist.

There were few firm divisions on the land – only long-collapsed walls which had once marked boundaries or confined sheep – until the fat man rounded a bend, and saw ahead of him a high fence of deer netting, which ran perpendicular from the road across country, splitting one of the orchards into two.

The fence was incongruous with the landscape, an eyesore intruding on an idyll. The fat man stopped the car, and reversing to where fence and road met, climbed out. The deer netting seemed illogically placed. It enclosed no land, and so was useless for containing livestock; it was simply a divider, running in a straight line, except at one point where it dog-legged, continuing shortly afterwards in its original track. There were no gates or openings, so anyone wanting to move from one part of the grove to the other would be forced to walk back to the road, or carry on to the fence's far end, hidden beyond a dip in the land.

The fat man rattled the netting, sending a metallic shiver down its length. The fence was sturdy, the posts and staples almost new. Whoever had erected it, had made certain it was solidly fixed.

He studied the divided land, finding no differences between the two tracts. The trees were all of the *Koroneiki* cultivar, their branches still laden with their distinctive dusty-green drupes; all were expertly pruned, and the ground between them was equally well tended.

He followed the fence along its left-hand side, orchard grasses brushing the hems of his trousers. The trees on both sides at first seemed healthy; but at the dog-leg, a number of trees were showing signs of disease.

The fat man approached an ailing tree. Running his fingers over the bark, he followed knots, whorls and fissures, tracing a distorted face in the aged trunk. He walked around the tree, and crouched down by its roots, then looked slowly up and down its length. Above his head was a daub of dried mud. He stood, and peering closely, found a ring of mud daubs around the tree. He scratched at one, and it flaked easily away. Licking the pad of a finger, he rubbed where the mud had been, and revealed a circle of bright copper set in the grey bark.

He took a Swiss army knife from his raincoat pocket, and prised out from its many attachments a petite pair of pliers. Applying the tips to the circle of metal, he eased out from the wood a long copper nail.

The mud daubs all hid nails. Painstakingly, he pulled all that he could find from the first tree, then moved on to the others that were sickly. When there were no more nails to be found, he gathered up his collection in both hands; there were perhaps fifty, the contents of a hardware merchant's bag. He searched amongst the tree roots for a hollow, and dropped the nails in, hiding them under handfuls of grass. Then, as if taking leave of a valued friend, he patted a tree on its trunk, and walked back to his car.

A kilometre along the road, the olive groves ended in rough pasture, where goats foraged amongst thorny shrubs for wild greens and herbs. A sign advertising olive oil for sale was hammered into the verge, and pointed down a dirt track, which the fat man followed.

The low-slung Tzen coped badly with the ridges and potholes, and the fat man drove cautiously to avoid damage to the exhaust. A line of stately cypress trees stretched skywards, the globes of their cones amber baubles in the sun, and around their feet was a builder's rubbish: a broken ladder, a cracked bucket, burst paper sacks of rain-hardened cement. Beyond the trees, the track forked. The fat man braked to a halt, and with the engine running, considered; then he put the car back into gear, and went left.

He passed through a gateway into a yard fronting a farmhouse and outbuildings. The place had age enough to be a curiosity, its origins lying in the house itself, where the door had once been central and the windows matched; but there had been extensions and renovations with no attempt to blend with the original, so the architecture of the elongated house flirted with styles and eras, and its façade was now set with an eccentric mix of windows – large and small, rectangular, square and round. The walls had been patched and restored, though the mortar was still crumbling in places, and more work was needed where the stone's natural weathering had deteriorated into decay. Here and there the red roof tiles had slipped, and crude repairs had been made to the chimneys where years of acid smoke had perished them; and on a chimney pot sprawled the great, precarious tangle of a stork's nest, a flamboyant woven disorder of sticks and twigs.

The yard's size suggested the farm had once thrived, though the stalls for livestock were all disused, piled up with rotting hay long past usefulness as feed, and fit only for nesting rats. A dilapidated lean-to was stacked to the roof with olive-wood logs. But where the bulk of the old farm-workings might once have been – the granary, dairy and presses – was now one single-storey building, with frosted glass in its windows and skylights in its roof, with the stones left over from its building stacked along its side, and lumps of hardened cement covering its forecourt.

Behind the new building, a young man at the wheel of an idle fork-lift truck was leafing through the pages of a newspaper; two others sat on full sacks of olives, smoking, flicking ash on to the empty sacks which lay around their feet and oblivious to the noise of a conveyor belt running unused at their backs. The fat man parked next to a silver Opel with rusted wheel arches and a dent in its driver's door, and taking his hold-all with him, waved a greeting to the men, and headed for an open door below a sign reading *Sales*.

Inside, the building was as broad and long as a warehouse, with no divisions from one end to the other, so the racket and clatter of machinery rebounded off every wall. The hospital-clean floors were painted functional grey, and all the steel and aluminium plant – vats, hoppers, pipes, valves – gleamed with polishing. Nowhere were there any olives to be seen, except on shelves above a counter and a cash register; there, various sizes of oil cans were displayed, all bearing a stylised view of olive groves, fronted by a cartoon-like picture of lustrous olives framed by branches of healthy green leaves, and in cursive black script, *D. Papayiannis & Son, Extra-virgin Olive Oil*.

Donatos Papayiannis sat in his wheelchair, his walking canes resting against its arm. On his knee lay a spiral-bound notebook where he had been making calculations with a blue crayon, now tucked behind his ear. Hard fluorescent lights emphasised the purplish flush on his face.

'*Kalos tou*,' he said. He slipped the notebook down the side of his seat-cushion, grasped his canes and heaved himself from the chair, struggling a little to do so and tangling his legs with the sticks.

The fat man stepped forward to help him, but Donatos balanced himself, and motioned the fat man back.

'Leave me,' he said, loudly enough to be heard over the machinery. 'I can manage. What can I do for you?'

The fat man looked around.

'This is an impressive operation,' he said, similarly raising his voice. 'Very impressive indeed. Everything is so . . . clean.'

'We pride ourselves on our cleanliness.' Donatos paused for breath before he went on, the machinery's din covering the wheezing in his lungs. 'My son polishes that floor himself, and does it better than any woman. I always say, if we ever spilled any oil, you could sit down with a piece of bread, and mop it up and eat it.'

'As it happens, I'm here to try your oil,' said the fat man, 'though I would prefer not to eat it off the floor.'

Donatos turned away unsmiling, and said something the fat man didn't catch. He made his way wheezing to the shelves, leaned his sticks against the counter, and from underneath took out a part-filled bottle of oil and a glass tasting cup. He unscrewed the cap from the bottle and prepared to pour oil into the little cup, but his hand trembled, and he hesitated.

'May I help?' asked the fat man.

Donatos shrugged, and conceded, holding out both bottle and cup. The fat man took them, and Donatos picked up his canes.

'Heart trouble,' he said, making his way painstakingly back to his wheelchair. 'I have good days, and bad days. Damn thing doesn't work the way it used to. If it were an electric pump in there, I'd have it out and put in a new one.'

'You could have a new one, or at least replace some parts,' said the fat man. 'Modern medicine can do almost anything, these days. What does your doctor advise?'

'Doctors? Pah!' Donatos grimaced, and might have spat, if the floors hadn't been so clean. 'I don't believe in doctors! A fast way to a quick death, putting your faith in doctors!'

He sat down heavily in his wheelchair.

'Of course there's a fair amount of quackery in the world,' said the fat man. 'And the medical profession is prone, these days, to treating symptoms and not causes.' He glanced covertly at Donatos's dark-red colour. 'Take high blood pressure, for example. Doctors will give you tablets, whereas by far the best prescription is sea water.'

Donatos leaned towards him, thinking he had misheard.

'Sea water?'

'My prescription is simple. Find a place by the sea which pleases you – a sandy beach, a promenade, a quayside if you like boats. Then sit down there, and watch the sea. I recommend three or four hours at a time, and the treatment must be taken daily. Within a month, most of your ailments will be cured.'

Donatos gave a bark of laughter.

'Whoever has so much time to spend looking at the sea? We have a business to run.'

'Your response to my prescription is a common one. People say they have no time, with no sense of irony at the fact that stress is shortening their lives, perhaps by decades. But I stand by what I say. In your case, though, I am surprised to hear you suffer from heart problems, since it seems probable you have pure olive oil running through your veins, and that should strengthen your heart. Is there a history of it in your family?'

'On the contrary.' Like a small boy, Donatos raised his chin to boast. 'My father lived till he was ninety-three, and never had a day's illness in his life. He went to bed one night after a good dinner and a glass of wine, and never woke up. That's the way we should all go. Not puffing and wheezing like some damned invalid.'

The fat man held up the bottle and the tasting cup.

'May I?'

'Yes, yes,' said Donatos. 'Try it. It's not the new season's, but the quality's still there.'

The fat man poured out a measure of oil. Its colour was brilliant green, and as soon as it left the bottle, its aroma bloomed – grassy, vital, swelling with the scent of the fruit. He took a drink, holding the silky oil in his mouth, enjoying the burst of intense greenness, the depths of ripe olives on his tongue; then he swallowed, and the pepperiness of the oil burned his throat. He coughed, and shook his head; he coughed again.

Donatos smiled.

'That's Papayiannis oil,' he said. 'As fiery and peppery as you'll find.'

The fat man nodded his appreciation.

'It's good. Very, very good.'

'You taste that bite?' asked Donatos, breathing hard. 'Those are *Koroneiki* olives, through and through. No blending, no dilution. That's the pure oil, as it should be.'

'It really is excellent,' said the fat man. 'And I must admit to being slightly surprised. Your place looks like a factory, yet this oil sings of the orchard, and if I were asked, I'd say it could only be the product of old-fashioned methods.'

'Pah!' Donatos waved a dismissive hand. 'People believe in the superiority of the old ways, but it's all a myth. The ignorant will tell you the best olive oil comes from millstones and donkey-power. Rubbish! What you get from millstones and donkeys is hard labour and waste. All the major prizes these days go to mechanically produced oils. Since we installed these machines, we've better quality oil and far better yields. In other words, we get old-fashioned flavour, but it's economically viable. Greek oil has always been the best in the world, and if more farmers would let go of their notions that quantity comes at the price of quality, the whole of the industry could be revitalised. But they can be stubborn and pig-headed, *kyrie*. They're frightened of change, and they dress up their fear as patriotism. They'll tell you Greek oil's always been made the same way, two men and a donkey, and that's how it should stay. But there's no one more patriotic than me! Greek oil for Greek people, that's what we produce here, the oil the heroes knew. Our oil is top quality, fit for the Hellenes, but we produce it cheaply enough that we stand a chance of not going bankrupt in the process. And let me tell you, the competition out there is fierce! They're flooding us with cheap oil from Spain and Italy, even Morocco, and we must all work together and refuse to sink under the tide. We all of us have a duty to stand up to the importers, and stop the flow. Those machines are my legacy to the next generation, and the generation after that. If we can do well as a family, we succeed both for ourselves and for Greece, by keeping our pride in a national industry. That's something money can't buy. The oil you have there . . .'

He stopped, and grimacing, bent forward in his chair; the colour of his face darkened, and he held his breath, as if to carry himself through pain.

'Should I fetch someone?'

Donatos shook his head vehemently. 'I'll do all right in a minute,' he said.

A metallic-red Nissan pick-up drove on to the yard, kicking up stones as it turned in a tight arc, and parked facing the gateway, showing the sign-writer's work on the driver's door – *Papayiannis Premium Oils*. 'Here's my son. Don't for God's sake say you've seen me unwell, or he'll be nagging me again to see doctors. I don't want doctors.'

'I shall say nothing.'

He watched Sakis Papayiannis as he crossed the yard, his hair uncombed and dishevelled, his work clothes scruffy and his boots dirty. Unlike many good-looking men, he moved without strut or swagger; instead, he walked with his head low, as if he might be shy, and quickly, as if he might be late.

He checked his watch, and a look of anxiety crossed his face; then he began to search his jacket pockets, pulling out a wad of scrappy papers, shuffling through them for one which eluded him.

As he came into the mill, he was still searching.

'Here I am, Papa,' he said. He found the paper he wanted, shoved the others back in his pocket, and looked up to greet his father. His eyes passed rapidly over the fat man, flickering as he noticed the white tennis shoes.

'*Kali mera sas*,' he said. He laid the paper on the counter, and spoke again to his father. 'I found Bouloukas's number, so maybe you could ring him. Tell him Tuesday's no good, it'll have to be Wednesday. You'd better use the phone in the house, it's too noisy in here. They're almost done picking in the far orchard, but they're running out of sacks, so I'll take them some of the empty ones from the yard.' He paused, and looked quizzically at his father. 'Are you all right?'

'Of course I'm all right,' said Donatos. 'For God's sake, stop worrying.'

'Here. I almost forgot.' Sakis dropped a paper bag into his father's lap. 'A gift for you.'

The old man smiled, and dipping his hand into the bag, chose a piece of almond praline. Before he put it in his mouth, he held the bag out to the fat man.

'Here,' he said. 'Try some.'

'Thank you,' said the fat man, and took a piece, enjoying as he ate it the crunch of the brittle caramel, and the slight bitterness of the almonds.

'My son says I eat too much of it,' said Donatos, choosing another piece, 'but I say at my age, a little of what you fancy does you good.'

'The word there is little,' said Sakis. 'You do eat too much.'

'If you don't want me to eat it, don't bring it to me. You're not logical.'

'I might as well bring it you. If I didn't bring it to you, she'd bring it to you herself.'

Donatos smiled again, a little archly.

'My son thinks the lady who makes it has a crush on me,' he said. 'And maybe she has. There's life in me yet, and the ladies can see it, even if he can't. By the way, Sakis . . .' He pulled the notebook out from the side of his seat. 'I still don't think you've got the setting right on that macerator. We'd be better on a slower setting. You said you'd look at it earlier.'

'And I did.'

'I never saw you.'

There was a fraction of a pause.

'If it will make you happy, Papa, I'll check it again.' Sakis turned to the fat man. 'Can I help you with something?'

The fat man held up the oil bottle and tasting cup.

'Your father has already been an invaluable help,' he said, 'and I'm about to buy some of your oil. But before I do, might you outline to me the process you use here? To the layman's eye, one machine looks much like another. And the place is so orderly, it seems to introduce the chaos of loose olives would be a crime.'

Sakis laughed.

'It's called progress, *kyrie*,' he said. 'And I'd be glad to show you, but the pickers are waiting for me back at the orchards.'

'They'll wait,' said Donatos, his mouth full of half-chewed praline. 'Show the gentleman what he wants to see. Those idlers will be only too pleased to have an extra five minutes on their backsides.'

Sakis opened his mouth to object, but changed his mind.

'Very well,' he said to the fat man. 'I'll give you the grand tour.'

'I'd be very grateful. The last time I saw olives pressed, they were using grindstones and hemp mats.'

'And the process was romantic, wasn't it?' asked Sakis. 'A taste of old Greece? If you want to see it again, you need go no further than our neighbours, over at the Kapsis place.'

'Kapsis,' mused the fat man. 'Kapsis. The name is familiar. Am I right in thinking it was one of the Kapsis family who was burned last night? The poor young man who fell into the bonfire? I myself was almost a witness, and I did see the aftermath. Were you there?'

'I wasn't there, no.'

'In fact it was suggested to me – and please don't take offence – but it was said that the boy might have been tripped, or even pushed, by a member of your family. Could that possibly be true?'

Donatos was studying his notebook, and didn't hear. Sakis seemed untroubled by the question.

'Gossip,' he said, 'nothing more. The boy missed his footing – that's easily done, when you're doing something as dangerous as jumping over a bonfire. There have been accidents before, over the years, and no one's tried to say anyone was pushed. People know of the rivalry between our families, and they build it into something it's not. Personally, I regard it as healthy competition. Kapsis's and Papayiannis's have more in common than they have differences. We're both in the same business, and both our fortunes rise or fall depending on the crop from our trees. A bad harvest doesn't recognise property boundaries any more than does a good one. We're brothers in this trade.'

'But you don't approve of their methods?'

'How can I disapprove? Their methods have been used for centuries. What I don't understand is, when better methods come along, why don't they embrace them? Maybe their sense of romance is overdeveloped, whilst I have none at all. I think what you'd call romantic is no more than ignorance. Though I admit those old ways have a certain picturesque appeal, a nostalgia which might be seductive. You should go and see for yourself, admire all their antiques. But believe me, there's no place for nostalgia in modern oil production. We may lack sentimentality, but our oils are better and better for you, more hygienic and more economical to produce. With our investment – and it was a big investment, as you can tell – we can take our business forward. If we insisted on sticking with traditional methods, there's no way we'd be producing oil in ten years' time. Those are the economic facts. As a sideline, yes, of course – if you're pressing oil for your family's use, for a few friends, then by all means stick with your donkeys. But we have no business but olive oil, and as such we owe it to ourselves, to our family, to stay in business. This is the only way we can do that. So go and visit them, and try their oil. Then come back and buy ours, when you've proven to yourself it's not only cheaper, but better.'

The fat man was thoughtful.

'Don't you find that in any way – sad?'

'There's nothing sad about making more of what God's given you,' put in Donatos, bullishly. 'God gave us ingenuity so we could improve our lot, not to sit around wondering how to put food on our family's plates.'

'We can't afford to find it sad,' said Sakis. 'We have bills to pay. And anyway, better to look forward in life, not backwards. Something old doesn't automatically have more value than something new. Is electric light not an improvement over candles?'

'Sometimes,' said the fat man, 'but not always. A romantic dinner, for example. In the glare of electric light, it isn't romantic at all.'

'But romance is overrated,' said Donatos, with a sly smile. 'There's many a poor sap fallen for a woman by candlelight, and when the sun comes up been horrified at what he's bedded! Candlelight's a woman's device, *kyrie*, and you'd be a fool to be sucked in by it. Never trust a woman who won't let you turn on the lights!'

'Maybe I might warm more to these new processes if I understood them,' said the fat man. 'Ignorance breeds mistrust, and I am not immune from that.'

'Come on, then,' said Sakis. 'I'll take you through it, from start to finish.'

He walked briskly towards the back of the mill. The fat man followed.

'May I ask,' he said, as they went, 'how much did all this cost you?'

'Look around you. You can see there's many millions of drachma in this operation. We had some savings – Papa has always been good with money – but there was a bank loan too. There had to be. But we proved to the bank's satisfaction that the new plant could pay for itself in six years. In year seven, we'll be in profit.'

'What year are you in now?'

'This is our second year. And thanks be to God, the harvest is good.'

'My congratulations to you. To have developed a plan and followed it through is admirable. You must be proud.'

Any answer Sakis gave was drowned out by the machinery at the back of the factory. Beyond the rear door, the fork-lift driver was still reading his newspaper, but the two young men the fat man had seen smoking had been roused by Sakis's arrival, and were busy now loading a steel hopper, using hunting-knives to slit the twine that bound the overfilled sacks, grunting as they took the weight and tumbled in the olives.

Sakis reached down into the hopper, and picking out an olive, held it up to the light to examine it. Seeming satisfied, he dropped it back in.

'Here's where we start.' He shouted over the noise of the compartmentalised conveyor belt, which was now carrying olives upwards, into the building. 'The olives go via these belts to the first stage of processing, which is washing, which takes place up here.' He pointed up at a great stainless-steel box, but from ground level there was little to see. 'The first step in the oil extraction process is cleaning the olives and removing any leaves and twigs. We wash the olives with water, and any debris is left behind in the bath.' He led the fat man on. 'When they come out of the washer, the olives are fed into this hopper here . . .' He slapped the hopper on its side. 'They go through this pipe here . . .' He pointed to a pipe leading almost vertically upwards. 'Then into the crusher.'

Sakis led the fat man back through the factory, all the way shouting explanations of how the process worked; and all the way there was nothing to see but pipes and metal boxes, nothing to hear but the whirr and clatter of machinery, and the slooshing and trickling of unseen liquid.

'Crushing releases the oil from the fruit. You can do it the old way, with millstones, or with metal-tooth grinders as we use here. We mix the paste in a process called malaxation, which combines the small droplets into bigger ones. Longer mixing times increase oil yield but allow a longer oxidation period that decreases shelf life, so we keep our malaxation process to a minimum. At this point the product looks very unattractive – it's a mush of crushed olives the colour of soldiers' camouflage. But then the magic begins. Now we come to separation.'

Sakis stopped in front of a huge metal cylinder.

'We used to do this with presses and hemp mats, but now we use a dual-phase centrifuge, which separates the oil from the wet paste. Here you see the first centrifuge; over there, the second, with these overhead pipes' – he pointed to them – 'carrying the oil from one to the other.' The fat man looked across at the second centrifuge, a complex arrangement of square tanks, gauges, pipes, and displays with lights and switches. 'And there, you see the baths the final product runs into. Around the back are the tanks where we rack the oil – the final separation which happens through gravity. What we end up with is the oil you tasted from that bottle over there.'

They made their way back to the counter. Donatos had turned to a clean page in his notebook, and was making notes in the awkward hand of one unused to writing.

'Did you check those settings?' he asked. 'I'm going to get the engineer to come over here and see what he thinks.'

'You've been very generous with your time,' said the fat man to Sakis. 'Let me take a litre of oil, and get out of your way.'

As Sakis reached a bottle down from the shelves, the fat man took money from his wallet.

'I notice you have a stork's nest on your roof,' he said. 'That's a token of good luck.'

'Luck?' Sakis gave a dubious laugh. 'You wouldn't say that if you were cleaning up their mess all summer. Sticks, and feathers, and muck! And the noise they make, fidgeting and flapping on the roof! If it were down to me, I'd shoot the damn birds, and pull that nest down and burn it.'

'Not while I'm alive!' objected Donatos. 'And not when I'm gone, either! They're beautiful birds, and that nest's been there since my grandfather's time. And the gentleman's right. The storks are lucky.'

'There's a stork's nest at the ruins of Ephesus,' said the fat man, accepting his change. 'On top of one of the pillars of the Temple of Artemis. It's been there for many, many years, and is quite remarkable to see. Storks are very faithful birds, when it comes to nesting.'

Outside, a small Datsun pick-up swept on to the yard; its front wing was battered and rusted from some long-bygone collision; the headlight was held in place with electrician's tape. The driver swung the Datsun round, pulled up along-side the red Nissan pick-up and gave three blasts on his horn.

'They need those sacks,' said Sakis. 'I have to go.'

The fat man picked up his oil.

'Thank you for this, and for the tour. You've shed light where I was ignorant. And I wish you the best of luck with your enterprise.'

The fat man walked slowly to his car. Sakis was loading empty sacks into the Datsun; when he was done, he climbed in beside the driver and slammed the door. As the Datsun drove away, the fat man raised his hand in farewell; but Sakis was in heated discussion with the driver, and didn't respond.

Donatos manoeuvred himself over to the counter, and found the phone number Sakis had left. He picked up the phone, and dialled. Pressing the receiver hard against his ear, block-ing his other ear with a finger against the machinery's noise, he heard the click of the connection being made, and the number he was dialling ring out. There was no answer. He broke the connection, and dialled again, taking special care to get the digits right. Again, there was no answer.

75

He dropped the receiver back in its cradle. Sakis had left the Nissan's keys on the counter. Donatos picked them up, and laying his walking canes across his knees, wheeled himself out into the yard.

Six

The fat man lodged his olive oil upright behind his hold-all, and drove as far as the point where the track forked. Checking his watch, he found there was an hour or two at least before lunchtime, and so he followed the right-hand road to the Kapsis estate.

The Kapsis's property had similarities to the Papayiannis's; the same high walls of old stone marked the yard's boundaries, and the farmhouse's origins lay in the same era, though its improvements were more conventional, and truer to a single architectural style.

The fat man parked the Tzen in the equivalent place to where he'd parked in the Papayiannis yard, between a once-black Citroën whose paintwork was sun-faded to an uneven gunmetal, and a run of ramshackle livestock pens where the original roofs had fallen in, and the woodworm-infested struts now supported tin sheets weighted with rocks. The pens held several milk-goats, and as he climbed from the car, the goats stopped chewing on the scraps of cabbage leaves littering their dirty straw, and watched him with their strange, slit eyes. A trickle of water ran into their trough, with the overflow draining through the foul-smelling straw and across the yard. Outside the pen was a milking-stool, a leather apron hanging on a nail and an overturned bucket. Chickens pecked at the weeds growing around an Italian scooter, whose windscreen was cracked from base to top; a rusting tractor had the field debris of its final outing dried deep in its tyre treads, and below its chassis a duck slept, its head hidden under its wing. On a heap of olive nets, a cockerel stretched its neck and crowed.

Taking care to avoid the chicken and duck droppings which littered the yard, the fat man made his way towards the farmhouse. Effort had been made to care for the old building – scented geraniums and mauve crocuses flourished in the window boxes, and the whitewash on the façade was reasonably fresh – but the whitewash didn't hide the bulge of a failing wall and a troubling crack which ran from ground to eaves. Outside the front door, a trellis supported a trailing vine, whose autumn-red leaves were thinning on its tendrils; and under the trellis was Marianna Kapsis, watching a small boy pump up the tyre of his bicycle.

'Give it a bit more elbow-grease,' said Marianna to the boy. 'You'll be here all day doing it like that.'

The boy's arm moved faster, but the pump's head came away from the tyre valve. The boy's eyes filled with tears.

'I can't do it, *Yiayia*,' he wailed. 'Can't you do it for me? Papa always does it for me.'

Marianna flicked ash from her cigarette, and looked down at the child's grubby hands and the bike's oil-clogged chain. She studied her rose-pink nails. On her right index finger, the varnish was chipped.

'Papa isn't here, *kamari mou*,' she said. 'And your *Yiayia* doesn't know anything about bicycles.'

'May I help?' asked the fat man, as he reached them. He gave the boy a warm smile, and held out his hand to Marianna. 'Hermes Diaktoros, of Athens. I'm here to buy some of your

78

oil, but if I can do this young man a service, I'm happy to do so.'

Indifferently, Marianna scrutinised him; but having taken in his bearing and the calibre of his clothes, she passed her cigarette to her left hand, and contriving a smile, held out her right. As he took it, he caught the sharpness of the hairspray holding her swept-back style. Under her dress and cardigan, her figure was spreading, and inside her sling-back shoes, the skin of her heels was cracked and pale; but her make-up, though unsubtle, flattered her face, and covered the inevitable wanness of middle age.

'Marianna Kapsis,' she said. '*Kalos irthate*.'

'Thank you,' said the fat man, and moving closer to the boy, he bent down and held his hand out again. 'And what do they call you?'

The boy was shy, and fiddling with the pump and the valve, lowered his head.

'Answer the gentleman, Yianni,' said Marianna, drawing on her cigarette.

'Yianni, eh?' said the fat man. 'If you don't want to talk to me, I don't mind. But I am rather good with bicycle pumps, so if you'd like me to help you, give me a little room, and I will.' In silence, the boy shifted back a metre or two, and the fat man crouched beside him, and fitted the pump to the tyre. With several quick motions, the tyre was inflated, and the cap screwed back on to the valve. 'Good as new. And that's a very smart bike. I wonder if you like nougat?' Again, the boy didn't reply, but the fat man stood, and reached into his pocket to draw out a long bar of pink nougat studded with pistachios. 'I had two of these, but I could only eat one. I'll leave it here on your bicycle saddle, in case you'd like it. And if you wouldn't, maybe you have a brother or a sister who would.'

The boy ignored him, and made a show of testing the pressure of his front tyre, squeezing the rubber between finger and thumb.

'Say thank you, Yianni,' said Marianna.

The boy remained silent. Marianna gave the fat man another smile.

'Children,' she said. 'You do your best. So, you're wanting some oil?'

'I am,' said the fat man. 'I hear good things about Kapsis olive oil.'

She dropped her cigarette, and ground it out under the toe of her shoe.

'I'll show you the mill,' she said.

In the position where, on the Papayiannis property, the new factory was built, on the Kapsis yard was a long barn of unworked stone and crude terracotta tiles. Bulging sacks of olives were stacked outside the great arched doors at its centre. Marianna pulled open the left-hand door, and led him into the barn.

There were no windows, only air-vents through which weak rays of sunlight lit motes of drifting dust. Under the naked undersides of the tiles, a fluttering sparrow settled on one of the old beams, where drifts of powdery cobwebs dangled from the struts.

Marianna snapped on a Bakelite switch, and the overhead lights flickered and faded before filling the barn with jaundiced light, which revealed at the barn's far end a colossal vat cut from a single piece of stone and mounted on a plinth. Over the vat, a haphazard collection of beams and poles were rigged to turn a system of iron cogs, which in turn revolved three millstones within the vat, set upright and attached to a central spindle. Around the vat, a shallow groove worn in the stone-flagged floor marked the track of generations of donkeys. Against the rear wall was a press, a rectangular arch of black iron pierced by a lengthy bolt, at whose base was a tall stack of round hemp mats. Nearby was an old-fashioned generator, set up to drive the engine for a system of canvas belts which brought some measure of automation to the old-fashioned mill, and the rest of the equipment necessary for oil production – troughs and storage tanks, sieves and sinks.

The fat man went to the vat, slapped the stone appreciatively, and looked up admiringly at the ingenious complexities of the machinery above it. Marianna followed him.

'This is a splendid piece of equipment,' he said. 'Do you know its date?'

'The year I couldn't tell you,' she said, 'but it goes back six generations at least. The Kapsis's aren't amateur oil-producers, *kyrie*. If there's anything to know about oil, this family knows it.'

'And you still employ the traditional methods. That's increasingly rare, these days.' He touched one of the millstones. Grinding had worn the cold surface smooth. 'I paid a visit to your neighbours before I came here.' He moved to the far side of the vat, and watched her as he spoke. 'Their operation is very different from yours. They seem to have embraced the new technology wholeheartedly.'

'A man may embrace a pig,' said Marianna, curtly, 'but it won't make for a happy marriage. You'd like to try the oil before you buy, I'm sure.'

'I would.'

By the doors was a table covered with the untidy mess of running the business: leather-bound ledgers and cheap invoice books, letters in coffee-stained envelopes, plates from bygone meals, loose papers, pencils and pens. Under the table were several boxes, irregular sizes and made for varied products – wine, biscuits and bleach. Marianna crouched to lift the flaps on a box, and lifted out a bottle of oil.

She sat down in a captain's chair, and ran her hands over the worn arms.

'This was my husband's chair,' she said. 'Every time I sit here, I think of him. He was a fine, tall man, strong, like you.' She looked at him, very directly. 'Are you married, *kalé*?'

'I? No. I'm not the marrying kind.'

'All men say that. Don't think you're too old. My husband was well over fifty when I married him, and I made him very happy. Maybe you should think about it. It isn't natural for a man to live alone. It isn't healthy. Maybe you just need to find the right woman.'

The fat man laughed.

'Maybe you're right,' he said, 'but I'm not quite the catch you might think. I'm here one day, and gone the next, and not marriage material at all.'

She opened a drawer in the table, and taking out a glass tasting cup identical to the one offered by Donatos Papayiannis, held it up to the daylight, revealing an oily fingerprint.

'Allow me,' said the fat man, pulling a paisley silk handkerchief from his pocket. He wiped the cup thoroughly, and put the handkerchief back in his pocket.

Marianna uncapped the bottle and poured a measure of oil into the cup.

'We've none of this season's bottled yet, but last season's is still in its prime,' she said. 'You've tasted their oil, now try ours. See what a difference tradition makes. You'll taste the history of Greece in Kapsis oil. Those stones give their essence to the oil, and you can't fake that with steel. Stones and olives are God-given gifts, meant to complement each other. Do we see steel occurring naturally in nature? No, we do not. Steel gives nothing to the oil. The oil slides off it. But those millstones that crush our olives came from the same earth that grew them. They were made to work together, and are *sympatico* with each other. The same with the press. Kapsis women cut that hemp, and wove those mats with their own hands. Hemp and olives, from the same soil. Papayiannis oil, what is that? Spun and forced from the olives in a centrifuge, all hard metal. My husband used to say our oil has soul, and everything we do here, we do with respect, and we use this method not because we are backwards, not because we are dinosaurs, but because we carry on the traditions of the land, because we respect quality and want the best product. Everything here has its place and its part, and you'll find that in the flavour of the oil. Here, taste.' She held out the glass. The oil's colour was striking, the yellow light giving an acid tint to its extraordinary greenness. 'Taste.' Her expression was intense, almost fanatical, her evangelism such that she might, had she been able, have tipped the oil down his throat herself.

He took a drink of the oil, played it over his tongue, and swallowed. Its flavour burst in his mouth, a distillation of grassy meadows and the olive groves, the essence, as she had said, of the olives themselves; and as he swallowed, his throat burned with a pepperiness so fiery, he coughed, and coughed again.

'There!' she said. 'You taste that fieriness, that burn! What do you think?'

'It's good,' he said. 'It's very good indeed.' He savoured the rest of the oil, working it round his mouth to draw out its subtleties.

'Better than mechanical oil, for certain,' she said. 'You'll acknowledge that, I'm sure. This oil is pure, oil as it was meant to be.'

'It is excellent, and I shall be pleased to buy a litre. I know my father would like to try it. He regards himself as a connoisseur of oils.'

'You should take two litres, then. One for yourself, and one for him.'

'No, no,' said the fat man. 'He has orchards of his own. A taste of mine will suffice.'

She named a price somewhat higher than Papayiannis's. As the fat man took out his wallet, sparrows fluttered overhead, and a small, brown feather dropped on to Marianna's shoulder.

'Those birds,' she said, brushing it off. 'It's impossible to keep them out. They get in under the eaves.'

The fat man looked up at white smears of excrement on the beams.

'I must say,' he said carefully, handing over his money, 'your neighbours' operation looks very prosperous.'

She laughed, and dug into a cash box for change.

'Appearances deceive,' she said. 'They're up to their necks in debt. They borrowed millions to turn that farm into a factory, and it'll take years before they break even. We make an honest living here, and pay our dues as they arise. My husband left me no debts, and I've incurred none since I lost him. Every year, we show a profit. Honest oil from honest people. How can it not be better than factory oil from a bunch of thieves?'

'Thieves?' The fat man slipped his change into his wallet. 'In what way are they thieves?'

'You'll have seen as you drove in that ugly fence between our properties. Through all the past generations, no fences were ever needed. That fence went up – and imagine what they paid for it, *kalé* – for one reason only. They wanted to claim trees that aren't theirs. The line is in the wrong place, and they know it. They're desperate people, *kalé*. They think stealing our trees will save them, but it won't. It'll take more than trees to save them from foreclosure.'

'When did the fence go up?'

'It was the old man's doing. He got into a dispute with my husband, and he's never put it behind him. I think worry about that man's malice helped my husband to his grave. Donatos Papayiannis is an evil and bitter old man.'

The fat man's eyebrows lifted.

'Really? He didn't strike me that way.'

'Because the man's a chameleon, a creature who changes his colours depending on his company. But he's bred them all to be spiteful and vindictive. Vindictive beyond belief.'

She turned her face away, but not before he saw the tears filling her eyes.

'May I ask,' he said, cautiously, 'vindictive in what way?'

'My grandson, *kyrie*! That fine young man, in the prime of his life, is at this moment in a hospital bed, horribly burned! His poor face!' She seemed about to break down; then she found strength, gathered herself and stood up. 'I must get back to Yianni. His mother is my granddaughter, Dmitris's sister. I have care of him whilst they're all at his bedside. And in the meantime, the mill is idle. My stepson supervises the mill, and of course he can't think of working, but every hour the olives aren't pressed, they deteriorate. That's what our neighbours have done to us – my grandson's life ruined, and a harvest and a pressing falling behind, maybe entirely lost.'

'Is there no possibility it was an accident? Boys who leap bonfires know they take a risk. They do it as an act of bravery.'

'It was no accident,' she said, fiercely. 'He was tripped.'

'Have you visited him?' asked the fat man, as they went outside.

She nodded.

'I saw him last night, and it broke my heart – his head all bandaged, his arm so red and raw . . . He wasn't conscious. They're keeping him sedated.'

'And are the police investigating your suspicions?'

'They say their hands are tied, that there are no witnesses. They're lazy, and want no trouble.'

'I'm very much afraid you may be right,' said the fat man. The day was moving into afternoon, and the sun was high; the flowers in their pots were fully open to its benign warmth. 'One thing before I go. The crocuses over there, below the window.'

She glanced across the yard.

'The mauve? They're pretty, aren't they?'

'*Colchicum autumnale*, the autumn crocus, sometimes called "naked ladies" because of their habit of flowering before they show their leaves. Where did you get them?'

She shrugged.

'I really don't remember. Somewhere out in the fields.'

'If you'll take my advice, you'll take them back there, as far away as possible from your family, certainly as far away as you can from any children. They might be pretty, as you say, but they are a deadly poisonous plant.'

On the road back into Dendra, the fat man found a phone box, and stopped the car. Searching in his pocket, he found change for a long-distance call, and from his hold-all, pulled out a little notebook with a tiny pencil tucked inside the spine. Flicking through the back pages to a list of contact details, he found the number he wanted, and dialled.

Within a moment or two, a woman answered.

'Ilias Mentis, legal services,' she said.

'*Yassou, koukla mou,*' said the fat man, in a light tone.

'*Kyrie* Diaktoros, *yassou*!' said the woman. 'Where are you? Are you coming to see us?'

'Alas, no. I'm a long way from home, and a long way from you. But I need Ilias to do something for me. Is he there?'

'He's here, but he's with a client. Shall I have him ring you when he's free?'

'I'm calling from a public phone, so that won't be possible. But what I need from him is straightforward enough, though as usual I need it in a hurry. Maybe you could take down the details, and pass them on to him?'

'I'll find a pen,' she said.

After the fat man left, Marianna lit another cigarette, and sat for a while smoking. In the breeze, the purple crocuses shivered on slender stems.

'*Yiayia! Yiayia!* Watch me! Watch how fast I can go!'

She turned to watch the boy as he rode full-speed along the side of the house, finding a smile for him as he came back and skidded to a halt near her feet. She stubbed out the cigarette, and rubbed his silky hair.

'*Ela, kamari mou,*' she said. 'Put it away now. Time for lunch.'

The boy wheeled his bicycle towards the barn. As he hauled open the door, a petite woman on a moped rode into the yard, and pulled up close to the front of the house. She cut the engine, pulled the moped back on its stand, and climbed off to untie the bindings holding a box to the rear luggage rack.

'Marianna,' she said. 'How are you?'

'*Yassou*, Meni,' said Marianna.

'I heard your terrible news,' said Meni. 'But look at you, always glamorous, even in a crisis. And look at me . . .' She glanced down at her trousers, sweater and boots. 'Still. I brought you something to eat.' She held out the box. 'It's just a chicken stew, and there's rice pudding, too.' She looked across to where Yianni was kicking stones as he crossed the yard. 'Maybe he might eat that. And I put in a bottle of wine. But tell me, how is Dmitris?'

Marianna took the box.

'Thank you,' she said. Her chin trembled as she held back tears. 'Thank you very much. There isn't much news. They keep him sedated. In a few days, we'll know more.'

'Have you seen him?'

'Yesterday. I shall go again, this evening.'

Meni touched her arm.

'You must be strong,' she said, 'for all their sakes.'

'I try,' said Marianna.

'Have the police said anything?'

Marianna laughed, bitterly.

'No proof, they say. Why not just arrest them all? They're all as guilty as each other. The men are talking about taking matters into their own hands.'

'That's a dangerous game,' said Meni. 'If they get caught, the police will throw the book at them. In those situations, it's always the wronged who suffer.'

'Not always,' said Marianna. 'Sometimes, just sometimes, there's justice in the world.'

Seven

Behind the wheel of Sakis's truck, Donatos drove as he always used to – slowly enough to scrutinise his own land and his neighbours', favouring the centre of the carriageway to give himself a margin for error. The window was down, his elbow resting on the sill, and the radio was retuned, away from the commercial music station Sakis favoured to an all-news broadcast, where a politician was stumbling over questions on government finances. Donatos's walking canes rested against the passenger seat. His wheelchair was left behind, in the yard.

His breathlessness had markedly worsened as he transferred himself from wheelchair to driving seat, and a small voice of rationality had almost persuaded him he was being foolish, but by the time he reached Dendra's outskirts, his breathing had settled back to its usual, almost adequate level. The sun felt good on his forearm; he remembered a song his mother used to sing, and whistled a few broken snatches. Driving by a *kafenion*, he caught sight of an old drinking partner he hadn't seen in years, and slowed down to pass the time of day, but complaining blasts from the traffic backed up behind forced him on. Arriving at a junction, he couldn't remember if Bouloukas's was to the left or to the right, so ignoring the green light, he stopped to consider. From behind, there were more blasts and beeps of annoyance. Donatos cursed other people's impatience, and turned right.

It was an error. He found himself on Dendra's main thoroughfare, heading away from Bouloukas's place. He pulled over to the kerb.

To make a U-turn, he needed breaks in the traffic in both directions, but the two seemed never to coincide. As he looked back over his shoulder, a motorcyclist pulled up to the pavement directly opposite him, and like Donatos, sat with his motor running. Donatos glanced across at him. The motorcyclist was looking back into the traffic, his long legs stretched to hold up the tall-framed dirt-bike.

Donatos felt the familiar, unwelcome tightening in his chest. Closing his eyes, he inhaled and exhaled as deeply as he could, and waited out the breathlessness. By the time he opened his eyes, the motorcyclist had been joined by two others, both on powerful machines, both wearing the American-style denim and leather the youngsters favoured. They were in discussion, shouting to each other over their engines. Then, they looked over at Donatos.

Did he know them? Without his glasses, he couldn't bring the young men's faces into focus. He was coping with the breathlessness, but now his heart was doing strange things, racing, then stalling for a beat or two, then lurching back into an undependable rhythm. The sensations were well known to him, but certainty they would settle did nothing to make them less frightening and unpleasant. He wished his wife were there. He wished he'd asked Sakis to drive.

The boulevard was briefly empty. Donatos wasn't ready to move, but the motorcyclists made smooth turns, and headed across the carriageway to position themselves around him – one centimetres ahead of his bonnet, one touching his rear bumper, the third so close to the driver's door, his handlebar scratched the paintwork. He looked through Donatos's window, and smiled unkindly. Kapsis. The young man was a Kapsis.

Donatos hastily wound up the window, and staring fixedly ahead, blasted his horn. The rider beside him tapped on the window. Out of the corner of his eye, Donatos looked across. The young man pointed down the road ahead of them, indicating that he should move forwards.

Donatos didn't comply; but the motorcyclist at the back revved his engine, and with smoke billowing from his spinning rear tyre, pressed up to the bumper to force him forward. Anxious about what Sakis would say if his truck were damaged, Donatos thought it better to submit, and so put the truck back into gear and moved off.

They had him pinned; there was nowhere to go but where they led. They moved him to the centre of the carriageway, and into the U-turn he had planned on making; but at the point where he was broadside across the road, they stopped, laughing as they revved their engines.

The lights at the end of the boulevard changed to green, and a stream of traffic headed towards them. The lead vehicle was a bus, and Donatos was in its path. The bus driver flashed his lights. In panic, Donatos hit the accelerator, but he raised the clutch too fast, and the truck stalled. The bus driver blasted his horn and began, at last, to brake. When one of the motorcyclists signalled to his allies to move, it was too late for Donatos. The motorbikes roared away, abandoning him in the bus's path.

When the fat man returned to the Hotel Byron, Lefteris was preparing the dining room for lunch. Four tables had been pushed together to make one large one; another was laid for two, and a third had a single place setting.

The fat man put his head around the door.

'*Yassas*,' he said. 'Do you know if your wife found time to press my suit?'

Lefteris was positioning a knife and fork alongside a folded napkin, adjusting them to be perpendicular.

'She's hung it in your room,' he said. 'Will you be wanting lunch?'

'Yes, I will. And I'm hoping you'll help me out with an experiment.' The fat man held up two bottles. 'I have samples of both Papayiannis and Kapsis oil, and if you will, I'd like both your and your wife's help in deciding which is best.'

'Gladly. But if we're doing that, you must sit with us.' Lefteris glanced over at the table laid for one. 'I'll move you over here. Shall we say in half an hour?'

The fat man's suit, beautifully pressed, was hanging on the wardrobe door. Taking off his unseasonal linen, he slipped into the suit trousers; but when he tried to fasten them, they pinched around his waist, spoiling and stretching the front pleats and detracting from the skill of the tailoring. With reluctance, he removed them, replaced them on the hanger, and put the linen back on.

In the dining room, a man and a woman were already seated at the table. Lefteris brought in a basket of wood-fire baked bread, and urged the fat man to join them.

'Let me introduce you,' he said. 'My wife's aunt, Katya, and my father-in-law, Tomas.'

The fat man inclined his head to them both.

'*Chairo poli*,' he said.

With slight surprise at the fat man's formality, Tomas returned the greeting in kind. Aunt Katya – elderly and bent-backed, severe-looking in widow's black – beckoned him to the seat next to hers.

'Come and sit by me, *kalé*,' she said.

The fat man placed his oil bottles under his chair. Aunt Katya clicked her false teeth, pushing them with her tongue from her gums to the back of her lips, then wriggling her jaw to settle them back into place. As she shuffled her own chair to give him more room, he caught a faint and unexpected perfume, which though stale through age, retained enough of its original sweetness to make it identifiable.

'Forgive me,' he said. 'I don't want to appear forward, but is the scent you are wearing by any chance French?'

She smiled at him.

'It is. My husband – may his memory be eternal – was a marine biologist, who travelled all over the world. He spoiled me with gifts, when he came home.'

A woman whose grey hair-roots didn't match the brunette of its lengths bustled in from the kitchen, and placed a covered dish on the table.

'She was a great beauty in her day, weren't you, Aunt?' she said. 'My uncle was her devoted slave.'

Aunt Katya touched the fat man's arm, and leaned closer to him, as if to impart a confidence.

'Do you know how long we were married?' she asked, and the fat man shook his head. 'Sixty-one years. What do you think of that?'

'Have you met my wife?' Lefteris asked. 'Stavroula, this is *Kyrie* Diaktoros.'

'You took good care of my suit,' said the fat man, as he and Stavroula shook hands. 'I appreciate it.'

'It was nothing,' said Stavroula, with a smile.

As she left them, Lefteris drew the cork on a bottle of wine, and with a hand behind his back in the style of a professional waiter, looked questioningly at the fat man, who held out his

93

glass. Lefteris filled it with dark red wine, and moved on to his father-in-law.

Stavroula returned with a dish of vegetables, and a soup plate filled with creamy slops, which she placed in front of Aunt Katya. Lefteris poured wine for himself and held up the wine bottle, and with a wink at the fat man, asked, 'Will you try a drop, Aunt?'

Aunt Katya shook her head vehemently, and placed her hand over her glass, even though it was already filled with water.

'You'll have me drunk,' she said. 'I don't want to disgrace myself by being drunk!'

Stavroula lifted the covers off the dishes, revealing chicken in a walnut and coriander sauce, a salad of lentils dressed with red onions and yogurt, and a spinach pilaf. She beckoned for the fat man's plate, and filled it with generous portions of all three.

'Papa, pass your plate.'

As she served her father, the fat man turned to Aunt Katya, who was taking her first spoonful of what he now saw to be semolina.

'Forgive my asking,' he said, politely, 'but your niece has prepared all this wonderful food. Are you not tempted to try it?'

'I'm always tempted,' she said, 'but my digestion's not up to it. So I eat what I can eat, and imagine the taste on your plates.'

The fat man took his first forkful of the food.

'This chicken is excellent,' he said to Stavroula.

'It's one of my mother's recipes,' said Stavroula. 'The walnuts come from the tree you see out there.'

'My compliments to you.' He tasted the wine, finding it dry and almost spicy with oak. 'But this wine – I have tasted something very similar, recently.'

'It's a local wine,' said Lefteris, taking his seat. He passed the bottle to the fat man, who read the rather plain label, where there was little more than the name of the vineyard – Lachesis – the grape and the year. 'And I suspect you've had plenty of it before, or of one of its near relatives, at the feast.'

'Ah,' said the fat man. 'The lady vintner. This is one of hers.'

'It is,' said Lefteris.

'Then I salute her too.'

The fat man cleared his plate, and accepted Stavroula's offer of more chicken and rice, but the amount she served him defeated him. He laid down his fork for the last time, and sat back in his chair. Aunt Katya was still spooning up delicate mouthfuls of semolina. Stavroula rose to clear the dishes, but the fat man stopped her, and produced the olive oil from under his chair.

'Before we leave the table,' he said, 'I'm hoping you'll all help me in an experiment. A tasting.' He looked at Stavroula. 'Do you think you might bring us some spoons, and more bread, and a couple of bowls to pour out some oil?'

Stavroula soon returned with what he'd asked for. Lefteris poured the remains of the wine into the fat man's empty glass; there was no more than a dribble.

'Shall we open another bottle?' asked Lefteris.

'Yes, open a bottle,' urged Tomas. 'Life is short.'

'I'd take another glass,' said the fat man. 'It's very pleasant drinking. I'm thinking I ought to invest in a bottle or two myself.'

Whilst Lefteris pulled the cork from a second bottle, the fat man poured measures of both oils into glass bowls, then picked up the bowls, and with his back to the company, passed them several times from hand to hand. Stavroula gave everyone a teaspoon, and a slice of bread.

'I don't know whether I should try the oil,' said Aunt Katya, doubtfully. 'Not with my digestion.'

'A little bread and oil will do you no harm,' said Stavroula. 'In fact it will do you good.'

The fat man replaced the bowls on the table.

'Now only I know which oil is which,' he said. 'I bought both this morning, one from the Papayiannis factory, one from the Kapsis press. I want to ask you which you think is the better oil.'

'It'll be Kapsis,' said Tomas, as Lefteris refilled his glass. 'You can't beat the traditional methods. The quality is bound to be better.'

'That may not be true,' said Lefteris, pouring more wine for the fat man. 'I've read the new methods produce a better oil, as well as more of it.'

'So which is which?' asked Stavroula.

'Let's see if you can tell,' smiled the fat man.

He gave the first bowl to Lefteris, who took a spoonful and sucked the oil over his tongue.

'It's good,' he said.

The others followed, tasting by spoon or by dipping their bread.

'That's a great oil,' said Tomas, following it with a slug of wine. 'That's the Kapsis oil.'

'So try this one,' said the fat man, and offered round the second bowl. They all tasted, and fell quiet.

'That's the Kapsis oil,' said Aunt Katya. 'At least, I think it is.'

Lefteris wagged his finger at the fat man.

'You're playing tricks on us,' he said. 'Those are the same oil.'

'No tricks,' said the fat man, dipping bread into the second oil. 'Both are essentially from the same trees, of course. But the methods of production could not be more different.'

'But the oils are the same,' said Stavroula.

'Does anyone have a preference?' asked the fat man.

'The second is the Kapsis oil,' said Aunt Katya.

The fat man shook his head.

'You'd be wrong,' he said. 'You tasted the Kapsis oil first. The fact is – and I am surprised myself – there seems to be no loss in quality through mechanical production. So we might say Papayiannis oil has the edge, since their yields are undoubtedly better. I am reluctant to suggest it, favouring as I tend to traditional, time-honoured methods, but maybe mechanical production is the way forward for Greece's oil industry.'

'Never,' said Tomas, draining his glass. 'Oil is like wine, and has no place in a factory. Do you think this wine we're drinking now could be made in a factory?'

'I agree about the wine,' said the fat man. 'But with oil, we may just have proved here that modern methods are at least equal to the old ways. And once initial set-up costs are paid back, they're a much better prospect for the farmer.'

Stavroula rose again to clear the dishes.

'Would you like dessert?' she asked the fat man.

'I really shouldn't. I had ice cream this morning.'

'Ice cream?' asked Lefteris. 'Where did you have ice cream?'

'At a *gelateria*, in the square behind the bank.'

Aunt Katya laid a concerned hand on his forearm.

'You shouldn't eat there,' she said. 'That place is dirty.'

'Aunt, you shouldn't say that,' said Stavroula. 'The gentle-man may eat anywhere he chooses.'

'But you and I wouldn't eat there,' objected Aunt Katya. 'And if it's dirty, he should know.'

'Why do you say it's dirty?' asked the fat man. 'It struck me as being a model of hygiene.'

'Now, maybe,' said Aunt Katya. 'But not always. I don't think you should eat there.'

'He may eat where he pleases,' said Tomas, rising from the table. 'Stavroula, thank you for lunch, *kori mou*. I'm off for my siesta.'

'Dessert?' asked Stavroula, again. 'There's fruit – fresh plums, or apples – or there's plum cake.'

'She makes an excellent plum cake,' said Lefteris. 'The plums from our tree are sweet, and she adds a little cinnamon. A little honey drizzled over the top, and a spoon of yogurt on the side – can we tempt you?'

But the fat man's stomach was beginning to trouble him, as if he'd eaten too much chicken, or too many lentils.

'Sadly, I must decline,' he said. 'Maybe later, at coffee time? In the meantime, if you'll excuse me, I'll follow Tomas's lead. I think a short siesta would help my digestion.'

Under the influence of wine and food, and in spite of the discomfort in his stomach, the fat man slept away the rest of the afternoon, to be woken by the slight chill which filled his room as the sunlight faded. His stomach was settling, to the point where it might tolerate an invigorating coffee, so he splashed his face with cold water, and ran a comb through his hair. Taking with him his suit trousers and his hold-all, he went downstairs.

He asked Lefteris to bring him Greek coffee without sugar and a bag for his trousers, and took a seat at a courtyard table. He lit a cigarette. The branches of the walnut tree moved in a rising breeze. In the street at the bottom of the steps, children shouted as they kicked a football against a wall, whilst overhead, a jet plane drew a white ribbon across the darkening sky. As he stubbed out his cigarette, the French clock in the dining room struck the hour in a tinkling melody of preparatory bells, followed by six bright chimes.

He finished his coffee, and as the evening was becoming cold, went inside the hotel reception, and studied more of the curiosities on display. There was a lithograph of the War of Independence hero Dimitrios Panourgias, his head wrapped in a turban like a Turk, and the fossil of a fish, each fine dorsal bone preserved in mud become stone. Behind the lithograph was a black and white photo of workmen with picks and shovels, and standing behind them, his hand on the shoulder of a workman, a man with the moustache of a Cretan and a resemblance to Panourgias himself.

A door banged, and there were footsteps along the corridor before Lefteris appeared, holding out a smart carrier bag from the Attica department store.

'Stavroula found this for your trousers,' he said. 'She wondered if you know this shop, since you come from Athens? She has a cousin who visits from time to time, and she always brings her a gift from there.'

'I know the place very well,' said the fat man. 'Your wife's cousin has excellent taste. But I've spent too long, in my time, eating pastries in their café. To my shame, I once ate three pieces of their exemplary chocolate hazelnut cake at one sitting, though only two of them served with the vanilla cream. It is those kinds of over-indulgences which send me on a mission to the tailor's now.'

'We can't keep the bodies of our youth for ever,' said Lefteris. 'And life is short. Better to indulge ourselves whilst we're able, wouldn't you say? I'd rather eat a slice or two of pastry and carry it on my stomach than eat nothing but semolina like poor Aunt Katya.'

'But her abstemious diet seems to do her no harm. On the contrary, she is remarkably fit, for her age. Maybe I should follow her example, at least for a while.'

Lefteris laughed.

'Put yourself on a milk and slops diet, and you'll lose your most important faculties,' he said. 'A man needs more than that to keep him functioning – red meat, and red wine, to give you vitamins where you need them.'

The fat man put his suit trousers in the carrier bag.

'You're right, of course,' he said.

'I almost forgot. What about your plum cake?'

The fat man's stomach gave a warning grumble.

'Later, perhaps,' he answered, and started down the steps towards the street.

Dusk was falling as the small Datsun pick-up pulled into the Papayiannis yard. The driver turned in a wide arc; the full beam of his headlights flashed across the gateway, and came to rest on Sakis's truck, highlighting the mica sparkles in the red paint.

'Thanks, *filé*,' said Sakis to the driver. 'I'll be there by seven tomorrow.'

He pulled the handle to get out; but with the door half-open, he hesitated. He had left the truck parked nose to the wall. Now its nose faced into the yard.

The driver squinted into the glare and gloom.

'Hey,' he said. 'What's happened to your truck?'

Both men climbed from the pick-up. The driver crouched by the Nissan's wheel arch, peering underneath to assess the damage. Sakis touched the huge dent on the wing, and gazed bewildered at the hole where the headlamp had been.

'Something's hit you hard,' said the driver, leaning under the vehicle. 'I reckon your chassis rail's going to need some straightening. What do you think, a tractor, maybe?'

Sakis shook his head.

'She wasn't parked this way round,' he said. 'Someone's moved her.'

He headed for the house, the Datsun's driver following close behind. Before he reached it, the front door was flung open.

'Sakis!' said his mother. 'Thank God you're here! Your father's had an accident!' She told the men the story: the collision with the bus which might have killed him, his refusal to go to hospital, the policeman who had driven the truck and Donatos home.

Sakis's face was grave.

'Where is he?' he asked, quietly.

'I made him go to bed,' said his mother. 'He isn't well, but he says he'll sleep it off. He says he'll be fine, but I don't think so. I think it's his heart, Sakis. I think the shock . . .' She wiped tears from her eyes. 'Talk to him,' she pleaded. 'Talk some sense into him, can't you?'

Sakis took the stairs two at a time. His father lay wide-eyed in the bed, his canes propped against the foot. In the lamplight, a shade of blue darkened the habitual redness of his face. He winced at every short breath, and there was bubbling in his lungs.

'What the hell were you thinking?' asked Sakis. 'What were you playing at?'

Weakly, Donatos shook his head.

'I'm fine,' he said. 'Don't . . .' He lacked the breath to finish the sentence. 'Son . . .' He lifted his hand from the blankets. Heavy veins stood proud on the yellowing skin. 'Son, I don't want . . .'

Sakis took the old man's hand, and squeezed it.

'Just rest a while, Papa,' he said. 'I'll be back before you know it.'

Downstairs, his mother was pouring whisky for the Datsun's driver. Sakis went to the phone.

'Do you think he's all right?' asked his mother, tremulously. 'The police said he was hit really hard, that another metre forward and he'd be . . . Who are you ringing?'

Sakis dialled, and didn't reply. His call was answered quickly.

'We need an ambulance,' he said. 'We need an ambulance now.'

He gave the details he was asked for, and hung up the phone.

'Your father'll be angry,' she said, wringing her hands. 'He told me I wasn't to call anyone.'

Sakis drew his mother to him, and kissed the top of her head.

'Sometimes, he's just a stubborn old mule,' he said. 'But that doesn't mean he knows what's for the best.'

Eight

In Dendra's back streets, few people were out. Behind a church, an impatient foot stamped on the kick-start of a temperamental motorbike, until the engine roared briefly, and died. Hot water trickled into a fouled drain, the laundry scent of ersatz lavender rising with the steam. A woman threw open a window, releasing the smell of frying fish, and the pop, sizzle and smoke of overheated oil.

The hotelier's directions had been convoluted, but the fat man came at last to a landmark that had been mentioned – a plaque commemorating the birthplace of an almost forgotten poet, where the fat man was to take the street opposite. Here, graceful buildings – once the homes of prosperous merchants – were falling into semi-dilapidation, the upper-floor windows boarded over or covered with filthy net curtains, the lower floors inhabited but neglected, or turned over to small businesses, workshops and shops whose frontages spilled light on to the lane.

A youth shouted angrily, '*Adé, malaka!*' and slammed a door, hard; a startled cat ran across the fat man's path. A seller of leather goods, opening up for the evening, was using a boat hook to hang handbags from his fascia. The fat man wished him *kali spera*, and browsed through a rack of belts until he found one a little longer than his usual size. He tried it round his waist, finding that only on its last hole was it a comfortable fit; somewhat abashed, he paid for the belt, and slipped it furtively into his hold-all like a troublesome secret.

Next door was a delicatessen whose signage claimed the shop's origins in 1925. In the window, the glass shelves were filled with bottles and jars – artichokes, sauerkraut and asparagus, fruits in syrup, vinegars and fine wines. There was a range of Italian pastas, and imported delicacies – pepper paste for Hungarian goulash, French *foie gras* and Polish bilberries. On the lowest shelf were trays of pâtisserie – croissants, gateaus and tarts – and samples of the twenty kinds of nuts roasted on the premises. A sign advertised fresh *taramasalata*. The fat man listened to his doubting stomach, and walked away.

The tailor's shop announced itself with a symbol of scissors hanging over the doorway. Inside, the place was musty from damp rising through the cobbled floor, and lit only by a low-wattage bulb, except over the workbench where an anglepoise lamp was extended to light a commercial sewing machine. Floor and bench were littered with scraps of material and snippings of thread; on the bench was an overflowing box of cotton reels, all shades of grey and brown. There were scissors and shears, and boxes of pins, and a miniature chest of drawers with Perspex fronts holding cards of buttons and zips; and in the corner, a dummy wore the loosely stitched pieces of a jacket, the sleeves missing but the lapels and pockets already in place. Bolts of cloth were ranged end-up behind the door, protected from the damp by sheets of polythene. An anorak was thrown over a chaise longue upholstered in fraying brocade; around the walls were photographs of models in suits, in styles contemporary in the cities a decade before.

Via a complex and amateurish system of wiring, the sewing machine was plugged into the light socket, whilst the open fuse box behind the bench showed several fuses blown. As the fat man entered, the sewing machine rattled on, run by the tailor with a pedal, as his hands guided the needle over black cloth marked up with tailors' chalk and long, white tacking stitches. The fat man closed the door noisily, but still the tailor didn't hear him; so when the machine finally stopped, and the tailor was adjusting the cloth to follow the next seam to be stitched, the fat man gave a light cough.

The tailor jumped round in his chair, and looked at the fat man over half-moon glasses. He was dressed for the cold, layered in a shirt, a sweater, and a down-quilted gilet, which did nothing to flatter his portliness.

'*Kali spera*,' said the fat man. 'Forgive me, I didn't mean to startle you.'

'I'm sure you didn't,' said the tailor. 'But this machine makes so much noise, when it gets going I can't hear anything at all. You could sneak up behind me and whack me on the head, or take everything you see in the shop, and if I were sewing, I'd have no idea you'd even been in. I used to have a bell on the door, but it made no difference.'

'Maybe you could set up some kind of lamp as a signal?' suggested the fat man. 'If a lamp lit up on the bench when the door was opened, your customers wouldn't take you by surprise.'

But the tailor looked doubtful.

'That would need electricity,' he said. 'And the electrics here are far from reliable. If I run any more than a forty-watt bulb, all the fuses blow. Still, I'm lucky to have electricity at all. My father ran this shop for decades with nothing but candles.'

He dipped his hand into an open drawer in the bench, and helped himself from a bag of chocolate raisins inside. As he tossed the raisins into his mouth, he remembered his manners, and held the bag out to the fat man.

'Help yourself,' he said.

But the fat man shook his head.

'Thank you, no.'

'They come from the delicatessen,' said the tailor. 'I got a taste for them when I was trying to give up smoking. I'm courting a widow who doesn't like the smell of cigarettes, and she bought me a bag to wean me off the tobacco. At the time, it seemed like a good idea. Every time I wanted a cigarette, I was to have one of these instead, as a little treat. I was only a twenty-a-day man, so that wouldn't have been so bad. But these things are so good, who can eat just one? I used to be thin as a stick of bamboo, and look at me now. She says I should swap the raisins for cherries, or plums, but who could eat that many plums without it taking its toll on the system? There's no lavatory here, and my house is streets away. So what's a man to do? I just keep eating the raisins. If you ask me, I was better off with the cigarettes.'

He helped himself to a few more raisins and popped them in his mouth, before returning the bag to the drawer and determinedly shutting it.

'You have my every sympathy,' said the fat man. 'I should introduce myself. Hermes Diaktoros, of Athens. *Chairo poli.*'

He held out his hand, and the tailor leaned forward to take it.

'Miltiadis Sloukas,' he said. 'What can I do for you?'

'I came for the feast, but it seems to have been the straw which broke the camel's back, as far as my waistbands are concerned. So I have a small job for you, if you can do it quickly. I shan't be in town very long.' He took his trousers from the department-store carrier bag. 'These will have to be let out. I have resisted for some time, but the truth is, I can no longer wear them.'

Miltiadis turned back to the bench and examined the trousers under the anglepoise lamp.

'This is beautiful cloth,' he said, rubbing it between his fingers. 'Wonderful quality.' He looked inside the waistband for a maker's label, but there was none. 'Was it made here, in Greece?'

'It's Italian. I have all my suits made there.'

'Why? What have you got against Greek tailors? I could make you a decent suit.' He looked the fat man up and down, struggling to gauge his size; on close inspection he seemed not fat, but powerfully built.

'I'm sure you could,' said the fat man, 'but I already have plenty of suits, if they did but fit me. If you can alter these trousers, that will help me a great deal. You see I am reduced to summer wear. I blame no one but myself, of course. When I'm presented with good things to eat, I tend to eat them. Just this morning, I ate a more than adequate breakfast, but then stumbled across a *gelateria*, and ate two scoops of ice cream. Small scoops, in my defence, and the ice cream was exceptional. An Italian made that too. Probably you know of him. His name – was it Rico, perhaps?'

'Renzo,' said the tailor. 'I know Renzo. If I were you, I wouldn't eat there again. The place has a bad reputation.'

He gave his attention back to the trousers, closely examining the seams. The fat man's stomach gave an uneasy rumble.

'Why do you say that?' he asked. 'What do you mean by a "bad reputation"?'

'I think I can get you a couple of centimetres on each side,' said the tailor, still peering at the seams. 'Maybe four, five centimetres in total. Will that be enough?'

'Whatever you can manage. Even two or three would help. I must say I found Renzo's ice cream delicious, yet you and others seem to think my eating there was foolhardy. Clearly you know something that I do not.'

'It's just my opinion, that's all. People should make up their own minds. All I'm saying is, if you eat there, make sure you have your doctor's number to hand. When do you need your trousers? I have to finish this suit before I can start on them.' He indicated the half-made jacket on the dummy, and the trousers he'd been stitching on the bench. 'The man's getting married in a couple of days. It's been a very short engagement, but the girl he's marrying is starting to show. Whether she's really his responsibility or not, is another matter. Some questions are better not asked.'

'If there are questions better not asked, I'm the man to ask them,' said the fat man. 'So tell me, why should I not eat the Italian's ice cream?'

'I don't like to repeat gossip,' said the tailor. 'All I'm saying is, I wouldn't eat there myself. People died, and dozens were ill. The newspapers were all over the story. Dendra was national news, for a while. Didn't you see it?' He pulled open the drawer, and helped himself to another handful of chocolate raisins. 'These things are too good to leave alone. I shut them out of sight, and I hear them calling my name. Are you sure you won't have some?'

'Quite sure, thank you. No, I didn't see that. I travel a great deal, and often I'm out of the reach of the daily papers. But people died, you said. How many, and what of?'

The tailor chewed his raisins as he spoke.

'There were four dead by the end, all poisoned. By what, remains a mystery. They suggested at first it might be something in the water, but if that were the case, everyone in the community would have been affected. Then they thought it was in some kind of food. What food was never proven. The bacteria were of animal origin, that's all they could say for certain. So they looked around for a common denominator, something everyone who'd become ill had eaten, and they couldn't find one. But the most likely candidate was Renzo's. As you say, his ice cream is second to none, and the whole of Dendra used to eat there, though no one local eats there now. Who'd eat something that might poison them? You'd have to be mad or stupid to do that.'

'Even though it was never proven?'

'There was speculation in the papers, and folks took that as proof. They wouldn't print something that wasn't true, would they?'

'But if he had poisoned all those people, surely the police would have arrested him, and shut him down?'

'I don't say the poisoning was *deliberate*. That would make him a psychopath, a madman. Maybe he just didn't keep the place clean. Foreigners don't have the same standards as us, do they? Look at the gypsies. Look at the Albanians. And I had a Turk come in here once wanting a suit, and he stank like a billy-goat. Say Renzo doesn't wash his hands properly, germs get in the food, it might be as simple as that. And the police did talk to him. I heard that from my brother. But like I say, there was nothing but the ice cream that was even close to being a common denominator. It was the only thing that made sense.'

'Almost made sense.'

'It was as close as they could get. Anyway, what does it matter, now? It's all water under the bridge, and folks' memories are short.'

'Not in my experience,' said the fat man. 'People remember for much longer than you might think. When did all this happen?'

'Not this summer just gone, the summer before. And speaking of time, when do you need your trousers? If I get on all right with this suit, I could have them ready the day after tomorrow.'

The tailor's lane led to a busier street where a *periptero* was lit up on the corner, and the fat man went in that direction. He passed a bar where the bartender, arms folded, watched a football match with a group of cheering, jeering youths; in a dark corner, on a leather sofa, a petulant girl lay her head on a young man's shoulder, whilst he craned his neck for a better view of the television, and watched with envy his friends seated at the bar. Steam from a kebab shop carried appetising smells of charred pork and garlic, and the fat man paused there long enough to read the menu before remembering the reason for his visit to the tailor's, and moving on.

The *periptero*'s owner was wrapped up for the depths of winter: fingerless gloves, a quilted anorak, a woollen hat pulled over his ears. Space was cleared on the plank-wide counter for a portable TV, where the football game played in grainy black and white, and the owner was watching it from his stool, his son seated beside him on an upturned crate, smoking and drinking from a can of beer.

'Just look at these *malakes*,' said the owner to his son as the fat man approached. 'Your mother'd make a better centre-forward.'

One of the players took a shot at the goal-mouth, and the TV crowd roared; the ball went wide, and the crowd groaned.

'*Poustis*,' said the son, and drank beer.

'*Kali spera*,' said the fat man, genially.

The owner gave him a curt nod, then his eyes went back to the television.

The fat man reviewed the *periptero*'s stock – bags of roasted nuts and seeds, packets of biscuits, chewing gums and bubble gums, magazines and next year's calendars – and chose, after some deliberation, two bars of chocolate, one of Pavlidis dark in its classic blue wrapper, one of Ion milk with toasted almonds. He laid the chocolate on the counter, and waited to be served.

But the owner, focused on the football, appeared not to notice him.

'That was never a foul!' he said, pointing at the set. 'There was absolutely nothing wrong with that tackle!'

'And look at him, lying there groaning like a baby!' said his son. 'Get up, *poustis*! The money they get paid, you'd think they could play the whole ninety minutes!'

'Excuse me,' interrupted the fat man, politely. 'I wonder if I might have some cigarettes?'

With some annoyance, the owner looked at him, his eyes flashing back to the TV.

'Get up!' demanded the son. 'Get up, *malaka*! You've only got a couple more minutes to play!'

'There'll be injury time,' said the owner, turning away from the fat man. 'At least five minutes, the way these *malakes* have performed.'

'I'm looking for these,' said the fat man, holding out a pack of his cigarettes to show the starlet's face. 'Do you have them?'

'What?' asked the owner, without looking at him.

'These,' said the fat man. 'Do you have any in stock?'

The owner glanced very briefly at the pack.

'No,' he said. His eyes went back to the television. 'Looks like they're bringing on Savevski.'

His son ground out his cigarette.

'About time,' he said. 'They should have played him from the first minute. Now maybe we'll see some action.'

But the TV was beginning to misbehave. The picture elongated itself from the middle, drawing itself into an arrowhead where nothing on the pitch could be made out; then the screen began to roll round, slowly at first but speeding up to a flickering blur.

The owner whacked the set on its side.

'Damned thing!' he said. 'What's wrong with it?'

'It's the aerial,' said his son. 'Jiggle the aerial.'

The fat man waited. The picture on the television flickered round, and the owner smacked the set again. His son stood up and twisted the two-pronged aerial in every possible direction, with no impact whatever on the faulty picture.

'If you wouldn't mind,' said the fat man, 'could you look for my cigarettes?'

'I told you, I don't have them,' said the owner, in annoyance.

The fat man smiled.

'Many people say that to me,' he said, affably, 'but they often find, if they look properly, that they have a packet or two hidden away.'

The son tilted the TV forward, and fiddled with the aerial lead in the back.

'Make sure it's in properly,' said his father.

'That's what I'm doing,' snapped the son.

The TV commentary was becoming eager, the crowd's excitement showed in its roar. With his attention on the commentary, the owner began a cursory search of his shelves of cigarettes, as the crowd's noise reached a crescendo, and the commentator shouted, 'Goal!'

'For Christ's sake!' complained the son. 'We missed it!'

'What a great goal for Savevski!' enthused the commentator. 'Just seconds after being brought on to the pitch, and he scores. Who could ever doubt that the old magic is still there?'

Behind a stack of boxes of Silk Cut was a torn packet the owner didn't recognise. He glanced inside.

'Well, I'll be . . .' he said, under his breath. Reaching in, he took out three packs of the fat man's cigarettes and placed them on the counter.

'Excellent,' said the fat man. 'I'll take two boxes of matches, too.'

On the TV, the final whistle blew. As the fat man turned from the *periptero* counter, the flicker on the screen was slowing down. By the time he'd put his purchases in his hold-all, the picture was restored to normal.

An ambulance was approaching, its siren blaring, the strobe of its lights flashing blue across walls and tarmac. It tore by, and the fat man watched it go, until its red tail lights were out of sight, and the siren faded to nothing in the night.

A little after ten, Miltiadis Sloukas put on his anorak, closed up his tailor's shop and locked the front door with a heavy key. Walking slowly, he followed his usual evening route, past the *gelateria*, which was still open for business. At one of the empty tables, Renzo stroked the terrier sleeping on his lap; seeing Miltiadis, he paused in his stroking and half-raised a hand, but Miltiadis pretended he hadn't seen, and hurried by.

At the *ouzeri* on Democracy Square there were men that he knew.

'Eh, *manka*!' called one (a sea captain who'd retired to a landlocked life and a wife he didn't love, and anchored his future firmly to the bottle; two years into retirement, he'd aged five or ten). 'Romeo! You old tom-cat! Are you off to see that woman of yours?' He gestured obscenely with his index finger and a fist, and the men with him all laughed.

Miltiadis didn't respond. On the far side of the square, he followed a side street as far as the Kokoras *souvlaki* shop.

At an outside table, four off-duty soldiers were finishing plates of *gyros*. A poster was stuck to the glass in the shop door, a rousing, bold-lettered message with a Soviet-style picture of bulbous-biceped, square-jawed men. Miltiadis read the poster – 'Unite with our tobacco farmers! Candlelight vigil for solidarity!' A date was given, and the address of the kebab shop. He shook his head, and pushed open the door.

Steamy air fogged the windows, and trapped the burned-oil smell of frying. Behind the counter, a woman was washing dishes. Hearing the door, she turned with a weary expression; but seeing Miltiadis, she took her hands from the hot water, drying them as she approached the counter between the range of steel griddle-plates and deep-fat fryers, moving carefully by the shaved roll of doner kebab rotating slowly on a vertical spit.

On his way through the shop, Miltiadis passed a young man seated alone at a table spread with papers and pamphlets.

'*Yassou*, Xavier,' he said.

The young man looked up, and smiled from behind round wire-framed glasses and a patchy untrimmed beard.

'*Yassou, Theié*,' he said.

Miltiadis took four lemons from his anorak pockets, and placed them on the counter.

'Dora, *kali spera*,' he said. 'I brought you these, from the tree at home. I picked them myself, this afternoon. I noticed you were running short, yesterday.'

She smiled, and was almost attractive. In front of the red-glowing grill, fat ran down the doner's close-packed meat into a drip-tray.

'Thank you,' she said, and ran a hand over hair made damp and shapeless from the kitchen's heat. 'Look at me, what a mess I am. We've been busy.'

With a questioning look, he glanced at the young man and his papers.

'Do you mean you've both been busy?' he asked. 'Or only you?'

'I mean the shop. Can I get you something?'

'I might have a beer.' She started to come out from behind the counter to go to the fridge, but he stopped her. 'I can get it.'

He chose a can of Heineken, and as he popped the cap, she handed him a glass.

'Will you come and sit a minute?' he asked.

But the door opened, and two of the soldiers came in.

'Two more *gyros*,' said one, reaching the counter. 'With onions, chips and sauce.'

The other was searching his pockets for change.

'Tomatoes on one,' he said.

As she dropped rounds of pita on to the griddle, Dora sighed.

The first soldier wandered over to Xavier's table.

'Oi, *malaka*!' he said. 'When are we going to see you at the barracks? It's time you got your fat arse slimmed down to size. We'll get you fit and pulling women in no time!'

Xavier looked exaggeratedly to either side of the soldier, and outside.

'What, like those women with you?' he asked. 'That's the only reason you were so keen to do your time, because boy genius there' – he thumbed at the second soldier – 'told you you'd be pulling women right and left in those uniforms. Now you're both puppets of the state, and still no women. I like your hair, by the way. It really suits you.'

He touched a curl of his own, thick hair. Self-consciously, the soldier slid a hand over his brutal cut.

'How do you avoid it, Xavier?' he asked, tetchily. 'No, really. How old are you now, twenty-four, twenty-five? No job, no university, and yet no call-up. You must be getting very creative with your excuses. How do you get away with it?'

'Haven't you worked it out?' Xavier gestured to the kitchen, where his mother held the pitas flat with a spatula to brown them, her face glowing from the griddle's heat. 'My mother's a widow, I'm an only son. Even our backward government realises she'd be sunk without me. Automatic exemption.'

'So why is it that she's back there grafting, and you're sitting on your arse?' The soldier called out to his friend. 'Eh, *malaka*. Get me a Coke.'

'My mother respects my ambitions,' said Xavier.

'Ambitions? What ambitions?'

'Ambitions beyond your grasping, *malaka*!' He laid down his pen, and looked over to where his mother was slicing hot meat from the grilling cylinder. 'Hey, Mama! Whilst you're doing those, do one for me!'

As Dora dropped another pita on the griddle, Miltiadis caught her eye, and gave a censorious frown. Dora looked away. Miltiadis picked up his beer and took a seat, away from Xavier's table. Above his head, the silent television was showing the news, film of the prime minister in a gilded chair, talking to a visiting foreign dignitary.

'Look at that snake!' said Xavier, bitterly, looking up at the footage. 'He sits in his golden chair, and he smiles, and shakes their hands. Nah! Here, *malaka*!' He stabbed at the paper he was writing on. 'Here are the flaws in your foreign policy!'

The soldiers laughed.

'So when you're prime minister, I suppose we won't see you sitting in a chair like that?' said one. 'And what will you offer the president when he comes to call? A kitchen chair? A bar-stool?'

'They should all stand,' said Xavier. 'The role of administering power should be uncomfortable.'

Dora shovelled the first pita from the griddle on to the waxed paper in her hand, layered it with browned meat, sliced onions and chips scooped from a fryer basket, and expertly twisted the paper to hold the pita in a fold. She shook on salt, added a squirt of sauce from a plastic bottle and handed the wrapped *gyros* to the soldier, then made another with the addition of tomato and handed it to his friend. She took their money, and gave them change. From outside, as the soldiers sat back down with their colleagues, there was a burst of laughter.

Dora rubbed at an ache in her shoulder, and turned her son's pita on the griddle.

'Xavier, what do you want on this *gyros*?'

'Everything,' he said. He crossed out a line in his letter, and wrote in new wording over the top. 'No, Mama, wait. I don't want mustard.'

Miltiadis drank his beer, and watched the mime of the prime minister's diplomatic efforts on the silent television. Dora made her son's *gyros*, laid the paper-wrapped food on a plate, and slammed the plate on to the counter.

'Xavier, come and get this,' she said. 'Miltiadis, let me get you something to eat.'

Miltiadis drained his beer, and went back to the counter.

Xavier glanced up from his writing.

'*Theié*,' he said, 'could you pass that over here?'

His face set, Miltiadis picked up the plate and put it in front of Xavier. He beckoned Dora to him.

'So what do you think?' he asked, quietly. 'You and me, later – how about it?'

Dora pulled an expression of hopelessness, and bent her head towards her son, subtly so he wouldn't see.

Miltiadis placed his empty beer glass on the counter, and turned to leave.

'Will you come tomorrow?' Dora asked.

Miltiadis's usual answer to this question was a smile, and a wink. But tonight, he only shrugged, and left her without a backward glance.

Nine

The fat man was breakfasting on Stavroula's plum cake. The window on to the garden was open; rain had fallen overnight, and the freshness of the lemon trees blended with the coffee Lefteris was brewing.

'Do you have plans for today, *kyrie*?' he asked.

The fat man swallowed a mouthful of ginger-spiced sponge.

'I was thinking I might play the tourist this morning,' he said. 'I passed a church which interested me, when I was on the way to the Papayiannis orchard – the church where you directed me to fork left. I thought it looked as if it might have some interesting history. It has a touch of the Byzantine, certainly, and I thought there might be parts of the structure which are earlier than that.'

'The chapel of St Laurentios,' said Lefteris. The *kafebriko* was singing, and the foaming coffee began to rise. Lefteris snatched the pot off the flame, and holding it high, poured an aromatic stream into the fat man's cup. 'It's old, all right. The oldest structure in Dendra, so people say.'

'St Laurentios, is it?' said the fat man. 'Your patron saint of cooks and chefs, and a man who met a very unpleasant end. Many of your Orthodox saints were unfortunate in their deaths, but I find St Laurentios's one of the most unpleasant.'

Lefteris carried the coffee to the fat man's table, and placed it by his hand.

'What happened to him?' he asked. 'My wife would no doubt know – the lives of the saints are her bedtime reading.'

'Laurentios annoyed his Roman captors by cheating them of the church's wealth, which even in those days was considerable. So they strapped him to a gridiron, and roasted him over a fire. He was greatly admired for his stoicism, but when the heat eventually became too much even for a suffering saint, he is said to have cried out – with remarkable fortitude and wit, given his circumstances – "I'm done on this side, turn me over and eat!" '

Lefteris grimaced.

'That is unpleasant,' he said. 'Can I get you more plum cake?'

'Thank you, no,' said the fat man. 'As you know, I'm struggling to maintain my figure. I shall drink my coffee, and take myself for a walk in the chapel's direction.'

Lefteris picked up the fat man's empty plate.

'Speaking of the Papayiannis's,' he said, 'you might be interested in this morning's news. You met the old man whilst you were over there, didn't you?'

'I did,' said the fat man. 'I talked to him for a while.'

'He's dead,' said Lefteris. 'According to the postman, his heart gave out. He died in hospital, during the night. Sad news for the Papayiannis's, but there'll be plenty of Kapsis's waiting to dance on his grave. There's a great gathering of the Papayiannis clan for the vigil and the funeral later on. We'll hope it goes off peacefully. There was some unpleasantness in town during the night, youths spitting and jostling.

The Kapsis boys reckon they know exactly who's responsible for poor Dmitris being where he is, and they want the Papayiannis boys to know they know. But nothing will ever be proved, and truth to tell, Kapsis's have behaved almost as badly, in the past. But you can bet there won't be many Kapsis's paying their respects to Donatos today.'

'Will you go?'

'I'll show my face. Stavroula's that rare woman who doesn't enjoy a good funeral, so it falls to me.'

'I'd appreciate you letting me know where and when the funeral will be,' said the fat man. 'I might decide to go along and pay my respects myself.'

'What about your brother?' asked Lefteris. 'Have you seen anything of him?'

'I have neither seen nor heard anything of him since the feast, and I am daring to take that as a positive. With a little luck, it may mean he's staying out of trouble.'

The fat man walked a while, heading in the general direction of St Laurentios. Two black-clad widows waited at a bus stop, their heads wrapped in scarves against the mild morning, and the fat man wished them *kali mera*; they mumbled their responses, and pressed their wicker baskets protectively against their thighs until he passed. A man in a baseball cap held a chihuahua on a lead, and unashamedly watched it defecate on the roots of a plane tree.

The fat man reached the main thoroughfare via a street bordering a park with a children's playground, where old tyres were strung from a pole frame to make swings, and the slide was without a ladder to the top. The playground was overhung by eucalyptus trees which sapped the autumn light, and made the place both dismal and forbidding. Behind the playground was a football pitch worn bare by many feet, where both goal posts were missing their cross bars. The refreshment cabin was boarded up for the season; short tarmac paths led between flowerbeds not replanted since the spring, and now overrun with weeds. At regular intervals, there were benches; on one, a white-haired man fed pigeons with seed from his pocket, whilst on another, a vagrant was sleeping off the night's excesses.

The route to St Laurentios's lay over the main road, but busy traffic made it difficult to cross; where a gap appeared, some vehicle would jump into it from a side road. The fat man was waiting patiently, when something about the park-bench vagrant struck him as familiar.

He made his way into the park, and stood over the man, who lay on his back, his hands behind his head, smiling in his sleep. There were wine stains on his yellow T-shirt, a smudge of lipstick on his neck and his sandalled feet were very dirty; stale alcohol came off him at every breath. Under his bench, pigeons pecked at the remains of a *gyros* in its wrapper, and the almost bare stalks of a bunch of grapes. An empty wine bottle lay on its side. The fat man picked it up, and read the label. The wine had been a poor quality factory blend.

The old man feeding pigeons was watching him.

'He's drunk, friend,' he said, tossing more seed to the flocking birds. 'He was singing, and waving at the cars. I fetched him out of harm's way, and sat him on the bench, and he went straight to sleep. He's out cold now, I reckon.'

'It would certainly seem so,' said the fat man.

He bent down, and shook Dino by the shoulder. At first, Dino didn't react, and seemed still contentedly asleep; but when the fat man shook him again, he opened one blue eye, and seeing the fat man, grinned, showing his wine-stained teeth.

'*Yassou*, brother,' he said. He closed his open eye, and shifted his position on the bench, making himself more comfortable before he went back to sleep.

But the fat man shook him again.

'Get up,' he said. 'You can't sleep here.'

'Ah, but I can,' said Dino, drowsily. 'I've been making this bench my home, when I've had nowhere better to go.'

'You have somewhere better to go now,' said the fat man.

'And where may that be?'

'You can come with me, and we'll find you some coffee.'

Dino opened both eyes.

'You know,' he said, 'that might be a good idea. That cheap wine has given me one hell of a headache.'

They didn't speak as they walked. Dino was yawning and lacked the inclination, and the fat man was content to be silent. But as the fat man turned down a lane which would take them to Democracy Square, Dino stopped him.

'I think we'd do better somewhere else,' he said.

'I presume you're worried about your unpaid bill at the *ouzeri*? I gave the patron my word you'd pay him.'

'You make it sound a fortune,' said Dino. 'What was it, a couple of ouzos?'

'A number of ouzos for your friends, and several carafes of wine.'

'A petty soul like him shouldn't keep an *ouzeri*. How can he put a price on companionship and enjoyment? And I seem to remember we did enjoy ourselves! But no, it isn't that. There was an incident, last night. It'll be fresh in people's minds, so I think I'm better staying away.'

'An incident? What incident?'

'Better you don't ask,' said Dino. 'And anyway, to be honest the details are a little hazy.'

The fat man sighed.

'We'll go elsewhere, then,' he said. 'I know a quiet place which will do very well.'

At the *gelateria*, Renzo sat alone reading a newspaper, his dog asleep by his feet. As the fat man and Dino approached, he folded the paper and stood up to wish them *kali mera*. The dog woke as he stood, and raised its head, and as Dino took a seat at an outside table, the fat man stroked the terrier under its chin; but the animal gave a low growl, and padded off to a safe distance, where it lay down again, head on paws, watching.

'What can I get you gentlemen?' asked Renzo.

'Alas, no ice cream for me today,' said the fat man, with obvious regret. 'My expanding waistline won't allow it.'

'I told you you'd put on weight,' said Dino. 'I'll have Greek coffee, sweet, a double. No, a triple.'

'And a Greek coffee for me too,' said the fat man. 'No sugar, thank you.'

Renzo gave a willing smile, and went inside the shop. The fat man took a seat opposite Dino, and watched the Italian through the window. As he lit the butane burner and spooned coffee into a pot, the smile had left his face, leaving him looking downcast and troubled.

Dino closed his eyes, and rubbed his forehead.

'My head!' he said. 'And every time I say the same thing – never again!'

'Don't tell me you're giving up drinking?'

Dino laughed.

'No, never that,' he said. 'Only the drinking of cheap wine. I've decided I'm going to go and buy some of that vintage we had at the festival. That was very drinkable, don't you think?'

'It was,' said the fat man. 'I had more of it yesterday, and I was impressed.'

'Then you should go and buy some for both of us,' said Dino. 'You have the car. And I still think she was your type, Hermes. Besides, you know if I go, I'll find it hard to leave. At least not until I've drunk the vineyard dry.'

'I agree, it would be dangerous. By the time you left, the poor woman would be bankrupt.'

'Get a case at least. Get two cases.' He massaged his temples with his fingers. 'You know, I swear my headache's getting worse. It would have been better if you'd left me to sleep it off.'

'On a park bench? Why haven't you got yourself a room?'

'Up to now, I haven't needed one. I spent most of last night with a lovely creature I found somewhere around here. In fact I have a rendezvous with her later on. But I've grown quite attached to that bench. It gives me a view of what's going on.'

'And what is going on, apart from the flow of traffic?'

'Sometimes the traffic doesn't flow so well. There was an accident, yesterday. Not so much of an accident, actually. I didn't say anything to the police because there's honour amongst bikers, but it could have been a whole lot worse than it was.'

Renzo brought out their coffee, in delicate cups decorated with gold Greek keys around their rims. There were glasses of iced water, and a hazelnut-studded *biscotto* in each saucer.

The fat man thanked him. Renzo went back to his seat at a nearby table, and picked up his newspaper. Dino moved his *biscotto* from his own saucer to the fat man's.

'I can't eat at this time of the morning,' he said. 'What time is it, anyway?'

'A little after ten.'

'So early! Really, Hermes, you should have left me to sleep. When I've drunk this, I shall go back to my bench.'

Two boys came into the square, one bouncing a basketball whose thump as it hit the cobbles echoed round the buildings.

Dino called out to them.

'Hey, lads! Do you want a game? I'll give you a game!'

The boys ignored him, and disappeared down a side street.

'They're afraid to take me on,' said Dino.

'Why don't you get a room where I'm staying, at the Hotel Byron?' asked the fat man. 'It's comfortable, and really, brother, you are in dire need of a shower and a change of clothes.'

'You're probably right. But there's no drama in a hotel. I'd miss all the excitement of my bench.' Dino tried his coffee. 'This is good. Maybe I will try one of those biscuits.' He took his *biscotto* back from the fat man's saucer, dipped it into his coffee, and bit off the end. 'There were three lads, on bikes,' he said, as he chewed. 'One had a very nice bike, actually, a Suzuki. I was thinking about one of those for myself.' He dunked his biscuit again, and ate a larger piece. 'I like these. Are they Italian?'

'I expect so,' said the fat man. 'What were they doing, these three youths on their bikes?'

'They were playing a dangerous game.' Dino dipped the last piece of his *biscotto* in his coffee, and as he ate it, reached out and took the fat man's. 'You won't mind if I have yours, will you, brother? I'm sure you've already had breakfast. I've never known you not have breakfast.'

The fat man waved his hand to consent, and reached into a pocket for his cigarettes.

'What game was it they were playing?'

Dino picked a hazelnut from the fat man's *biscotto* and popped it in his mouth.

'They pinned a truck, a red Nissan, with an old man at the wheel. They were only playing. Boys will be boys. We all love to be boys. But even so, they went too far. The old man looked distressed, even before they scared the life half-out of him.'

The fat man found his lighter, lit a cigarette and drew on it.

'How did they do that?' he asked.

'They forced him into a U-turn, across the boulevard, and held him there – one at the front, one to the back, one to the side – in front of the oncoming traffic. At the last moment, they moved off, but he wasn't quick enough getting out the way. He took a blow right on the wing. That did damage enough, but he almost took it broadside. Of course the bus driver braked much too late, but those lads were wicked. If I see them again, I shall tell them so.'

He finished the fat man's *biscotto*, and sipped his coffee. The fat man, seeming thoughtful, drew again on his cigarette.

'The old man,' he said, as he exhaled. 'What happened to him?'

'He was in a bad state, very shaken up. A policeman got in the driving seat, and took him away, back to the oil mill, I suppose. My head isn't getting any better. Have you got any of those special powders in your bag there?'

'What oil mill?'

'That's where the truck had come from, some oil mill. It said so on the side. What are you thinking, Hermes? You've got that look on your face.'

'I was thinking about what you said, about scaring the life half-out of him,' said the fat man, resting his cigarette on the edge of the ashtray and picking up his coffee. 'What if they didn't scare the life half-out of him? What if they scared him so badly that it killed him?'

'They wouldn't have done that,' said Dino. 'They were just youngsters, having a joke.' He yawned. 'Time for bed. And you're right, I should find somewhere more comfortable than that bench. Where did you say you were staying?'

'The Hotel Byron.'

'The Hotel Byron it is, then. Don't forget to fetch our wine, brother. You've seen how poorly I tolerate the cheap stuff.' He rose from his chair. 'Thank you for the coffee.'

As he walked away, not quite in a straight line, the fat man called after him.

'Don't you want directions to the hotel?'

Dino raised a hand.

'I'll find it, when the time comes,' he said.

After Dino left, the fat man smoked the rest of his cigarette. Renzo turned the page of his paper. The little dog wandered over to Renzo, sniffed the hem of his trousers and lay down.

The fat man stubbed out his cigarette, and began to look in his pockets for change. Renzo folded his paper.

'Can I offer you something, before you go?' he asked, picking up the ashtray. 'Another coffee? Maybe something stronger? I have brandy, but only three star. I have a bottle of *grappa*, if you'd like to try it. My brother brought it from Italy, when he came to visit.'

'You're very kind,' said the fat man. 'Thank you.'

As Renzo went inside to fetch his drink, the fat man reached over for the newspaper – that day's edition of *To Vima*. The headline was of Athenian politics, and he read none of the lead article; instead, he went through the paper quickly to the last pages of news, the *In Brief* stories warranting only a line or two of print.

The square was quiet, and the fat man heard the noises inside the *gelateria* – the hum of fridges, the click of the dog's claws on the tiles as it followed Renzo inside, the clink of the bottle as the *grappa* was poured.

Renzo set an elegant, antique liqueur glass before the fat man, and a clean ashtray painted with a map of Italy, with Rome and Venice, Milan and Naples marked in red.

'The *grappa*'s on me,' said Renzo, 'in case you don't like it.'

'I'm sure I will. Are you going to join me?'

Renzo shrugged, and went inside to pour himself a glass of the spirit, and joined the fat man at his table.

The fat man tasted the *grappa*, and nodded approval.

'It puts me in mind of the best of our *raki*,' he said.

'It's intended as a *digestif*,' said Renzo. 'They make a lot of it, where I come from.'

'A *digestif* is perfect,' said the fat man. 'My stomach has suffered too much abuse of late. Do you miss your home? Do you ever think about returning?'

A distant look came to Renzo's eyes, and perhaps the watery beginnings of tears.

'I think about it,' he said. 'And then I put the idea aside. I have the business here. To go back, I would have to sell it, and selling it at present wouldn't be easy. And Italy isn't kind to people like me, and though they never say it, I know I am a disgrace to my family. Here, of course they call me names, and whisper and laugh behind my back. But they are respectful, mostly, to my face. Though I've done you no favours, sitting down at your table. If you're seen with me, there'll be talk.'

'I choose my own company,' said the fat man. 'I have never allowed anyone to choose for me.'

A silence fell between them. The fat man seemed to be reading, and sipped absently at his *grappa*.

'There's a story here,' he said at last, his finger marking a place on the page, 'an anecdote almost, a "fancy that" piece about a street in Patras being blocked to traffic for some hours by a dead horse. No doubt there was chaos. Here it is as an amusing aside, a page-filler – yet I doubt it was amusing to the horse's owner. What was the animal doing in the city, I wonder? Was it one of those carriage rides for tourists, or pulling some sort of cart? I think I would assume it would be a working animal. That being the case, this was quite possibly a catastrophe for the owner, if the horse was his livelihood. Imagine it – his distress at losing the animal which he may have been fond of, dealing with the police who were no doubt called, the rage of inconvenienced motorists, the difficulty of finding someone to take away the carcass. Such a drama it must have been! In two lines, this is an amusing story, but extrapolate the story behind the words, and it's potentially a very sad little tale. Isn't that always the way with newspaper stories? The context, the human factor, is so often missed.' Renzo was silent. 'I took my trousers to your friend, the tailor, by the way. Miltiadis, I believe they call him, Miltiadis Sloukes. He was telling me you were in the news, quite recently.'

'Not recently,' said Renzo. A touch of colour rose in his cheeks, and he glanced over to the cutting in the window, where he was smiling as he received his award. 'That clipping's an old one. And sadly, Miltiadis and I are no longer friends.'

'Miltiadis wasn't referring to your prize-winning,' said the fat man. He folded the paper, and laid it down. 'He was telling me about an outbreak of poisoning.'

Renzo left the table, and picked up the watering can which stood against the wall.

'What is it they say, that there's no such thing as bad publicity?' he said, as he dribbled water from the can on to a pot of lavender. When he'd poured only a dribble, he touched the soil to check the moisture level. 'You have to be careful with these. It's so easy to drown them.' He moved on to the next pot, his back to the fat man. 'I wouldn't agree with that. Twice now I've been in the papers. Once was a cause for celebration, as you see from the piece in the window. It brought people from all over the district, and business boomed. Then, there was that other business, and there I was again. No names were mentioned. They only said the suspected source was an ice-cream shop in Dendra. But there's only one *gelateria* in Dendra. Within two days, my local trade dried up, and it has yet to come back to life.'

'But there were people dead, weren't there?' asked the fat man. 'Four, according to Miltiadis.'

'I'm sure he couldn't wait to tell you,' said Renzo. He trickled the last of the water on to the lavender, and broke off a head or two which were past their best, taking them with him inside the shop. He returned with the bottle of *grappa*, and refilled the glasses before he sat down. 'Miltiadis felt I implicated him,' he said. 'As did one or two others. Before the outbreak, everything I used to make my ice cream was local. My eggs came from Miltiadis, amongst others. He has a bit of a smallholding, and keeps a few chickens at home. I used to have some fruit from him, too. After the outbreak, I switched to eggs from factory chickens, chickens not fed on the scraps from someone's table but on a control-led diet. I stopped taking local cream, and ordered in sani-tised, pasteurised stuff, which I still use. I changed all my suppliers, and most haven't forgiven me. Apart from the loss of business, they see the implication – which I can't deny – that it was their products that were tainted. But what else could I do? The health inspectors took my shop to pieces. They tested everything down to the last teaspoon looking for anything suspicious, hunting for the fatal bacteria, but they found nothing, not a trace of anything that would kill a fly, let alone four human beings. But my turnover was fast, then. I couldn't rule out the possibility that I *had* produced a bad batch, which was sold, and eaten. I was a factor most of those people – most of them, not all – had in common. I have no idea if I was guilty, or not. In my heart, I don't believe so. Everything I make, I taste, and taste, and taste, but I wasn't ill. My detractors say maybe I *was* ill, and hid it, and of course I could have done that. But people *died*! Was it my fault? Did I poison them? I live with that question every day. Meanwhile, they isolate me. They don't come here, they don't speak. I rely almost entirely now on summer's tourist trade, out-of-town customers who don't know my reputation as a poisoner. Without them, I'd be finished.'

'Was no one else under suspicion?'

Renzo shook his head.

'Look at me,' he said. 'I'm foreign, and I'm a *poustis*. I've never hidden what I am. So maybe I am guilty, but whether I am or not, I'm their scapegoat. In a small town like Dendra, what more perfect scapegoat could there be than a foreign *poustis*?'

The fat man sipped more *grappa*.

'In fact you make a poor scapegoat, because you are still here, in Dendra,' he said. 'The original idea of scapegoats was to carry bad luck or plague far away. In ancient Athens, the city kept a supply of undesirables – criminals, drunkards and paupers – to perform the role of scapegoats, and when they were needed, they were fed figs and cheese, beaten with branches and then burned, limbs first, before their ashes were scattered to the four winds. A very unpleasant fate indeed. The name for these poor souls was *pharmakoi*, from which we derive our modern word pharmacy, where we find cures for our ills. But as time went on, and we supposedly became more civilised, the sacrificial role was taken on by goats, who were driven out of towns or villages, taking misfortune with them. If they returned, they brought the bad luck back.'

'They'd be happier, then, if I would go,' said Renzo. 'And if I could, I'd be only too glad to leave this place.'

'I'm sure you would. The people here have treated you badly, because as you say, you are subject to their prejudice, and so an obvious target. But I think you, and they, are missing a crucial point. Scapegoats are made to shoulder the blame, but scapegoats are not the guilty.'

After the fat man had left, Renzo sat on at the table. The bottle of *grappa* was by his hand, and he reached out to refill his glass, but changed his mind and instead put the bottle down by his feet. A pigeon took flight from a balcony rail above the watch-seller's, circled and disappeared over the rooftops. The lingerie shop's matronly owner was dabbing at the window cobwebs with a feather duster, but disappeared when Renzo looked her way.

Xavier wheeled his bicycle into the square, carrying a batch of leaflets under his arm. When he saw Renzo, he walked in his direction, and leaned his bicycle against the *gelateria* wall. He held out one of the leaflets.

'How's it going?' he asked.

'Eh,' said Renzo. 'Not so bad. Could be better, could be worse.'

'I was wondering,' said Xavier, 'if you might put one of these up in your window. I'm holding a candlelit vigil, and I need to get the word out.'

Renzo took the leaflet, and read through it.

'Why not?' he said. 'Good for you, trying to change the world.'

'Not the world,' said Xavier. 'Just one small part of it.'

He crouched down, and rubbed the terrier's head; the dog sighed, and rolled on to its side, encouraging Xavier to rub its belly.

'Since I'm here,' said Xavier, 'have you got any of that banana and coconut in the freezer?'

Renzo smiled.

'I made some yesterday,' he said. 'Come on inside.'

A distant church bell began to toll the sad rhythm of the passing bell, and was joined, within moments, by a second.

Renzo listened.

'Who died?' he asked.

'A Papayiannis,' said Xavier. 'The old man, Donatos.'

Renzo led the way inside, and went behind the freezers. He took the scoop from its bowl of water.

As he was wiping it dry, he said, 'He wasn't so old, was he? Sixty, sixty-five?'

Xavier was peering down on to the display of ice creams, searching out the banana and coconut.

'I've no idea,' he said. 'Could I try a taste of the double chocolate?'

Renzo picked out a wooden spoon, dipped it in the ice cream and held it out to Xavier.

'What did he die of?'

'This is great,' said Xavier, licking the spoon. 'I don't know. Heart failure, I think. The funeral is this evening. I'll have a scoop of that as well. With a swirl of chocolate syrup.'

'He was a difficult man,' said Renzo. 'Still, we shouldn't disrespect the dead. Have a scoop of the *panna cotta* to go with it. It's on me.'

Ten

The chapel of St Laurentios was a humble building of unworked stone, whose only embellishment was a modest belfry mounted on the tiled roof. The door had been left ajar, as though someone had just left and might soon be returning, but though the fat man looked up and down the road, no one was in sight. Ducking his head under the low arch of the doorway, he went inside.

The chapel had no windows, and the place was dark but for the light of a slender candle bent from the heat of its own flame, and a wick burning in a glass of oil and water before the largest icon of the saint. The chilled air was frowsty with mildew. Somewhere behind the modest iconostasis, water dripped on to stone.

The fat man put nothing in the offertory box, but helped himself to a candle from the stack, lit it from the oil lamp and moved closer to the icon of St Laurentios, who stood bearded and indifferent with his gridiron and the palm leaf which signified his martyrdom. The fat man raised his candle, spreading shadowy light across the sooty walls and ceiling, and – shrouded by centuries of blackening smoke – a panoply of faded frescoes: a once-blue sky turned to night, peopled by a crowd of haloed saints, with fire-dancing demons prodding pitchforks at their feet.

He lowered the candle, and studied the floor, a plain arrangement of flagstones worn into shallow dips where trodden most. Before the 'beautiful door' in the iconostasis – where only the priest was allowed to pass through into the inner sanctum – was a carving in the stone.

He crouched to examine it, running his fingers over the simple design, eroded by time and impossible to make out in the weak light. But as he traced it, the curving lines made sense, and the fat man smiled. It was a crescent moon, the sacred symbol of the huntress goddess, Artemis.

The Lachesis vineyard spread across the sloping sides of a ridge, from where the eastern view was of Dendra and expanses of olive groves, and to the west, a hinterland of pine-wooded hills. The narrow three-storey house seemed an anomaly, similar to the tower houses built as defences in the bleakest coastal villages of the Peloponnese. The grey stone had never been rendered, and made the house forbidding; tiny windows set high in the walls would make the interior oppressive.

The fat man parked on the raked gravel surrounding the property, and climbed from the car, intending to approach the house; but somewhere behind, music was playing, and so instead he followed a well-worn path over grasses regenerating in the season's coolness.

The vines grew in rows running down the hillside, supported by wires strung between posts. The green growth of summer had all fallen away, and the vines were pruned back almost to the stubs of their trunks. Amongst them, on hands and knees with a hessian sack half-filled with weeds nearby, a slight figure in cord trousers tucked into wellingtons was digging with a hand fork; an old cassette player, once black but faded with clay dust, was turned up to full volume, broadcasting a moody nocturne.

The fat man followed the line of the vines, expecting to be unheard over the music and that he would take the digger by surprise; but as he drew close, the figure, still kneeling, looked up at him, the eyes hidden by shadow cast by an old man's cap.

'*Kali mera*.'

At the fat man's words, the digger shoved the hand fork into the stony ground, and standing, pulled off the cap, revealing grey hair cut short but very chic, and a woman's face tanned dark as a fisherman's.

'I'm sorry if I startled you,' said the fat man.

'You didn't startle me,' said the woman, with a smile which showed white teeth. 'Maybe it's I who surprised you?'

The fat man returned her smile.

'A little,' he said. 'From a distance, I took you to be a man.'

'That's the fate of the older female. We lose our charms, and our curves droop to less desirable places. And I don't help myself by dressing in a man's clothes and labouring in the fields. How could you not mistake me for a man? Except now you stand beside me, you'd never make the same mistake, seeing I barely come up to your shoulder. I wouldn't make much of a man, at my height.'

Over the smell of turned earth, he caught a trace of her floral perfume: iris and musk.

'Now we're face to face, I see my error is absurd,' he said. 'I didn't mean to be ungallant, and I apologise unreservedly. Allow me to introduce myself. Hermes Diaktoros, of Athens.'

'Meni Gavala.'

'*Chairo poli*.'

She repeated his formal greeting.

'You have such lovely manners,' she said. 'Good manners are rare in Dendra. My mother was French, and spent a lifetime trying to instil French manners into the population here, with no success whatsoever. And to make her task more difficult, she married my father, who came from the Mani, where the manners – then, at least – were about as rough as they possibly can be without people actually killing each other. When we moved here, he built this house in the Mani style. He never forgot his heritage of vendettas and constant in-fighting. I suppose he thought if we ever went to war with the neighbours, we could be safe from attack on the third floor.'

'And are you at war with your neighbours?'

'I'm pleased to say I have no near neighbours, though in Dendra, the war between certain neighbours keeps the gossips entertained for hours. But I'm sure you're not here to gossip. What can I do for you, *Kyrie* Diaktoros?'

'I've been drinking your wine over the past couple of days, and I'm impressed. I'm here hoping I might buy some.'

The music came to a climactic end, beyond which the everyday sounds of the place – the whisper of a breeze, bird calls, the distant sound of machinery in the olive groves – were amplified.

'The music was beautiful,' said the fat man. 'Was it Debussy?'

'No, Fauré. The vines prefer him.' Meni laughed. 'You'll think me mad, of course, but my mother taught me the value of playing music to the vines. She came from a Burgundy family. Some of these vines are imported from there, cuttings from old family rootstock, but they don't flourish. The soil here isn't ideal for French varieties. I have a few grapes from them, and they add interest to the vintage, but it's my

Agiorghitiko grapes which are the stars of this vineyard. They're of this place, and everything is perfect for them, both soil and climate. But all the vines do better with music. An hour or so a day lifts their spirits as it lifts ours. This time of year, when the vines are resting, I play them something soothing, like the Fauré. In spring, I wake them gently with Mozart or Vivaldi, and in summer when they're working their hardest, I rouse them with Greek dances, their native music. That in part gives the wine its quality. You may not agree, but I'm convinced of it.'

'And does your husband go along with your unorthodoxy?'

The smile left her face.

'My husband, sadly, is not here to approve or disapprove of anything I do. The vineyard was always my work, my family's work, though he was always happy to drink his share. But it's been a long time since he and I opened a bottle together.'

'Forgive me. Are you a widow, then?'

'You think I'm unorthodox because I don't wear black?'

'Unorthodoxy is generally something I applaud.'

'If I knew for sure he was dead, then I'd wear black. But I've no proof. He was, or is, an engineer, and took a contract out in South America. Six months, he should have been gone. That was sixteen years ago. They tell me he and a friend went exploring the jungle, and never came back. The friend, they say, was blonde. Which is extraordinary – I never knew him to show interest in blondes before. He always said he preferred brunettes. So I may or may not be a widow. Maybe I should have claimed the status, but I hate to wear black – it's so unflattering on a woman my age. And in a corner of my heart, I hope the vines will call him home. I still write to him. Every month, I write to where I know he last was.' She looked towards the distant hills, and was lost in thought, until she seemed to come back to herself. 'Enough of an old woman's ramblings! We need more music!' She bent down to the cassette player, reversed the cassette and pressed the play button. A fresh piece of music began, the gentle lilt of a piano. '*Les romances sans paroles*. They'll enjoy this. Now, to business. Shall we?'

He followed her between the rows, but she led him not towards the front of the house, but to the back, through an orchard of mixed trees all picked clean of their fruit. The fat man stopped beneath one, and looked up at a single plum withering on a high branch, just beyond his reach.

'This plum,' he said, 'what is it?'

'An old variety of damson,' said Meni. 'The flavour's excellent – you can make jelly with it, or eat it as a dessert, and it goes very well with goats' cheese – but it's very susceptible to blight. I have an interest in preserving old varieties, the traditional fruits our grandparents knew. I planted all these trees myself. You'll see they're all quite young, only adolescents of the tree world, but they're old enough to produce decent crops. The fashion for hybrids disturbs me. In the search for quantity, we have sacrificed so much quality.'

'Isn't that the crux of your local feud?'

Meni considered.

'I suppose in a way, yes. The argument there though isn't over varieties. They've both got what their ancestors planted, and are lucky for it, I'd say. Their dispute's over maximising production. I can't see how the traditional way can't be best. You see this apricot? Its ancestors were around at the time of Jesus. The fruit's not as sweet as modern taste likes it, but again the flavour is superb. And can we not add a little sugar or honey ourselves?'

'And this looks something like an almond.'

'Again, an old cultivar. You see I have several of its modern counterparts, over here. The nuts are very flavourful, but the yield is low. I think it's so important to see beyond profits, and keep sight of what has value. I've made this orchard my life's work. I'm proud of it, and it will be my legacy. I've no granddaughter to carry my name, as in the Greek tradition, so I shall carve my initials in these tree trunks. Everyone should have a legacy. Don't you agree?'

The fat man considered.

'If only it were so,' he said. 'Too many souls who spend time on this earth are left with no lasting memorial, not even a stone to their name. Maybe we should do no more than ask to be remembered for our deeds.'

'But what about those who die too young to have deeds to remember? What about them?'

'Then we should remember their smiles, and their joyful innocence.'

'You're a wise man, *Kyrie* Diaktoros,' she said. 'Come inside, and let's find you some wine.'

Meni led him into an untidy kitchen, leaving open the door to supplement the weak light from a small window. The room smelled of good things, both sweet and savoury. A cake dusted with icing sugar was cooling on a board; on the stove, over a flame so low it was barely visible, a pot of lamb was stewing with onions and herbs.

'You'll see I'm no typical Greek housewife,' she said. 'I'm one of nature's untidiest creatures. I drove my husband almost mad with my messiness. Still, I was and am a decent cook. My daughter'll be here in a while. I don't see her as often as I'd like, and I like to feed her well whenever I get the chance. She's quite capable of feeding herself, of course, but I love to have someone to cook for. I cook for everyone.'

'It smells delicious,' said the fat man. 'Your daughter's a lucky woman.'

She went to a small door in a corner of the kitchen, turned the Yale lock and slipped the catch to keep it open.

'Here's the main reason this house was built here,' she says. 'There was a cave in the hillside, big enough to make a decent cellar. My mother insisted she could never live in a house without a cellar in this climate, and I agree with her. In summer, you must have somewhere cool, but not so cold as a fridge. Fridges have their place, but they destroy the flavour of some foods, fruits especially. The entrance wasn't here, it was away down the hill. My father had a new entrance excavated here, and blocked the natural entrance from within the cellar, at the back. My father was no fool. He knew that to build a wine cellar with public access was to invite everyone in the district to come and help themselves. But the steps are steep, and a little uneven. I think it might be better if you waited here.'

'Whatever you suggest.'

On a shelf inside the cellar door was a clay bowl, moulded in the shape of a mussel shell, with wings drawn up at one end to form a hole through which a string poked. The bowl was half-filled with oil. Meni patted her trouser pockets, and found a book of matches carrying the name and number of a firm of roofers, struck a match and lit the end of the string.

'That's an intriguing lamp,' said the fat man.

'It's one of my treasures, bought for me by my husband on one of his trips. It's supposed to be genuine Mycenaean, but I salve my conscience from guilt regarding hoarding antiquities with the thought that it's probably a fake. It's an ingenious thing, so simple yet so effective, and quite safe. Olive oil won't burn without a wick, so if I spill a little here and there, it doesn't matter. It's much cheaper than batteries, and more reliable than a torch. There're no electrics down there. For years I ran this place off a generator, and when they installed mains electricity, they forgot all about the cellar. The old generator's still down there. I crank it up if the power goes off, which it seems to do almost every time it rains.'

He watched the pale glow of her lamp as it descended the stairs, then looked around the kitchen. The chair-backs were draped with cloths and clothes, and a half-worked piece of knitting in pale blue wool. On the window sill were photographs: one of a man, not handsome but intelligent-looking; another, more recent, of a young woman holding a toddler, the woman laughing as the beaming child reached out to touch her face.

From the cellar, he heard the rattle of bottles and Meni's muttering as she climbed back up the stairs. When she reappeared in the kitchen, the lamp's wick was out.

'I shouldn't try and carry so much,' she said. 'I let the lamp spill, and drowned the wick. But the stairs are awkward, and I like to make as few trips down there as possible.' She placed four bottles on the table. 'My vintages are small, but I think they're special. Where did you try my wine?'

'I'm staying at the Hotel Byron. Lefteris served a bottle – two, actually – at lunch yesterday.'

'Lefteris is a good customer. And the wine you had must have been last year's. I used a little less than usual of the French stock. My mother would turn in her grave to hear me say it, but I think it worked very well with less. I'm afraid I can only let you have a few bottles. I supplied the wine for this year's feast, and that made a large hole in supplies. I have my regular customers to look after, and the cellar stock is getting low. But if you'd like to try something else . . .' She picked up one of the bottles from the table. 'You might like this.'

She opened the bottle, and poured the wine.

'Sit,' she said, handing him a glass, removing the knitting from a chair so he could do so. 'Taste.'

He did so. The wine was heavy, dense and syrupy.

'What do you think?'

He tasted again.

'Is it fortified? It reminds me of a wine my father had from Portugal.'

'If you like it, why not take a bottle to go with the other three?'

'I will. You have real talent in this arena. How does your success go down with the men?'

She laughed.

'They make excuses for me because they see me as a mad foreigner, and they accept it because they like my wine. Shall we have a little treat to go with it?'

She found clean plates, and cut two slices of the cooling cake, one large, one very small. She put the larger portion in front of the fat man, and gave him a cake fork and a napkin.

'Orange and almond,' she said. 'A flourless cake, a recipe of my paternal grandmother's. The secret is in the boiling of the oranges. I boil them for two hours, then they just melt into the mix. The almonds, of course, are all my own.'

The fat man tried the cake.

'The almond flavour is intense.'

'I have too many of them,' said Meni. 'I spend my days trying to think of things to make with them. You see over here, I'm going to make almond *skordalia*, another family recipe. I make biscuits, and praline . . .'

'I tried your praline,' said the fat man. 'I had a piece from *Kyrie* Papayiannis.'

'Really? From Donatos? You do surprise me. Don't take any more. He's very careful of his praline, and he won't be happy if you eat it.' She gave a laugh. 'I suppose at his age, he must guard his pleasures.'

The fat man laid down his fork.

'You haven't heard the news,' he said. 'And I, as a stranger, am the wrong man to be carrying it. Are you close to the family?'

'I know them all, of course. I buy their oil, they buy my wine. Tell me, what's the news?'

'I'm afraid Donatos Papayiannis is dead.'

Meni sat up very straight and looked directly at him.

'Dead? How so? I saw him, only . . . Recently, this week, and he seemed . . .'

'Not well, in my estimation,' said the fat man. 'I spent a few minutes with him myself, and he was not at all a well man.'

'The cause of death . . .' she asked. 'What did he die of?'

'His heart, I gather. He told me himself it was failing, and I wonder if he was put under a degree of stress yesterday which may have been the final straw.'

'What kind of stress?'

'Some harassment at the hands of a group of youths. That is my own reading of the situation, at least.'

'And the funeral?'

'Later today, I believe. Will you go?'

'With my daughter being here, I don't know. But it's a shock. I didn't expect . . . It brings it home, doesn't it, the fragility of life? One moment here, another, gone.'

'He had refused to see a doctor,' said the fat man. 'I myself don't advocate the current fashion for running to the doctor for every cough and sneeze. But in his case, I thought he would do well to seek medical care, and yet he never did. Not until he reached the hospital, at least. By which time I assume it was too late.'

'I expect so.'

'I wonder if some good may come of his death,' said the fat man. 'Whether the old feud might abate somewhat, with the head of the clan gone.'

'The head of the clan will be replaced with another,' she said. 'Sakis.'

'He struck me as being a reasonable man. But I wonder about Marianna Kapsis, whether she might be more stubborn. You know her, of course. She is, like yourself, a strong and successful woman. Dendra seems to breed them.'

'So you've met Marianna, and have lived to tell the tale.'

'What do you mean?'

Meni smiled.

'I'm only teasing you. But the town gossips would have you believe an attractive man like you who wears no wedding ring is lucky to have escaped from her clutches. They'll tell you she's a gold-digger, who married old man Kapsis for his assets, such as they were, and that he didn't last long after she got her hands on him. There were whispers about her when he died, whether she speeded him along. But she's more a Kapsis than those who are Kapsis by blood, and though some of them don't like it, she rules them with an iron rod. She's made her stepchildren afraid of her, and in the main, they do as they're told. And if she's the man-eater they say, which men have been her prey, I couldn't tell you. Still, they paint her as a black widow, always on the look-out for her next victim, so if you're unmarried and want to stay that way, maybe you should watch out for her.'

'Whatever her reputation with the opposite sex, she seems to know her business. I tried their oil, and found it excellent. I tried the Papayiannis too, in a blind-tasting experiment, and my tasters could find no difference between them. Which do you prefer? Which would you recommend?'

She shrugged, and offered to refill his glass.

'If you've tried only those two, you haven't begun to taste our olive oil,' she said. 'There are far more producers than Papayiannis and Kapsis in this area, some better, some not so good. You should look beyond Dendra, *Kyrie* Diaktoros. Oil is like wine, and what I like may not be what you like. It's a very personal preference. You should broaden your horizons, taste all this region's got to offer. Oil is an adventure, an uncertain craft. Like wine, a slight difference in soil, a degree or two in temperature, a different blend – all affect the flavour. There's a wholesaler in Neochori, where all the growers take their crops. He could take you through a whole spectrum of flavours, from the mildest to the hottest of the peppery. If you're serious about your oil, you should go there. Dendra oil is good, but you may find another you prefer.'

The sun had passed its noon peak, and as they drank, the kitchen fell into shadows.

Meni apologised for the lack of light.

'It's galling,' she said. 'But the views from upstairs go some way to compensating for the gloom. Let me show you.'

She led him up a wooden staircase, highly varnished but dusty, to the top floor, and a room used as an office. At one end of the room, a ladder led up to a trap-door, and picking up a pair of binoculars from the desk, she led him upwards again and out on to the flat roof, where beyond the carelessly scattered materials for repairing a leak stood a single chair.

The view was magnificent – of Dendra, of hills and valleys, and the distance beyond.

'The best is after dark, when the stars come out,' she said. 'I sit up here for hours sometimes, watching the heavens. In the moonlight it's so beautiful, it brings tears to the eyes. And something else.'

She handed him the binoculars, and brought his attention to a stand of trees on a rocky crag, some distance off.

'Look carefully, and you'll see an eagle's nest,' she said. 'All spring and summer, I watched them raise their young. Two chicks. Such noble creatures. I'm hoping they'll breed again, next year. I think they will.'

'Eagles, the most venerated of birds,' said the fat man. 'So much so, in ancient times they were the symbol of Zeus himself. I hope you're right, and that they'll return. Now, I should leave you to prepare for your daughter's visit. How much do I owe you for the wine?'

Meni wrapped him cake and pie to take away. As he was putting his parcels and wine on the passenger seat, a battered little Fiat driven by a young woman turned into the gateway. A small child was secured in the back. The woman lifted him out, and settled him on her hip.

'*Yassas*,' said the fat man.

She cast an eye over the foil-wrapped packets on top of the wine, and gave him a broad smile.

'My mother has been plying you with gifts,' she said.

'She's very kind. I came to buy wine, and I'm leaving with food for a week.'

'No preserves?' asked the young woman. 'No eggs?'

'I declined the eggs,' he said. 'And there's a jar of marmalade in there, somewhere.'

'I'm well prepared for my visit,' said the young woman. 'I haven't eaten for two days. She likes to spoil us. Doesn't she, *kamari mou*?' She chucked the smiling baby under the chin.

'You're lucky to have such a caring parent,' said the fat man.

'I know I am,' she said, and went smiling into the house.

*　　*　　*

148

As the funeral bells began to toll, a pall of dove-grey cloud was sapping light from the late afternoon. The Papayiannis house was smoky with incense and scented with white lilies, mingling with the tang of whisky and the steam of brewing coffee.

The shadow of his mourning beard was already dark on Sakis's cheeks. He gave the command to lift, and he and his three relatives – uncle, brother-in-law and cousin – heaved Donatos's coffin from the dining table on to their shoulders. Either whisky or the weight made the uncle stagger, and to a gasp from the onlookers, the coffin slipped; but in a minute or two they were settled, and with Sakis at his father's right shoulder, Papa Kostas the priest led them out into the yard.

The women in their best black followed on. Haggard with shock, Sakis's mother Tasia was supported by her sister and Amara. Behind them, wailing and dabbing their eyes, came neighbours and relations. A young girl hushed a babe in arms, whose crying was drowned out by the women's laments.

Outside, the men ground out their cigarettes and came forward to help with the coffin, sliding it on to the back of a black truck valeted for the occasion. The majority of the mourners climbed into other vehicles, ready for the drive to the cemetery; but Sakis had chosen to walk, and as the make-shift hearse moved slowly through the yard gates, he and his fellow bearers followed on foot, heads bowed, with the cortège crawling behind to match their pace.

From an upstairs window of the Kapsis house, Marianna watched the procession move down the road.

'*Adios*, old man,' she said, under her breath, and without even the shortest invocation for his immortal soul, she turned away.

The service in the cemetery chapel was brief. From there, Donatos's coffin was carried to the family grave, and lowered in with ropes. Papa Kostas said the necessary words, splashed holy water from his aspergillum, made crosses in the air and stood aside to wait for his fee.

Sakis held his weeping mother's arm, supporting her as she dropped a white rose on to the casket. The clods of earth she and Sakis threw into the grave thudded like portents on the coffin lid. Amara stood alongside her mother-in-law as one by one the other mourners approached the grave, scattering in handfuls of earth before wandering away to pay respects at memorials to their own relatives, or joining hushed conversations, both serious and banal: the suddenness of Donatos's passing and the fickleness of Fate, or the extramarital affairs of their neighbours.

The fat man had come late to the ceremony. Once the coffin had been carried out of the chapel, he strolled up to the portico, and smoked a cigarette as the funeral came to its end.

Lefteris was talking with two men, demonstrating, perhaps exaggerating, the length of something between his hands; the disbelief of his listeners was obvious, though one turned his face away to hide his doubt. Renzo stood alone behind the open grave, ostracised or self-excluded from the gathering. Meni had arrived in her daughter's Fiat but never came beyond the cemetery gate, keeping, like Renzo, to herself, whilst her daughter waited for her in the car.

As Miltiadis the tailor left the graveside, he touched Sakis's elbow and said a few appropriate words, then moved away to join a group of his contemporaries, passing close to Dora as he did so but giving her only a cursory nod, as if he and she were barely acquainted. Dora offered condolences to Tasia, who seemed bewildered at being a centre of attention, and baffled as to why she herself was there.

The fat man finished his cigarette, stubbed it out on the wall and put it back in the box for later disposal. The crowd was thinning. Sakis noticed the waiting priest, fumbled for money and paid him, whilst Amara led the compliant Tasia away. The sexton was keen to finish his work, and asked Sakis if he might begin the filling-in, but Sakis was reluctant and shook his head, telling the sexton he wanted a little more time.

The fat man reached the graveside, and looked down into the grave, on to the pine box and the stem of the half-buried rose. Very faintly, he smelled the coffin's barely dry varnish. He reached deep into his pocket, brought out a small coin with the glint of old gold and tossed it into the grave, where it landed with no noise, and slipped unseen between the clods of earth and stones. For a few moments he bowed his head; then he walked away between the graves, following the other mourners to the gates.

Eleven

The next morning, the fat man set off early for Neochori. Lefteris had told him there was a new road, a black-topped dual carriageway stretching away between the acres of olive groves, but the fat man preferred the old route, through the mountains.

The road was steep and strewn with rockfalls, and wound in sharp hairpins deeply shadowed by larch and pine. Gorges dropped to breathtaking depths, and the carriageway skirted their rims, with only the flimsy panels of damaged barriers between road users and the chasms. The road signs had all been targets, and were dented by shotgun pellets, or shot into holes by rifle bullets. From time to time, the fat man stopped the car, and climbed out to admire the views: a bridge high over a fast-flowing river which foamed between crags and rocks; soaring buff peaks where the first snows had already fallen; in the far distance, a glimpse of cobalt sea. Beyond the mountains, burgeoning clouds signalled a coming change in the weather.

At the outskirts of Neochori the road levelled out, and at the head of the main street, alongside a church dedicated to the apostles, the fat man pulled over to get his bearings from the plan Lefteris had drawn for him. According to Lefteris, it was by the church the fat man should turn left, and he moved off cautiously from where he had stopped, positioning the car correctly on the centre line and indicating before making his turn. From this street, he would find the oil wholesalers along the third street on the left, but before he reached it, he saw a sign on an office block for the *Neochori News*; and since there was a space outside with only a single yellow line forbidding parking, he left the car there.

The reception area at the *Neochori News* seemed long deserted. An arrangement of dusty-petalled silk tulips stood on the desk; a plainly mounted certificate and a black and white photograph hung on the wall.

The fat man studied the photograph – a head-and-shoulders shot of a cheerful man looking into the camera with amusement – and read the brass plaque screwed on to the frame: *Panayiotis Dimas, Proprietor*. The certificate was embossed with a wax rosette, and under the elaborately inscribed heading of *The Pan-Hellenic Federation of Journalists*, it announced Panayiotis as the Best Investigative Journalist of 1964.

The opening and closing of the outer door had drawn no one's attention. Out of politeness, the fat man waited a minute or two, then went through the door beyond reception.

He found himself in an office, where the woman seated at the only occupied desk drew on the remains of a Marlboro, and looked at the fat man through heavy-framed, cat's-eye glasses.

'*Kali mera sas*,' she said. 'Can I help you?'

The fat man put on a genial smile.

'*Kali mera sas*,' he said, as he approached her. Her hair was black, but not naturally so; her skin was made more sallow by crimson lipstick. Despite her being some years past the age customary for marriage proposals, he saw no wedding ring. He held out his hand. 'I am Hermes Diaktoros, of Athens. I'd like to talk to someone about your archives.'

'Esmerelda Dimas,' she said, and placed her cigarette in the notch of an ashtray to touch, very briefly, his hand; her own was cold, the nails long with chipped red varnish, the insides of the index and middle fingers stained the ugly amber of tobacco. Immediately she let go of his hand, she reached out for the burning cigarette, and drew on it gratefully, like one reunited with an old friend. Smoke trickled down her nose and from her mouth. 'You'll have to talk to me, Jill-of-all-trades that I am. Owner, editor, reporter, photographer and archivist. What do you need?'

'I've been spending some time in Dendra,' said the fat man, 'and I've made the acquaintance there of a businessman who's fallen on hard times. I understand there was some kind of calamity which would undoubtedly have been reported in your newspaper.'

'What calamity?' She picked up a coffee mug decorated with the slogan of a minor Socialist party, but finding it empty, she frowned, and she put it down.

'An outbreak of food poisoning.'

The journalist inhaled long and deeply from the cigarette, then stubbed it out, taking her time to bend and break the butt, and using it for a few moments to stir the grey residue in the ashtray.

'So you're interested in that. Who's your businessman?'

'An Italian gentleman, by the name of Lorenzo Rapetti.'

'Are you a lawyer?'

'I? No. Why should I be a lawyer? Do you know Signor Rapetti?'

'I know of him.'

'And you remember the story, of course?'

She shrugged. From a capacious handbag by her feet, she found a pack of Marlboros and a cheap lighter.

'How could I forget? It was the biggest story to hit this prefecture for years. Four people were dead. The nationals were all over it.' She smiled a bitter smile. 'It seemed like the only time the phone's rung since my father passed on.' As if choosing from a box of chocolates, she dithered over the cigarettes before drawing out her selection and lighting it, and dropping the pack and the lighter back into her bag. 'But I'm sure Signor Rapetti has told you the whole story. What do you need from my archives?'

'Signor Rapetti hasn't told me a great deal, nor have I had much detail from anyone else. I was troubled by the sorry state of his business when his product is so good.'

Her eyes grew wide.

'You ate at his place?' She made a triple cross over her chest, drawing a vague crucifix in blue smoke with the burning cigarette. '*Kyrie*, you are a braver man than many.'

'As you see, I have lived to tell the tale. What I'm looking for is indisputable evidence that his shop was the outbreak's source. I assume it was never proven, or Signor Rapetti would be in jail as we speak, on a charge of manslaughter.'

With some reluctance she stood, leaving her cigarette in the ashtray.

'I'll show you what we have. Remind me, when was all this? A year ago, two?'

'I'm afraid I don't know exactly,' said the fat man. 'I knew nothing of this affair until I arrived in Dendra. I travel widely, sometimes to places where newspapers don't reach.'

She made her way between the desks to a bank of tall steel cabinets, and opened one to show racks of the *Neochori News* hung horizontally on spindles. She lifted one out to check the date.

'You could start here,' she said. 'Fortunately for you, we're a weekly and not a daily. I keep meaning to put all these on microfiche and have a bonfire with the back issues. It would make everyone's life easier, but microfiche machines cost money I don't have. Anyway, help yourself.'

The fat man lifted half a dozen papers from their spindles, and carried them to an empty desk. Esmerelda filled her coffee mug from a dripping filter pot.

'I'm afraid I can't offer you coffee,' she said. 'I only have the one cup.'

'No matter.'

'I drink far too much. But it seems to make the day so much brighter.'

As she sat back down at her desk, she drank a mouthful from her mug, and picked up her cigarette. The fat man glanced across at her, and saw her expression was more hopeless than bright. He read the front page of the first newspaper before him, from the last week in December of the previous year. Its headline was, predictably, *Happy New Year*. He skimmed the news pages of that edition, stopping when he came to the features pages. There was nothing relating to the drama in Dendra, and the three previous editions drew a similar blank; but in the fifth paper he opened, dated late in November, at the bottom of page six he found something of interest: an apology and retraction of inaccuracies published against Lorenzo Rapetti.

The fat man glanced again at Esmerelda. Cigarette in mouth, she was transcribing shorthand from a reporter's notebook into longhand.

He put the newspaper to one side, and read the headline of the next: *Four dead: Poisoning source set to be confirmed*. There was the same photo Renzo had in his window, of him receiving his award, over a report that a source had named

Dendra's *gelateria* as the likely origin of the fatal bacteria, and claiming an arrest could be expected any time soon. The story ran over the front cover and most of page two, detailing the outbreak, those affected and including photographs of those who had died. The fat man read the story carefully, twice; then he took out a small notebook with a pencil in its spine, and copied down the names of the victims.

He closed the paper.

'*Kyria* Dimas,' he began.

'*Despinis*,' she said. 'I'm not married.'

'I saw a photo and an award in your reception – your father, I assume?'

She took the cigarette from her mouth, and replaced it in its cradle in the ashtray.

'That's Papa,' she said, and made more crosses, this time with the point of her pen. 'This paper's founder. When he ran it, all these desks were full, and the paper sold in tens of thousands. He had such a nose for a story! They'd ring from Athens almost daily, asking whether there was anything they should know about. And he'd give them tips, but this paper always published first, and broke the story. Scoop after scoop fell into his hands. When he left us, somehow the news dried up, and I had to let the staff go. Now there's just me, and Stefanos who runs the presses. Me, him and those racks of old editions.'

Like a lush with a bottle, she tipped coffee down her throat, and drew again on the shrinking Marlboro.

'It seems he trained you well, though,' said the fat man. 'This article is well drafted, and your writing has flair. It's a good piece of journalism. Except, of course, for its obvious flaw.'

'What do you mean?'

'That the facts are not facts. In the way of too many newspapers, you haven't let the lack of proof stand in the way of

157

your story, and now Signor Rapetti's business and his life are in ruins, because of your speculation that his shop was the source of the outbreak.'

'I had it on good authority.'

'Whose authority? A police officer? A doctor? A public health official? Why is your authority not named and quoted?'

'You must know no journalist reveals their sources.'

'If your sources are reliable and official, why should you not? Give me a name, and I shall speak to them myself.'

He held his pencil ready over his notebook. Behind her glasses, Esmerelda's eyes narrowed.

'Are you sure you're not a lawyer?' she asked. 'Well, you can tell Rapetti there's no point in suing me. I've nothing to be sued for, as you can see.'

'I've told you, I am no lawyer. But why protect someone who's fed you false information?'

Esmerelda shook her head.

'You're assuming the story's wrong. But Rapetti remains the likeliest culprit, in my view.'

'I've been there,' said the fat man, 'and the place is spotlessly clean, his working practices beyond reproach.'

'Maybe,' she said, 'but aren't you overlooking the obvious, that he has improved his habits since those people died?'

'Are you not overlooking the obvious, that his business was very successful? Whose business did he damage when it became so? Have you not considered that his business might have been sabotaged? I suspect your father's secret was an understanding of the unpleasanter side of human nature, and I think he'd have followed up every possible line of enquiry. The best journalists share traits with the best detectives. You, by contrast, went to press without proving anything, and so were forced to issue an apology which did absolutely nothing to repair the damage your libel caused. You are lucky indeed that Signor Rapetti hasn't sued you. You broke a basic tenet of journalism, printing a story based on hearsay, digging out a photograph from your files, putting the piece together without ever leaving your desk. That's not journalism, that's laziness. Your father would have turned in his grave.'

His words brought colour to her sallow cheeks.

'My information was much more than hearsay. And we had the photo on file. What was the point?'

'The point was, if you'd gone out like your father and poked your nose where it wasn't welcome, who knows what you might have discovered? You might have had a scoop, and there might have been two awards hanging on that wall, instead of one. You might have made your father proud. Instead, you brought his paper into disrepute by publishing an unproven story which ruined a man's livelihood.'

'I only printed what people were saying.'

'Do you know nothing of people, *Despinis* Dimas? You took tittle-tattle, and repeated it to thousands. That is unforgivable.'

'I think it's time you left,' she said.

'Since I have what I need, I shall do so.' He slipped the pencil into the notebook's spine, and tucked the notebook away. 'I shall leave you to contemplate how your father would feel if he knew how lazy a journalist you are. A newspaper should be an instrument of good, not a rag for repeating gossip. I shall discover for myself whether Signor Rapetti was guilty or not. But before I say anything to anyone on my findings, I shall be very sure of my facts. My view at the moment is that someone has tried to shift blame on to an easy target, and that Signor Rapetti has been something of a scapegoat, with your paper whipping him through the streets. Please, think about what you have done, and what you might do to make reparation. *Yassas.*'

He made for the door; but as he reached it, she stopped him.

'*Kyrie* Diaktoros. Wait.' She ground out the second cigarette, and stood up again from her desk, brushing flakes of ash from the lap of her skirt. 'If I was wrong about Rapetti, then I'm sorry. But I'm not as convinced as you are of his innocence, and if he was responsible for those deaths and has got away with it, then I'm not sorry at all. You might yet find his tears are crocodile's. Let me show you something.'

She turned to a filing cabinet behind her, and searched a drawer until she found a collection of photographs, blown up to the size of a sheet of writing paper. She offered them to the fat man, who studied them in silence. The pictures were taken at early dawn, and the poor light affected the quality; but they clearly showed the *gelateria*, and in each one, the reflection in its window of a camera's flash. Taken in sequence, the first showed a man with his back to the camera, washing the shop window with a sponge. In the second picture, the man had turned towards the lens, clearly startled by the flash; in the next four, he was approaching the photographer. The last was almost a close-up of Renzo Rapetti, but not the gentle, disheartened man the fat man had met; in this picture, Renzo Rapetti was angry and aggressive, baring his teeth at the photographer, and threatening with his fist. And in all the photographs, what he was trying to erase from the window was easily read: sprayed in black, the word *Poisoner*.

'Where did you get these pictures?' asked the fat man.

'I took them,' said Esmerelda. 'I might disagree with your saying I'm no journalist, but you'll see from those I can't defend my photographic skills. They weren't good enough to print, hence our using the file picture of Rapetti receiving his award.'

'He looks very angry.'

'He was livid. I thought he would hit me, but he didn't, in the end. He tried to snatch the camera, but I ran away. He didn't follow me. I wasn't expecting to come across him. It was very early in the morning, as you can see.'

'So why were you there?'

She shrugged.

'I was doing what any newshound does. I was following a tip-off.'

'From whom?'

'You know,' she said, 'I don't think you've said why you've come here, or why you're asking your questions. You say you're not working for Rapetti, that you're no lawyer, and you don't strike me as a policeman. So what exactly is your interest?'

'Truly, I am no lawyer, and there's no police force in this country that would employ me. My methods are too maverick, too unorthodox for them. I work for the highest Authorities, whose interests lie in justice where there's been none. I act on their behalf, in the capacity of what you might call an investigator. So you could help me a great deal by telling me who it was who gave you your tip-off.'

'You've a low opinion of me, but I respected and trusted my source. She's the valued asset of any journalist, the fount of local knowledge. And what I know about local knowledge is that people round here know everything there is to know about one another. When I saw what was written on that window, I took that to mean someone in Dendra knew something, knew the truth, but didn't know how to prove it. I didn't run that article out of laziness. I ran it out of frustration. I could see how it was going to be. Time was going by, and no one was coming up with anything new – not the police, no one in public health, not the medical profession. Someone was going to get away with it, and no one was going to take responsibility for the deaths of those poor people. And I'm far more my father's daughter than you know. I couldn't bear that fact. So I gambled, with my reputation, with this paper's reputation. I gambled it all on what my father taught me – that somebody, somewhere always knows. I took that writing on Rapetti's window to be local knowledge. And you know what? I stand by it. The woman who saw the writing was my aunt. She keeps long hours, and saw it on her way to work. You should talk to her, hear what she has to say. You'll find her in Dendra, at the sign of the cockerel.'

The fat man handed back the photographs.

'Thank you,' he said. 'And my apologies if I have given you offence.'

'If you're sorry, you might make it up to me by doing me a favour,' she said. 'There's little enough happens in this backwater, so if you find a decent story, let me be the first to know.'

Twelve

The road where Lefteris had shown the oil wholesalers on his plan was a dead end, still paved in last century's cobbles and littered on its pavements with dumpster waste scattered by feral cats. The fat man drove slowly past a repair shop for heavy vehicles, and raised his hand to a grimy mechanic who stopped work to watch him pass. Alongside the repair shop, a site had been cleared, and an estate agent's billboard showed an artist's impression of new offices to be built there; but investors had not come forward, and only the concrete bones of foundations poked through clay studded with the broken bricks of demolition. At the road's end was a high wall set with shards of bottle-glass, and tall wooden gates standing open, splitting the signage painted across them – *Zysis & Co AE*.

The fat man drove through the gates, into a yard fronting a warehouse, and parked between an unmarked transit van and a tanker rig. The place seemed quiet. From the repair shop along the road came the whine of an angle-grinder.

A middle-aged man sat on a stack of empty pallets, eating a sandwich overfilled with meatballs and fried aubergines. The fat man climbed from the Tzen, and wished him *kalo mezimeri*.

'Can you tell me where I'll find whoever's in charge?'

The man had just bitten into his sandwich, and his mouth was too full to speak. Instead, he pointed to the open roller-shutter which was the warehouse entrance.

Beyond the reach of daylight from the yard, the warehouse was dark. The concrete floor was slick with greasy spillages, and over everything hung the soapy smell of crushed olives. The space inside seemed diminished by its division into bays, each one identified by a white number on the wall. Many of the bays were empty; others were filled with aluminium barrels, or with cases of oil in five-, two- or single-litre bottles, shrink-wrapped and ready for shipping. Nailed high overhead was a red-lettered sign: *No shipments in or out without management approval.*

In the near corner, two half-glazed stud walls made an office with no roof, where a man was talking on the phone, carrying the base with him and pacing up and down to the extent the phone wire would allow. The fat man studied him through the glass. Unshaven for several days, he wore jeans which were too big for him, and a cable-knit sweater. On a silver chain around his neck was a deep-bowled silver spoon, and tucked into the waistband of his jeans was a creased white cloth marked with oil stains. The man turned, and seeing the fat man, raised a finger to him to ask him to wait, and continued talking animatedly into the phone.

'Two-four, and not a cent more,' he said. 'I didn't say it was good, I said it's what I can pay . . . Last year was different. Five years ago it was three-six. I don't have to tell you how the market is . . . Fine, if you think you'll get more there, be my guest. I've heard he's paying two-two, two-three. Try there, and then come back to me.' He glanced again at the fat man. 'I have to go. We'll talk later.'

He replaced the receiver on the base. Immediately the phone began to ring. Again, he raised a finger to the fat man, and answered it.

'Yes? Michaeli, how are you, how's the family . . .? Good . . . Two-four, my friend . . . It's not great, I know. I'd pay more, but it's down to my brother, and he's a hard man, as you know. But tell me, what have you got? . . . Sounds good. Listen, I'd have to try it, of course, but maybe I could go two-six, two-seven . . . You'll get no joy there, my friend, they're saying he's paying lower than ever . . . OK, a firm two-seven, if the quality's right . . . Tomorrow, the day after. I'll be here . . . See you then.'

He banged the receiver on to its base, and slammed the phone down on a cardboard file thick with papers. When it rang, he snatched off the receiver, cancelled the call and laid the receiver alongside the phone. The silence seemed to please him, and the muscles of his face relaxed. He beckoned the fat man through into the office, but though he mustered a smile of welcome, his attention was distracted; he lifted the receiverless phone base from the file, and began to search through the papers inside.

'What can I do for you?' he asked. He pulled a sheet from the file, glanced at it, replaced it and continued his search.

'*Kali mera sas*,' said the fat man. 'Hermes Diaktoros, of Athens.'

Surprised at the fat man's beautifully enunciated Greek, the man looked up from the file.

'Athens,' he said. 'I would have guessed so. Spiros Zysis.' They shook hands. 'How can I help you?'

'I see you're very busy,' said the fat man. 'I was wanting to try some of your oils.'

Behind the desk was a shelf of oil samples in green bottles, each labelled with a name and a code. Spiros looked at the samples, then at the silenced phone.

He hesitated.

'*Kyrie*,' he said, 'I'm going to be honest with you. I don't have time to taste oils with you today. Tasting these oils is a job for half a day at least, and today I don't have half an hour, let alone half a day. It's harvest, and every farmer for miles around is trying to screw me on price. There's no one here now, but only because they're all off drinking coffee, whilst I, as you see, am so up to my neck, I can only dream of having time to drink coffee.' Through the open doorway, they heard a vehicle pull on to the yard. 'See, we speak of the devil, and here he is. So, although I would love you to taste my oils – I have some beauties here, absolute top quality – please, come back next month. Come back in January, February. Then I have all the time in the world.'

'Maybe your brother could help me?'

For a moment, Spiros was puzzled. Then he laughed.

'You overheard my phone call. Tell me something. Are you here to try and sell me any oil?'

'On the contrary. I'm interested in buying.'

'Then I'll let you in on a secret. I have no brother, only a sister, a wonderful woman who's a housewife in Patra. She has a small share in the business, which my father left to her. People see we trade as Zysis & Co, and assume I'm in business with a brother. I let them make their assumptions, because my phantom brother is very useful to me. He's a tough businessman who drives a hard bargain, and I'm always the nice guy.'

The fat man smiled.

'Ingenious.'

'A practicality. If it weren't for my brother, these people would drive me crazy.'

In the yard an engine revved and then slowed, and a voice shouted, 'Whoa! That's far enough!'

'You'll have to excuse me,' said Spiros. 'I must see who's here.'

He grabbed a clipboard and a pen, and left the office.

The fat man crossed to the sample shelf, and studied the row of green bottles, but there was nothing to distinguish one from another but their handwritten labels. He followed Spiros as far as the warehouse doorway, and looked out on to the yard.

Around a three-wheeled truck – a primitive contraption with an uncovered bench seat, and handlebars rather than a steering wheel – Spiros was in conversation with two men. One was very elderly, bent-backed and emaciated, formally dressed in a jacket and tie, his sparse hair combed and oiled, though his grooming was spoiled by open-toed sandals made necessary by the bandaging of ulcers on his calves and feet. The other was his middle-aged grandson, lank and lean from hard work, who wore a farmer's filthy clothes. On the back of the truck was a hunting dog, a black Labrador unhappily pressed up against the truck sides by a plastic barrel lashed in place with baling twine. The old man was unsteady, relying for balance partly on his grandson, who kept a hand under his elbow, and partly on a handsome antique cane.

The lid was off the barrel. Standing on the rear bumper, Spiros took the spoon from round his neck and dipped it into the oil. Drawing out a spoonful, he sniffed and sucked, and, eyes closed, swilled and drank and coughed; then he refilled the spoon, and did the same. The old man and his grandson waited tensely.

Spiros's face gave nothing away.

'How much have you got?' he asked.

'Only this,' said the grandson, 'plus what we've kept for ourselves. There's only me to harvest. I did my best.'

'What's he say?' asked the old man, putting his hand to his ear and leaning towards his grandson's mouth.

'He wants to know how much we have,' shouted the younger man in his ear, and the old man sadly shook his head.

'Only a little,' he said. 'Just a little.'

Spiros looked inside the barrel.

'It looks a little short on measure,' he said, 'but let's call it a hundred and sixty litres.' He dipped his spoon again, and took a quick taste. 'What blend do you say this is?'

'No blend,' said the grandson. 'Only *Ladolia*. What do you think?'

Spiros stepped down off the bumper, and for a few moments faced the two men in silence.

He smiled, broadly.

'I think it's superb.'

'What does he say?' asked the old man.

The son was grinning with relief.

'He says it's good, *Pappou*,' he shouted in the old man's ear. 'He says it's really good.'

The old man mumbled under his breath, made three crosses with the head of his cane, and turned away his face to hide tears.

'But the market's low,' said Spiros. 'Market price even at this quality is only two-six, two-seven. Every year, the foreigners put us under more pressure. In Spain, they're giving oil away.'

'Two-seven!' objected the grandson. 'Last year we got three! It's not worth my time at two-seven!'

Spiros shrugged his sympathy. The grandson touched his arm, and spoke quietly.

'Listen,' he said. 'This will likely be my grandfather's last harvest. Please, give him something good to remember.'

'I know what you're saying,' said Spiros, wiping his spoon on the white cloth and hanging the chain back around his neck, 'but if I give you three, I'll take a loss on it.'

With watery eyes, the old man was watching.

Spiros sighed.

'You know what?' he said, at last. 'The oil is top quality, and I'll take the barrel at three-ten.'

The son beamed, and clapped his grandfather on his bony back.

'Three-ten,' he shouted in the old man's ear. 'He says he'll give us three-ten.'

The old man smiled, showing his empty gums, and gripped Spiros's upper arm.

'Thank you,' he said. 'Thank you.' He looked at his grandson. 'I told you it was worth doing, boy. I told you it was good.'

'Come into the office,' Spiros said to the grandson, 'and we'll sort you out.' He called out to the man with the sandwich, who had finished eating and was now enjoying a cigarette. 'Tasso! We'll have this in number twelve.'

As the grandson helped the old man back aboard the truck, Spiros made for his office, passing the fat man in the warehouse doorway. By the time the grandson joined him, Spiros was seated behind his desk, writing on the next available line in a ledger, across the page in green ink: the family name, the variety, the quantity, the date, the price, the location of their farm. When the details were complete, he stood and took a wad of cash from his back pocket, counted off a number of notes and handed them to the grandson, who thanked him profusely.

'I won't forget this,' he said, offering an enthusiastic handshake. 'You're a gentleman.'

'You take care of your grandfather,' said Spiros. 'And take care of your trees. They deserve it.'

As the grandson drove the old man away, a forklift truck was bringing the oil barrel into the warehouse. Spiros seemed to have forgotten the fat man, who was waiting patiently whilst Spiros made entries in a cash book.

'I see how busy you are,' said the fat man at last, 'and I appreciate you're not free to give me a lot of time. But I would appreciate your answering me one question. I've tried two oils from this region, both from Dendra. Is Dendra oil some of your best?'

Spiros seemed not to have heard. He finished writing in the cash book, then flicked through the ledger, running his fingers down the entries, pausing at three or four. Then he stood up, efficiently picked three bottles from the sample shelf behind him and placed them in a row on his desk.

'How can I not make time for a customer?' he said. 'Not as much time as I'd like, but let me show you something. These are last year's oils, and they're past their best. Soon the new crop will be in, and you should buy from that. But let's try these.'

He found a plastic spoon in a drawer, and filling it with oil from the first bottle, handed it to the fat man, who tasted it.

'Forgive the spoon,' he said. 'It isn't the way it should be done. When you come back, we'll do this properly, but you'll get an idea at least. What do you think?'

The fat man was reluctant to answer, and tried the oil again.

Spiros laughed.

'Not so good, eh? Industrial oil. Lamp oil, as the Italians call it, the very dregs. This oil is rancid, fusty, made with rotten fruit and the second pressing of the leftovers from virgin oil. You taste in there maybe something metallic, something vinegary? Not fit for pigs! But let me tell you, this oil made it on to the market, and was sold in supermarkets as extra-virgin olive oil! Yes, truly! And how? Because there are unscrupulous men out there – too many of them, my friend, far too many! – who will take a cheap oil like this and bastardise it – filter it, blend it, deodorise it and colour it, and *voilà*! To those who know nothing – and that, I am afraid, is the majority – it becomes first quality, extra-virgin. This oil might fetch good money in Frankfurt or Amsterdam. But virgin? Pah! This oil, friend, is a whore. It's a whore which is destroying the true oil business, and putting quality growers like the gentlemen who have just left us out of business. Now, please. Forgive my little trick, but I wanted to make a point with you. What I sell from this warehouse is only the purest olive oil. What happens to it when it leaves here, I have no control over. But if you buy direct from me, I guarantee you oil you would be proud to serve to your family and to your guests.' At the edge of the desk was a bowl of green apples. Spiros picked one out, and opening a blade of the penknife, cut off a slice of the tart fruit and passed it to the fat man. 'Here, eat this and clean your palate.' The fat man did so, and Spiros wiped the plastic spoon, and opened the second bottle. 'Now try this.'

He filled the spoon, and held it out to the fat man, who hesitated to take it.

'I've made you nervous,' said Spiros. 'But I promise you, no more tricks. As you taste it, suck the air over it, as if you were tasting a fine wine.'

The fat man took the spoonful of oil into his mouth, and drew in air through puckered lips. He held the oil on his tongue for a moment, then quickly swallowed it as he began to cough, and tears came to his eyes.

'There you have it!' said Spiros, excitedly. 'There you have the best oil I could sell you! It's peppery, and it burns! But tell me, what flavours are you getting now?'

The fat man wiped his eyes, and licked his lips.

'It's wonderful,' he said. 'It's green, and grassy . . .'

'Exactly! Fresh-cut grass and green tomatoes, maybe a little artichoke? It's bitter, and it's hot, yes? This is a wonderful oil. Unfortunately I can sell you none of this. I sold all of it I had, early in the year. It's a connoisseur's oil, and I have my special buyers who take it every season. Do you find that pepperiness unexpected? It's not to the general public's taste, so the big companies blend the heat from decent oils, mixing them with milder olive oils, canola oil, anything to disguise what the public isn't used to. But this is the real thing – this is extra-virgin olive oil as it should be, not the abomination you buy off the supermarket shelves. Imagine it, my friend, on your table. Now, another.'

He cut the fat man another piece of apple; the fat man ate it, and took the spoonful of the third oil Spiros offered him.

'What do you think to that?'

The fat man took the oil in his mouth, sucked air in over it, and savoured it on his tongue before swallowing it.

'It's good,' said the fat man. 'It's very good. It has a burn to it, and the same grassiness as the last.'

'You're right, it is a good oil,' said Spiros. 'It's a little past its best now, but it's still good.' He tried a little himself, as an indulgence. 'Does it seem familiar to you?'

The fat man was doubtful.

'You're not sure, and I don't blame you,' said Spiros. 'When you taste several oils, it becomes difficult for the novice to tell them apart. But I think you have tasted this oil before. This is Kapsis oil, from Dendra.'

'How do you tell them all apart?'

'It's a craft I've learned, from being a boy. I understand the oils' nuances. But even I have days when it's difficult. The first sign of a cold, and my palate is useless. So just to be sure, I code them in my ledger.'

'And which one of these is from the Papayiannis mill?' asked the fat man, pointing to the bottles on the shelf.

'None of them. I had no Papayiannis oil last year. All their oil went for export. I couldn't blame them, really. They were offered an unbeatable price. Though it might have annoyed me, if I hadn't done all right out of the deal myself. This company has dealt with the Papayiannis family for decades, and there has to be a place in business for loyalty.'

'What happened?'

'They brought me a lot of oil. Their new machinery has upped their yields. We agreed a price, I bought the oil into the warehouse. But a few days later, here came Sakis, wanting to buy it all back. All of it, and more on top, as similar as I could give them, he said. He'd got a contract from someone in London or New York, someone passing who'd loved the oil and wanted to buy the lot for a chain of restaurants. Well, it was no skin off my nose. I took my cut, and sold them back their own oil, plus the extra they were wanting.'

'Where did the extra come from?'

'It was from their neighbours in Dendra. They wanted a close match, and that was the closest I could get.'

'How did they feel about that?'

Spiros smiled and shook his head.

'I didn't tell them. I know how things stand between those families. I told them it was from elsewhere, and they were happy. From the barrels alone, there's no way of telling which producer an oil's from. The only way is through my coding system, in my ledger.'

Outside, another vehicle pulled on to the yard, blasting its horn for attention. Spiros glanced at his watch.

'If you know the family, have you heard of Donatos Papayiannis's death?' asked the fat man.

'I have,' said Spiros. 'The oil community's tight knit, and bad news travels fast. I'd have gone to the funeral, but I couldn't spare the time. As you've seen, the place is bedlam, and I must excuse myself, and get on.'

'Of course,' said the fat man. 'My thanks to you. You've been most helpful.'

'I mean what I say,' said Spiros. 'Come back after harvest, and I'll introduce you to a few more of our oils.'

He replaced the receiver on the phone. Immediately, it rang.

'Before I go,' said the fat man, as Spiros reached out to answer it, 'the barrel you just bought from those two gentlemen – is it a good oil?'

'It's a different oil to these last two you've tasted, but excellent in its way. *Ladolia* olives are harvested black, not green, and the oil is milder, paler in colour. With the best ones, like the barrel out there, you get a distinct flavour of almonds. Yes, it's an oil I wouldn't hesitate to recommend.'

'Then I'll buy it from you. I'll give you four-ten for the whole barrel.'

'Four-ten? That's far too much. I've overpaid on it myself. Give me three-twenty, and I've turned a profit on it.'

'Four-ten,' said the fat man. 'I insist. I'll send someone to pick it up in the next few days, and he'll bring cash. It's been a pleasure meeting you, Spiros.'

Spiros offered his hand.

'Likewise,' he said, and answered the ringing phone.

It was close to the traditional hour for lunch, and traffic in Neochori was thinning out. The fat man parked near the Church of the Apostles, and wandered for a while along the main street, reading every name carved on the war memorial, looking over the titles in a bookshop window where a new guide to the island of Thiminos took pride of place. Coming to a restaurant where the food smelled appetising, he glanced only briefly at the menu, preferring to judge by the number of diners the likely quality of the food; and seeing through the condensation-misted window that the place was nearly full, he went inside.

He was shown to a table by a young girl whose hair was bleached almost white, and cropped short to show off the earrings dangling from her lobes – three in each ear, all silver drops, spirals and hoops. Her tight-fitting jeans were tucked into ankle boots, and her black T-shirt had a clenched, red fist on the chest, over the slogan, *Eat the Rich*.

She left him to take his seat, and returning with a basket of warm bread and a jug of water, handed him a menu.

'I hope,' he said, as he opened it, 'that your T-shirt is not an advertisement for what I shall find in here?'

She looked down her front, reminding herself of what she was wearing, and smiled.

'We're short of volunteers for the pot,' she said. 'We don't get many of the rich coming in here. Can I get you something to drink?'

'An ouzo,' he said. 'And before I spend time on the menu, can you tell me what I should order?'

'That depends,' she said. 'Are you hungry, or not so hungry? If you're hungry, there's braised veal with pasta – that's good – or there's slow-roast lamb, or rabbit with onions. If you're not so hungry, there are octopus *keftedes*, or there's squid stuffed with spinach and feta. Papa does them on the barbecue. The squid is fresh today.'

'Your father's chef here, then?'

'He is.'

'And does he share your politics?'

'He has his own politics. He's taught me to think for myself. But he was at the Polytechnic uprising in seventy-three.'

'Was he? I witnessed those events myself.'

She looked at him, scrutinising his face, unselfconsciously trying to determine his age; but though there was grey in his hair, close inspection showed no wrinkles to support a diagnosis of middle age.

'You don't look old enough to have been there,' she said, mistrustfully. 'You must be younger than my dad.'

'Maybe time has been kinder to me than to him,' said the fat man. 'Is he a good cook?'

'One of the best.'

'Then tell him I'm hungry, and to send out whatever he thinks I should eat.'

She brought him, first, his ouzo, then a dozen tail-on prawns, fried in crisp cauls of *kataifa* pastry, with garlicky dips of yogurt with dill, and roasted aubergines with fennel seeds. When he had cleared his plate, she brought him the braised veal, a crumbling of *kefalotyri* cheese added as it was served, and melting into the sauce.

When she came to clear his second course, he was sitting back in his chair, hands on his stomach.

'Truly excellent,' he said. 'Your father's a very good cook.'

'I'll tell him you said so.'

From the kitchen came a shout.

'Arethusa! Table four!'

She picked up his plate and the bread basket.

'That'll be your dessert.'

'Is there dessert?' asked the fat man, doubtfully. 'I don't know whether I should.'

'You should,' said Arethusa. 'I make the desserts.'

'Then it would be ungallant of me to refuse. I shall be wanting Greek coffee afterwards, no sugar.'

'*Amessos.*'

Dessert was a cinnamon-sprinkled rice pudding, served with poached quinces in orange-flower syrup. The fat man ate very slowly, but by the time Arethusa brought him his coffee, his bowl was empty.

'How was it?' she asked.

'Delicious,' he said. 'I promised myself I would eat only a taste, but as you see, that taste led to my finishing the whole dish. You make a creditable apprentice to your father.'

'My future's not in cooking,' she said. 'I want to make a difference in people's lives.'

'And can you not do that here, by giving them the pleasure of food?'

'Life's not about pleasure, when so many don't have money to eat at all. They need champions to fight on their behalf. That's what I want to do.'

'And what does your father say about that?'

'He says I should find myself a husband, and settle down.'

'His ambitions for you are rather modest. Will you go along with them?'

She gave him a smile, which – despite the severity of her haircut and her unfeminine clothes – made her very attractive.

'I'm not the dutiful type,' she said, and left him to his coffee.

Thirteen

After lunch, the fat man dozed away an hour at the wheel of his car, undisturbed by passing traffic and the shouts of schoolboys kicking a football between themselves as they made their way to the nearby park. Refreshed, he roused himself, and drove with his usual care to the outskirts of Neochori.

The entrance to the St Panteleimon hospital was flanked by palm trees. Opaque glass orbs – which had, at one time, lit up – were mounted on the gatepost pillars, and on the orbs were painted red crosses, and serpent-entwined staffs of Asklepios, the god of healing. Beyond the driveway, the post-war hospital building was four storeys of cheap construction and peeling paint. The hedges lining the footpaths were straggly with unchecked growth; cars were parked on the flattened clay of what had once been flowerbeds.

The fat man parked in a tight space by a statue of the hospital's most generous benefactor, and locked the car. The benefactor's marble shoulders were spattered with pigeon droppings, and his pedestal was scribbled with graffiti: the rising green sun of PASOK socialists, a football fan's support for AEK. In a freshening wind, a plastic cup blew along the edge of the kerb. Below a notice ordering *Ambulances Only* stood two taxis, whose drivers were relaxing on a nearby bench. One was eating a *gyros*, wiping up with a finger a dribble of oily liquid which ran from the wrapper on to his leg, and oblivious to the other, who was declaiming against the poor treatment his wife had suffered at the hospital when admitted for an emergency hysterectomy.

'In agony she was,' he was saying as the fat man passed, 'and they gave her nothing for the pain. When they cut her open, everything popped out like a champagne cork.'

In the reception area, the soles of the fat man's tennis shoes squeaked on the polished floor. On banks of uncomfortable chairs, people were waiting. A young mother comforted a grizzling, feverish toddler, whilst her own mother nursed a teated bottle of water and a box of rusks. A brawny man was holding his hand vertical, his middle three fingers voluminously bandaged, his work-boots caked in dirt. A woman with a gauze patch over one eye was picking at hangnails. And with his arm in a new sling, asleep in the corner, was Dino.

It had been the fat man's intention to speak to the receptionist, but instead he made his way between the rows of chairs. Dino's mouth was open, his head back, his breathing loud and guttural. His clothes were still the same (though the yellow T-shirt was very dirty now, and he had acquired from somewhere a knitted hat, which he was clutching to his chest), and the odour coming off him of stale alcohol and sweat overrode even the hospital smells of carbolic, boiled greens and frying fish.

The fat man frowned. He put out a hand to shake Dino awake, but changed his mind, and crossed to the reception desk.

The receptionist had squeezed herself into a uniform sizes too small, and the blouse buttons gaped across her chest. On her overloaded desk was a vase of radiant flowers – purple iris, scented roses, frothy sprays of gypsophila – but the vase was inadequate for both their quantity and quality, and whilst the flowers were fresh, a number were already wilting from broken stems. Tucked behind the vase was a packet of expensive biscuits – German wafers covered in dark chocolate – and on the receptionist's breast, above her name badge, was a tell-tale crumb of the same chocolate. She was searching a stack of patient files, some holding only a page or two, some bulging with paperwork. As he reached her, she pulled a folder from the stack, placed it to one side, and looked up at him expectantly.

'*Yassas*,' he said.

An ambulance drew up outside; finding his parking space taken by taxis, the driver gave a blast on the siren. Dino shifted in his chair. One of the taxi drivers reluctantly stood, and prepared to move his car.

'May I help you?' asked the receptionist.

'I'm here to see a patient of yours,' said the fat man. 'Dmitris Kapsis.'

But his last words were lost, as a determined woman in a blue overall started up a floor polisher, and began gliding it over the gleaming floor. The receptionist gave the cleaner a look of annoyance, and was leaning forward to ask the fat man to repeat himself, but her phone rang, and she answered it.

'I've found it,' she said into the receiver. 'It's here, on my desk, but you'll have to come and get it. I can't leave reception.'

Outside, the ambulance parked in front of the doors. The co-driver jumped out, and walked smartly to the rear of the vehicle. The cleaner drew closer to reception, and the receptionist hung up the phone. She seemed distracted; her plump hand was on the patient file.

'Dmitris Kapsis?' prompted the fat man. 'Where will I find him?'

Still not hearing him, the receptionist shook her head impatiently, and leaned towards him.

'Dmitris Kapsis.'

Understanding at last, she reached out for a clipboard, and searched the ward lists for the name.

'Are you a relative?' she asked.

The fat man hesitated.

'A friend to the family,' he said.

'In that case, you can't see him,' said the receptionist, and she laid down the clipboard. 'Dr Fitanidis has said close family only.'

The fat man cupped his ear.

'I'm sorry?'

'Close family only,' she repeated. 'Dr Fitanidis says so.'

The ambulance's rear doors were open, and the driver was putting a ramp in place. The co-driver strode into the reception area and glanced around.

'Eh, Toula!' he shouted to the receptionist. 'I need a wheelchair!'

'We haven't got any,' she called back. 'They've taken them all up to the wards, and they never bring them back.'

'They've got three on B ward,' remarked the cleaner, moving the polisher close to the fat man's feet, 'standing about doing nothing, getting in my way.'

'You'll have to fetch one from there,' the receptionist told the ambulance man. 'And tell them to return the rest.'

The ambulance man headed for the hospital's interior. After a moment, the receptionist picked up the patient file and called after him, 'Adonis! Wait! Can you take this up to Dr Fitanidis's office? He's asking for it urgently.'

But over the floor polisher, the ambulance man didn't hear, and disappeared.

The receptionist looked anxious. She reached out for a biscuit.

'Those look very good,' said the fat man. 'I have something of a sweet tooth myself. Do you have a cafeteria here?'

'Second floor.' She bit into her biscuit.

'May I help out?' he suggested. 'I'm sure it's highly irregular, but I assure you I am trustworthy. Might I be your messenger, and carry your file to Dr Fitanidis?'

'I'm afraid not,' she said, sharply. 'These are confidential records.'

'As you wish,' he said, and turned away. But the phone on her desk rang again, and rather than answer it, she picked up the file.

'*Kyrie!*' The fat man stopped. 'If you wouldn't mind just saying you're family. His secretary's on the first floor, straight ahead at the top of the stairs, second door on the right.'

The fat man made his way along the first-floor corridor, stepping aside for shuffling patients in bathrobes and slippers, one pushing his own drip-stand on squeaky wheels, another clutching his stomach as if afraid of losing his guts if he let go. Two doctors in shirtsleeves and stethoscopes puzzled over a patient's chart. In a janitor's closet, someone was clattering buckets and mops. A nurse with a drugs trolley leaned, arms folded, against the wall, unable to wheel the trolley past a stepladder whilst the electrician at its top fiddled with a screwdriver in an overhead duct.

Dr Fitanidis's name plate was engraved in loud capitals; alongside his name, it listed his degrees, memberships and qualifications, which the fat man noted, and with an expression suggesting he was impressed, he entered the office.

The doctor's secretary was an extremely attractive girl with long, black hair put up in an elegant chignon; she was typing, listening to dictation through a set of earphones, and noticed the fat man only when his shadow fell across her desk. The door between her office and the doctor's was closed. She pressed a button to stop the dictaphone and removed the earphones.

'Can I help you?'

'I'm playing messenger,' said the fat man, with a smile. 'I brought this from downstairs.'

The file was labelled with Dmitris's name and a code, B14. She took the file and read the label.

'At last.' She left her seat, walked gracefully and with a slight sashay to the doctor's office, knocked briefly and without waiting for a response, went inside. There was a murmur of voices.

When she returned to her desk, the secretary picked up her earphones, preparing to go back to her work.

'I wonder if I might have a brief word with Dr Fitanidis?' asked the fat man.

'On what matter?'

'Regarding a patient of his, Dmitris Kapsis.'

'Are you a relative?'

'I have an interest in his case.'

'But are you a relative?'

'No.'

'Then I'm afraid it's out of the question.' She replaced her earphones, taking care not to disturb her chignon.

'Perhaps I could wait, and ask him myself if he would talk to me?'

'Impossible. His schedule is very tight. He has a patient with him now, and he's due in theatre in half an hour. If you'll excuse me, I have work to do.'

'What if I had the family's agreement? He would speak with me then, no doubt.'

'I expect so. If you had an appointment. Otherwise, I'm afraid the answer's no.'

Back in the corridor, the fat man stopped at the foot of the stepladder. As he looked up, the screwdriver fell from the electrician's hand. The electrician swore; the fat man picked up the screwdriver, and held it up to the electrician.

'That's awkward work,' he said. 'And complicated. The logic of electricity has always baffled me.'

The electrician looked down on him, taking in his hold-all, his clothes, and his shoes.

'There's not much to it,' he said, 'once you've mastered the basic principle. Which is that, if you get it wrong, at best it'll sting a bit, at worst it'll kill you.'

'It sounds as if you have a healthy respect for it. Has it ever caught you out?'

'Once, in my early days.' The electrician descended a couple of steps. 'Here, take a look at this.' He pushed up his sleeve to show a large patch of his forearm skin, which was hairless, very smooth and pink. 'Like a fool, I set myself on fire. And let me tell you, there's no pain like it. It was burned right down to the bone, so badly there was talk of my losing the arm altogether. Even when it healed, it was so hideous my own wife couldn't bear to touch it. But that man in there . . .' He pointed his screwdriver at Dr Fitanidis's door. 'He's a miracle-worker, a magician. He saw it one day after I started working here, and we got talking. He wanted to know what butcher had worked on it, and offered to do me a better job. I was reluctant, but he persuaded me, and the result's what you see here. He put it right, almost as good as new.'

'It was Dr Fitanidis I wanted to see,' said the fat man, 'but understandably, he's a very busy man. As it happens, it's a burns case I'm interested in, but not being a family member, I can't get an appointment. Yet your story confirms that he's the man I should talk to.'

The electrician considered.

'I probably shouldn't tell you this,' he said, 'but if it's in someone's best interests . . . The doctor has his diversions, as we all do, and he takes his pleasures very often up at Argiri Lake. I'm not saying you'll find him alone. If you've been in there, you've seen the girl who works for him, and if she's providing other services, he's a lucky man. But when he's not here, if the weather's decent, that's where you're most likely to find him.'

Bed B14 was not on the open ward but in a side room. A handwritten note taped to the closed door warned against entry, and of the risk of infection. In the passageway outside the room, despondent members of the Kapsis family – a young woman with the child the fat man had seen in Marianna's care, a youth not much older than the boy in the bed, a man who from his looks was father to both Dmitris and the youth – sat on a row of chairs with their backs to the wall, with the necessities for their vigil around their feet: water and fruit juice, blankets and newspapers, gifts of food from relatives and neighbours, toys to entertain the child.

The fat man greeted the family respectfully and glanced through the window separating the passageway from the side room. Dmitris Kapsis lay motionless in the bed. A mask of gauze was tied over his face; the square-cut holes for his eyes, mouth and nose gave repugnant glimpses of scabbing flesh glistening with ointments. From the waist down, he was covered in a carefully folded sheet and blanket; above the waist, he was naked, except for gauze wrapping his right arm and shoulder. A drip fed fluids into a vein on his left hand, and to his stomach through a feeding tube threaded into his nostril. At the bedside, his mother sat on a hard chair, her hair tucked into a paper cap, a hospital gown over her clothes, holding his hand between her own, on which she wore surgical gloves.

'I saw his accident,' said the fat man to the relatives. 'How is he?'

'Accident!' The youth drew in his cheeks to spit his disgust, but remembered where he was. 'Since when is a shove in the back an accident?'

'Leave it,' said his father. 'The gentleman's good enough to ask after your brother. He's as you see, *Kyrie*.' His eyes were swollen from tears, and he wiped away more. 'They're doing all they can. But the pain he's in when they do what they have to do! Every time they change the dressings, he's in agony! We're going this evening to offer prayers, to ask for some relief from his suffering.'

The fat man looked in again at Dmitris, who was moving his head and becoming restless. His mother let go of his hand and came to the window, pointing to her wrist where a watch would be and mouthing her words so as not to disturb her son.

'Tell them it's time for his morphine,' she said. 'Tell them to be quick, he's in pain.'

'If I can do anything to help him, I shall,' said the fat man to Dmitris's father as he left. 'In the meantime, I hope your saints will respond to your prayers.'

In reception, the seat Dino had occupied was empty. The ambulance was gone. One of the taxi drivers sat alone on the bench, chewing open-mouthed on a piece of gum, a foot crossed over his thigh.

'You wanting a taxi?' he asked, when he noticed the fat man.

'Thank you, no. I have my own car. I was wondering if you saw a relative of mine leave a short while ago? Scruffy, long hair and a yellow T-shirt, arm in a sling?'

'Your relative, is he?' asked the taxi driver with a smile. 'He's a live wire, isn't he? Had us both in stitches, he did.'

'I'm sure he did. Did you notice which way he went?'

'He went through the gates, same as everyone else. He went with my cousin.'

'Your cousin?'

'In his cab. Your relative asked him to take him to Dendra.'

As he approached the Hotel Byron, the fat man was surprised to hear laughter from inside. In the dining room, he found Lefteris, his father-in-law Tomas and Dino sitting at a table, each with a glass of wine poured from a bottle carrying the Lachesis label and all in stitches at some joke. Tomas was laughing so hard, he was wiping away tears.

Seeing the fat man, Lefteris got to his feet.

'*Kyrie* Diaktoros,' he said, 'come and join us.'

'Yes, come and join us, Hermes,' said Dino. 'The wine and the company are good.'

'You two know each other?' asked Lefteris.

'I should say so,' answered Dino. 'He's my brother.'

Tomas pulled a fourth chair up to the table.

'Come, sit, sit,' he said. 'You enjoyed this wine, and we're just going to open another bottle. Lefteris, open another.'

'I did enjoy that wine,' said the fat man, 'enough to go to the trouble of visiting the vineyard and buying some, so I know that the vintage is far from limitless, and that it would be a crime to drink it without savouring it, and giving it due respect. I mean you no offence, brother, but you'll admit you're not always particular about what you drink, so might I suggest, Lefteris, that if you're going to open a second bottle, you open something more in the factory-bottled line.'

Dino gave a bark of laughter.

'Hermes,' he said, 'you're the life and soul, as ever! Don't be so pompous! Why is it for you to tell these gentlemen what wine they may or may not drink? And if you've bought some anyway, why not open a bottle of yours? Come on, live a little!'

Lefteris placed a fourth glass on the table, and the fat man sat down.

'It seems you at least have been living, in your usual style,' said the fat man. 'I saw you at the hospital. What did you do to your arm?'

Dino grinned, and took a drink which emptied his glass. Lefteris was removing the foil from another bottle.

'The details are sketchy, as I was just saying,' said Dino. 'I remember I was getting on well with a lady, who wasn't perhaps quite as young as I'd like, though she wasn't the worst you've seen, by any means. I bought her a drink or two . . .'

'Did you buy her a drink or two, or merely lodge the debt on some unpaid bill?' interrupted the fat man.

Dino went on as if he hadn't heard.

'We had a couple of drinks,' he said. 'We were in one of those places that sells wine from the barrel, and they keep a barrel out in the street as advertising.'

'I know the place,' said Tomas. 'I've had a glass or two there myself, in my time.'

'I liked it there,' said Dino, 'and the wine wasn't bad of its type. Anyway, we had a drink or two, and then she made me a bet.' The fat man looked up to the ceiling, and sighed. Lefteris filled his glass with ruby wine. 'She bet me I couldn't roll that barrel to the end of the street.'

'That's not so difficult, surely,' said the fat man.

'It is when you're standing on it,' said Dino, and he jumped up from his chair, and mimicked his precarious balance on a rolling barrel. 'Like this I was! But I didn't get far. Down I came, right on this wrist, and I knew from the pain it was broken. But that old barrel just kept rolling and going, and the street was more downhill than I thought. It stopped in the end, all right! Right through a shop window! You should have heard the noise, and the commotion! I was in agony, but I didn't hang about. I took myself off sharpish, and found a taxi to the hospital, where I ended up like this.' He held up his plaster-cast inside its sling. 'I need another drink for the pain. Medicinal purposes only!'

'And what happened to the young lady?' asked Tomas.

'When I left her, she was laughing so hard she couldn't stand. It's a sad day for a man when all he can do is make a woman laugh.' He sat back down. 'Hey, Hermes, if you saw me at the hospital, why didn't you give me a lift?'

'You were out cold, or so it seemed. By the time I left, you'd got yourself a taxi. Did you pay him, by the way?'

'I had no cash on me. I told him to call in here when he was passing. I'll be staying here tonight. Lefteris has given me a room.'

'I'm pleased to hear it,' said the fat man. 'Maybe before you have another drink, you could go and make use of the shower.'

'All in good time,' said Dino. 'And by the way, I think "out cold" is a bit strong, when I merely closed my eyes for a while. The place was warm, and I was tired from the pain-killers they gave me. Anyone would have dozed off. Though it wasn't easy to sleep there, with all the noise. Still, I was pleased to be awake to see the cat-fight. That at least was entertaining. Lefteris, my friend, I wonder if you'd mind pouring me another drop?'

'What cat-fight?' asked the fat man.

'Two women at each other's throats. One had brought in flowers for some patient, and they ended up all over the floor.'

'Tell us,' encouraged Tomas. 'This sounds a good story.'

Lefteris refilled Dino's glass, and Dino took a drink.

'I was still waiting to be seen,' he said. 'Even with my broken wrist, they kept me waiting. But I was taking an interest in my surroundings and my fellow patients. A woman came in – not bad-looking, actually, in a mature kind of a way – and she'd brought gifts for someone. She'd got a huge bouquet of flowers, expensive-looking, all out-of-season irises and roses, and a box of chocolates or biscuits, something foreign. So she goes up to the little receptionist and gives the patient's name she's come to see. And as she's standing there, another woman comes in behind her – a harridan of a woman, a bottle-blonde in high heels – and she marches up to this woman at reception, and taps her on the shoulder, and says, *Yassou*, whatever her name was. Well, the woman with the flowers nearly jumps out of her skin. Red as a beetroot, she goes. And the blonde asks her what the hell she's doing there, and she holds out the flowers and says, *These are an apology and a peace-offering, for poor someone-or-other*. And without further ado, the blonde snatches the flowers out of her hands, and drops them on the floor, and stamps on them two or three times, and mad as Medusa, spits on them! She spat on the flowers!'

Tomas and Lefteris were spellbound; the fat man was listening closely.

'What happened then?' asked Tomas.

'The blonde said, *We don't want you here, or any of your tribe*. And she spat on the flowers again, and said, *Now I've returned your compliment. An eye for an eye*, and went marching off into the hospital. So the other woman – quite calmly, it seemed to me – handed the box of chocolates or whatever they were to the receptionist, gathered up the flowers, dumped them on her desk and walked out.'

'Well, well,' said Lefteris. 'You'd think they'd behave better, in a hospital. Can I get any of you gentlemen something to eat? There's chicken pie from lunch. My wife makes it Cretan style, with feta and pine-nuts. You'll find it tasty.'

'I could manage a little something,' said Dino.

'*Kyrie* Diaktoros?'

'Thank you, no,' said the fat man. 'I have an errand to run. Brother, think back if you can. What name did your Medusa use to the woman with the flowers?'

'I can't remember,' said Dino. 'You know I'm not good with names.'

'Try,' said the fat man. 'What did it begin with?'

Dino considered.

'It was a name like someone else's,' he said. 'A name like someone else I've met recently. A-something. Ariana. Amanda.'

'Amara?'

'That's it, Amara! You're a genius, Hermes! How did you know that? Were you there?'

'Not at the time, no,' said the fat man. He stood up. 'If you'll excuse me, I must leave you. But before I go, I wonder if I might borrow your typewriter?'

'Typewriter?' Lefteris looked across at the antique machine on the window sill. 'You mean that one? I doubt whether it works. It's many years since anyone last used it.'

'I'll give it a try, if I may. And I'd appreciate a sheet of paper, if you have one.'

*　　*　　*

191

Dark had fallen quickly, and as premises reopened for the evening's business, Dendra's mood moved upbeat from the torpor of autumn siesta.

But the fat man seemed in no hurry to find the sign of the cockerel the newspaper editor had mentioned. He wandered at a leisurely pace through the lanes, gazing in the shop windows at whatever took his eye – a vase hand-painted with flying birds and lines of poetry, the imaginative arrangements of flowers in a florist's window. He spent a little while at a coffee merchant's, breathing in the smell of the hot beans as they turned in the drum of a roaster, discussing the optimum blend for his taste as the owner ground him a quarter kilo of Colombian. Along the street, he found a shop tiled floor to ceiling in white, where white cheeses – blocks of sharp feta, aged and salty *anthotyros*, sweet and nutty *graviera* – were displayed on marble slabs. He asked for a portion of *touloumotyri* – made the old way inside a cured goatskin – and the shop keeper scooped it from the hide with a wooden spoon, giving him a fork to eat it from the pot. As he enjoyed the cheese, he caught a whiff of smoke and grilling pork, and tempted, followed his nose down a side street, where he found the Kokoras kebab shop – the sign of the cockerel.

The fat man paused to read the poster publicising the candle-lit vigil on behalf of the tobacco farmers, and went inside. At the sink behind the counter, worn and weary in rubber gloves, Dora was scrubbing a pan. Xavier sat amongst the few customers, a notepad and pen and a letter on official government stationery close to hand.

As the fat man approached the counter, Dora mustered a smile, dropped the pan into the greasy dishwater and pulled off her gloves.

'*Kali spera*,' she said. 'What can I get you?'

The menu on the wall had been there some years, and the prices had been altered several times.

'*Kali spera*,' said the fat man, as he read. 'I think a chicken *gyros*, with *tzatziki*, chips and tomatoes. A few onions, maybe, but no mustard. And I'll have a lemonade to drink.'

'Help yourself to lemonade.' Dora placed a glass on the counter, and pointed to the drinks cooler. Opening the kitchen fridge, she took out a plate of skewered chicken-breast pieces, and frowned a little as she sniffed them for freshness. With a scraper, she swept the burnt debris of *souvlakia* from the griddle and sprayed olive oil on to the cooking surface. Taking the topmost chicken skewer from the stack, she sniffed it again before laying it on the heat, where it sizzled and began to smoke. She dropped a pita beside it, and pressed the bread down with a spatula so it would colour from the oil.

The background music changed, from a rock ballad to a love song. Dora turned the chicken, and looked troubled.

'If you don't mind my asking,' said the fat man, 'aren't you a relative of Esmerelda Dimas, the newspaper editor?'

'She's my niece.' Dora lifted the edge of the pita to see if it was browned.

'I met her the other day. She seems a bright young woman.'

'I suppose so.

'Was it your brother who founded the paper?'

'My brother?' Dora seemed confused. 'Oh, you mean the *News*. No, not my brother, my husband's. No one on my side of the family can string two words together.'

'Really?' He glanced at Xavier, but the contradiction of her statement was lost on her. She turned the chicken again, and flipped the pita. 'I believe Esmerelda reported on the food-poisoning outbreak here in Dendra. When was that, a year, two years ago?'

'About that.'

'She and I were talking about the damage something like that might do to a business's reputation.'

She looked at him, and something like a shudder ran through her.

'Trouble like that could ruin you for good,' she said. 'I live in dread of the health inspectorate. If they'd said the outbreak came from this shop, I don't know what I'd have done.'

She lifted the pita off the griddle, and laid it on a plate.

'They came here, then?'

'Oh yes, they came here more than once. They took samples of everything – swabs from the fridge, from the sinks, from the toilets. I do my best to keep things clean, and it was a great relief when they didn't find anything.'

'But they did at the *gelateria*.'

She looked at him closely.

'Are you from the papers yourself?'

'I? No, I'm not from the press. But I had some excellent ice cream at Signor Rapetti's shop and was sorry to hear his story. As you say, a positive result might ruin a man, as it has almost ruined him.'

'I don't know that they ever did have a positive result,' she said.

The shop door opened; Miltiadis, the tailor, came in, and the troubled expression left Dora's face, and was replaced by brightness. The fat man turned, and recognised him.

'*Yassas*,' said Miltiadis, approaching the counter. 'Xavier, how are you?'

'*Yassou, Theié*,' said Xavier. 'I'm very well, thanks. I had a reply from the Ministry of the Interior.'

'And what did they say?'

Xavier held up both pages of the crest-headed letter.

'A great deal, and nothing,' he said. 'A lot of words to say damn all. I'm writing to the minister now to challenge his so-called facts.'

Miltiadis nodded.

'You keep it up, son,' he said. 'You keep it up.'

'How are you, tailor?' asked the fat man as Miltiadis joined him at the counter.

Miltiadis placed a ribbon-tied box beside the bottles of ketchup and mustard.

'Just a few lemon biscuits,' he said to Dora. 'I made them myself.' She smiled.

'I'm sure they'll be delicious,' she said. 'Help yourself to a beer. I wasn't sure you'd come tonight.'

'Oh, you know me,' he said, choosing a Fix. 'I'm a creature of habit.'

'I must collect my trousers from you, if they're ready,' said the fat man. 'Though I'm afraid if I don't cut down, they may need to be let out again.'

Dora popped the cap off Miltiadis's beer.

'The gentleman was asking about Renzo,' she said. A look passed between them.

'I was enquiring how he coped when the bacterial tests proved positive at his shop,' said the fat man. 'But the lady suggests there were no positive tests. Which makes me wonder, how come the finger was pointed there?'

Dora began to assemble the fat man's *gyros*.

'That's a good question,' she said, 'and I don't think I know.'

'But you knew enough to tell your niece with certainty that the fatal outbreak came from there. False certainty, as it seems.'

'Yes.' Thoughtfully, she put his plate on the counter. 'But I was told with certainty myself. An arrest was imminent, that's what I heard. But who told me? Miltiadis, I think it was you.'

'Maybe. It might have been.' Miltiadis sipped his beer. 'I knew it for fact, at the time. That's why he and I fell out. He stopped taking my eggs, so who was going to look like the source? I might have been arrested myself! And I was only doing him a favour, letting him have the eggs cheap. Someone told me it was him for certain. But who was it? I can't remember.'

The fat man left him to think, and ignoring the empty tables in between, took his *gyros* to a seat very close to Xavier. The young man was absorbed in scenes of scuffles on a picket line, and seemed indifferent. The fat man began to eat, and as he did so, the smell of his food caught Xavier's attention, so his eyes moved surreptitiously between the TV screen and the fat man's plate.

'This is very good,' said the fat man between mouthfuls. 'I recommend it. You should try one.'

Xavier tucked a strand of his long hair behind his ear. A crumb of pita had caught at the foot of his beard. He squeezed a roll of belly fat through his T-shirt.

'I know they're good,' he said. 'I grew up on them. I grew up in here, and I eat too many of them, as you can see. That's my mother, behind the counter.'

'Really?' The fat man was about to take another bite, but he hesitated, and with a puzzled expression, looked across to where Dora was peeling onions, wiping away tears with the back of her hand. 'It's not my business, of course, but she looks like she could do with some help.'

The young man sighed.

'I agree. I keep telling her she should hire someone, but she insists she can cope.'

The fat man laid down what was left of his *gyros*, and smiled as he dabbed the corners of his mouth with a napkin.

'You miss my point,' he said. 'I was referring to you.'

196

'Me? If I had the time, I would. But I have my work here.' He indicated the spread on the table beside him: his note-book, the letter from the ministry, a newspaper with para-graphs ringed in red ink. 'My mother understands the work. My father was an activist. He was Dendra's top official in the Socialist party.'

'And that was his only job?'

Xavier didn't answer.

'Maybe he ran this shop too?'

The fat man pointed to the poster on the door.

'Is it you who's organising the vigil?'

'It is.'

'And are you expecting a good turn-out?'

Xavier shook his head.

'Last month, I was involved in action for the electricians' union, and no one came, not a single soul. There's no one here with any kind of political conscience.'

'Then perhaps you should be somewhere where there is.'

'Like where?'

'Athens. Thessaloniki. Your enthusiasm does you credit, and your lion-like zeal for your causes is to be applauded, but a *souvlaki* shop in Dendra is no place to start a revolu-tion. Activists are effective in groups, and those groups gather in the cities, to challenge power where it resides. You may support those men on the picket line' – he pointed up at the television – 'but actions speak louder than words, Xavier. Your letters may needle a few politicians, but from this distance you're easily dismissed. You'll win no battles with letters. I'm afraid it's all too rare that the pen's mightier than the sword. If you really want to support those men, go and stand by them, shoulder to shoulder. And if you want to change the world, you'll need to get out there and find your tribe.'

Xavier's face fell.

'How can I go?' he asked. 'I'm all my mother has.'

'Really?' The fat man looked over to the counter, where Dora scraped sliced onions into a Tupperware box; Miltiadis watched her with a certain light in his eyes, and when Dora noticed, she mimed a flirtatious kiss.

'Ah,' said Xavier.

'You may be freer than you think. And I think you have fire in your belly, and might do Greece some good. Give it some thought. Keep up your good work and be a thorn in the government's side. And don't be despondent about your vigils. See how it goes this time. Maybe attendance will improve on this occasion.'

He ate the last of his *gyros*, and rose to leave.

'It's been a pleasure, Xavier. But we are never as tied as we think. May I take one of those?'

Xavier handed him a leaflet. The fat man called out his thanks to Dora.

'I'll be in tomorrow, tailor, to pick up those trousers,' he said to Miltiadis.

'Right you are,' said the tailor. 'And by the way, I've remembered who it was told me about Renzo. It was Sakis Papayiannis.'

In Neochori, the last diners were late leaving the restaurant. Arethusa put the chairs up on the tables, and fetched the broom and dustpan from the closet. In the kitchen, her father clattered pans and plates, whistling the folk tune that had been her favourite when she was a little girl. Wearily, she swept dirt into the pan, and went out on to the terrace to drop it in the dumpster.

The wind was freshening; leaves from the overhead vine were dancing in mad circles, the telephone lines were singing between their poles. A sheet of paper had blown in from the street, and was pinned against the dumpster. Arethusa lifted the dumpster lid, and tipped the pan inside, knocking it against the hard plastic to loose all of the sweepings, then bent to pick up the paper. As she was about to screw it up and drop it in the rubbish, a few words on it caught her eye. She read it through; then she tucked it into the pocket of her apron, and slammed the dumpster lid shut before going back inside.

Fourteen

The next morning, with the day promising a little warmth in the sunshine, the fat man asked Lefteris if he might breakfast on the terrace outside. He took a seat on an ornate but cold cast-iron chair at a cast-iron table, and in a few moments Lefteris followed him out. He asked the fat man to stand, and slipped a welcome cushion on to the chair, then brushed away a few fallen leaves from the table, and with a flourish covered it with a cloth.

'Have you seen anything of my brother?' asked the fat man.

'He was out late,' said Lefteris. 'I gave him a key, but I don't know what time he came in. I believe he had company, from the giggling and whispering on the stairs. I can't help but wonder how he'll be feeling this morning. I was suffering with a sore head myself, and he left me and Tomas to go out and drink more. I've seen nothing of Tomas yet, either. We got through a few bottles between us. We finished every drop I had of the Lachesis. I'll have to go up there, and see if Meni's got any more.'

'Take what I've got in the car,' said the fat man. 'I don't have much, but I feel guilty for foisting my brother on to you. Everywhere he goes, he drinks them dry.'

'Ah, but he's such good company, isn't he? I haven't laughed so much since I can't remember when. I'll get your breakfast.'

Whilst Lefteris was gone, the fat man enjoyed his surroundings: the freshness of dew on the rose leaves, the cool green of the walnut and lemon trees. The last swallows were gone; in the eaves of the old building, the mud nests were deserted. Down below, a motorbike roaring up the lane braked sharply at a warning shout. The shutter on the back of a delivery van rumbled shut, and as the van drove off, the music blasting from its radio faded away. In the remaining quiet, a donkey's hooves clipped along the cobbles.

Lefteris brought out breakfast, including a few slices of sausage steaming from the pan.

'The butcher just brought this, and Stavroula thinks you should try it,' he said.

The fat man picked up his fork and tried a piece of the dark meat, which was salty and well spiced with paprika and pepper. He chewed, swallowed, and tried another piece.

'This pork has an interesting texture,' he said.

'That's because it's not pork,' said Lefteris. 'It's wild boar. Made, I'm proud to say, from an animal I shot myself. There're plenty of them, up in the mountains. In fact my cousins and I are going hunting, later on today. Your brother said he'd like to join us. He tells me he's a crack shot, even with one arm. Maybe you'd like to come, too?'

The fat man laughed.

'Lefteris, take a piece of advice from me,' he said. 'Fetch your gun, and your dogs, and get out of here before my brother reappears. One-armed or two, Dino and rifles are a potentially fatal mix, for obvious reasons. And apart from the unlikelihood of his being sober, he's too fond of talking to be anything but a hindrance to you. Every animal and bird would hear him coming from miles away. As for me, I have things to do that won't wait, and so I must decline, though I wish you the best of luck.'

'Thank you,' said Lefteris. 'We'll do our best. Maybe tonight we'll have something good in the pot for you to try.'

When the fat man called in at the post office he'd named to his lawyer's secretary, the delivery he was expecting had arrived, and was sitting in the pigeonholes of the Poste Restante.

Outside, he took the papers from the envelope, looked them over and nodded with satisfaction; then he slipped them into his hold-all, and went on his way.

The fat man found the turning for Argiri lake without difficulty, and followed the road as it led upwards to the high hills, into a landscape recovering from the devastation of forest fires, where blackened stalks of Aleppo pines poked from the green of shrubs and grasses already re-establishing themselves. At the road's summit, he caught his first view of the lake, a near oval of water made silver by the reflections of clouds, met along one shore by marshland, on the other by healthy trees which had escaped the fires. A kilometre further on, an unsigned track led off in the lake's direction, but finding the track too rough for the low-slung Tzen, he pulled over under a myrtle tree and continued on foot.

The afternoon was cool, the foliage on the track's verges still wet from the previous night's rain. A breeze tickled a stand of towering bamboo, raising a rattle from the leaves and rigid stalks. Hold-all in hand, the fat man walked briskly, until he rounded a bend to find a BMW saloon parked with its nearside wheels in the long grass, its wheel arches and the lower panels of its doors splashed with mud. He looked through the driver's window, but there was little to see: a road map in a seat pocket, a sweet wrapper in the open ashtray, a woman's umbrella on the rear seat.

He walked on, following the track down into the gloom of the pine woods lining the northern edge of the lake. The track narrowed to become no more than a footpath. As he made his way through the trees, he heard the mellow splash of water on the shore, and the breeze carried the dankness of the marsh, and the malodour of waterlogged vegetation. The path had been churned by others' feet, and in places he stepped off it to avoid sinking into a mire, finding drier routes over the fallen pine needles.

At the water's edge, black-headed terns ran in the shallows; a long-necked egret prodded the reeds for frogs. Along a stretch of rock-strewn sand, a man sat on a low camping stool, his knees folded almost to his chest. He was thin, and losing his dark blond hair; he wore rimless glasses and an unclipped goatee, which together with his khaki slacks and tweed jacket gave him a Scandinavian air. He had made a table of a broken branch, and balanced on it was a jar of water, and a well-used paintbox whose blocks of colour were all worn hollow. A sketchbook was open on his thighs as he worked on a watercolour view. He glanced up at the fat man, then his eyes went back to the lake.

'Dr Fitanidis?'

The doctor dipped the bristles of his fine brush in water, swirled the brush in paint, and put a tiny detail into his impression of the far shore. Reviewing his painting, he asked, 'Who wants to know?'

'My intrusion on your private time is unforgivable,' began the fat man.

'You're right, it is. So please, don't intrude.'

'I wouldn't think of it, if it weren't necessary,' said the fat man. 'But you're very well protected at your place of work.'

'With good reason. My time there is extremely valuable.'

He rinsed his brush, dabbled it in green paint, then in brown.

'I understand how valuable your time is,' said the fat man. 'And I would under no circumstances intrude there either, were it not a question of life and death. Or maybe I should say, of quality of life, and death.'

The doctor's focus moved between his paper and the view.

'So what's so important that you've come all this way?' he asked.

'It concerns a patient of yours, Dmitris Kapsis.'

The doctor looked at him, and looked away.

'Are you a relative? I haven't seen you at the bedside.'

'In all honesty, I am not.'

'Then you'll understand I can't discuss his case with you. Now, if you wouldn't mind. My time here is both short and precious to me.'

'I'm not a relative, but I'd like to be his benefactor. I did try to see you this morning, but your secretary did an excellent job of despatching me.'

The doctor smiled.

'My niece. A highly capable girl. The common view at the hospital is that I hired her for her beauty, and to some extent that's true. I see some very ugly things in my work, *Kyrie* . . . I didn't catch your name.'

'Diaktoros. Hermes Diaktoros, of Athens.'

'*Kyrie* Diaktoros. In my work, I move through a world of disfigurement and pain. My niece is a cheerful reminder that there is beauty, too. My staff take her to be my mistress, and the reason for my disappearance, most afternoons. Their explanation for my absences flatters my male ego, especially since the truth, as you see, is far more pedestrian. Here I commune with nature, and find solace for the world's woes. That, and not an adulterous affair, is my weakness.'

'I would call such a pastime more strength than weakness.'

The doctor applied paint to paper, working on the details of the trees.

'So, since you've found me, if you have the boy's good at heart, question me, and if I feel able to do so, I'll answer,' he said. 'But allow me, please, to continue with my little effort here. It's coming out quite well, but if it dries, all will be lost.'

'Please do,' said the fat man. 'And I won't keep you long. I merely wish to know what Dmitris's prospects are.'

The doctor rinsed his brush, and dipped it in discoloured white paint.

'You'll have seen the effects of fire on the way to the lake,' he said. 'Two years ago, parts of these hills were decimated by a blaze which smouldered for days. Fire is cruel enough to solid wood and bark, *Kyrie* Diaktoros. On soft human skin – well, you don't need me to paint you a picture. I don't mean to be flippant. Happily, sometimes I can be of help to those afflicted. I have a gift for healing, which I used to think came from God. There was a time when I believed in God as someone, or something merciful. Now I see my calling as a means to thwart Him. My life's work is to undo some of the miseries He causes, especially the miseries caused by fire.'

'But weren't Dmitris's burns the work of human hands? I heard he was tripped, or pushed.'

'Perhaps. But what of babies coming deformed from their mother's womb? Fine minds destroyed by stroke and dementia? Accidents which put athletes in wheelchairs and take limbs from children? Blindness, deafness? Are these from human hands?'

Briefly, the fat man was silent.

'I have no answer to give you,' he said. 'But in Dmitris's case, what can be done?'

The doctor shook his head.

'What can be done and what I can do are not the same. I supervise the practical necessities of his care. Burn victims lose a great deal of fluids from leaking capillaries and open wounds, so we're hydrating him, though that's a process which needs careful management. Over-hydration causes swelling, which leads to problems of its own. Skin and tissue are a natural barrier to bacteria, and when they're lost, the patient becomes vulnerable to infection, so we're giving him intravenous antibiotics and, distressing and painful though it is for the boy – and his family, who watch him suffer – his bandages are changed several times a day. We're feeding him the large number of calories he needs for the tissue to repair itself, as far as it's able. Before long, there'll be grafts, and I'll do my very best for him. But burns are traumatic injuries and psychologically damaging, especially when they're disfiguring. Dmitris will need plenty of support, or he may give up trying to recover. And in all this, I'm hamstrung by my budget, by a lack of equipment and by my staff, who are well meaning and committed but trained to a certain point and no further. I'm afraid he won't be handsome again, whatever I can do. That was his worst piece of luck, to be here instead of London, or New York, or Switzerland. In any of those places, he might do better.'

'Why so?'

'Their facilities are vastly superior to ours. A special burns unit might do wonders for him. The Americans especially are way ahead of us.'

'So if he were in America . . .?'

The doctor laid down his brush.

'I've seen what they can do there. Alas, as so often, Dmitris's outcome will depend on money, or lack of it. That's why I come here. Look around you. Here in this place, money has no influence. These wild things – plants, animals, birds – will live or die, without help or interference. As underfunded doctors, that's our tragedy. We know what may be done, but lack the resources to deliver the very best care.'

'But if you had those resources? If they were made available to you? Could the Kapsis boy be helped, then?'

'If the facilities and staff were in place, of course. Though it would not be a quick job, even so. Deep scarring may take years to heal. But with state-of-the-art equipment, medicines, the right nursing care, he might do very well.'

'Then I must see what I can do.'

'And so must I. Be assured I will do whatever's in my power to help him.' He leaned back from his painting. 'Finished, I think. As much as any creative piece is ever finished. Painting is a little like reconstructive surgery, in that regard. I'm always tempted to go back, change and improve, if the first results are not entirely satisfactory. It's usually possible, at least up to a point.'

'I like it very much,' said the fat man. 'You have a real eye for the landscape.'

'Because the landscape talks to me, and I listen. If you like the picture, take it, be my guest. I'll do another before I leave.'

'Thank you.'

'Was there something else? You said matters of life and death. The Kapsis boy is poorly, but in no danger of dying.'

'But there was a death at the hospital, last night,' said the fat man. 'A much older man, Donatos Papayiannis.'

'I wasn't there last night, so I'm afraid I know nothing about him. What did he die of?'

'Almost certainly, the cause would have been recorded as heart failure. But I wonder if that was correct. He had symptoms which mimicked heart failure to an extent, but I have another idea, and if you think I'm right, I wonder if you might instigate the appropriate tests.'

'What were his symptoms?'

'Chronic shortness of breath, a redness in the face, general malaise.'

The doctor frowned.

'And what were you thinking?'

'I met *Kyrie* Papayiannis, and his symptoms reminded me of a case I saw many years ago,' said the fat man. 'I don't want to be overly dramatic, but I've been wondering if it's possible he might have been poisoned.'

Fifteen

At the Papayiannis estate, the idle machinery was silent behind the closed mill doors; on the yard, the olives in their ranks of bulging sacks were past their prime. Except for an out-of-date newspaper in the abandoned fork-lift truck, there was no sign of the men who worked the oil press, and there were no voices, no whirring pickers to be heard from the orchards, where only the wind disturbed the silver-leaved trees.

The fat man parked next to Sakis's red pick-up. The dent from Donatos's accident was still conspicuous on the wing.

Up on the roof of the house, straddling the ridge, Sakis was pulling sticks from the stork's nest, throwing handfuls to the ground, where they broke and scattered. Bedraggled quills and white down from the nest's soft lining blew around the yard.

From the bottom of the ladder, the fat man shouted up. Sakis – in leather gauntlets, with a hat pulled down over his ears – appeared not to hear, but the fat man was persistent, and raised his voice to such a volume he was impossible to ignore.

Sakis dropped a handful of fouled twigs by the fat man's feet. Shards of soiled bark peppered his toecaps.

'We're closed,' Sakis shouted. 'The mill is closed!'

'I haven't come to the mill,' called the fat man. 'I've come to talk to you.'

'Another day.' Sakis wrestled more sticks from the nest.

'It must be today, and soon. Or you're likely to have other visitors who are less welcome than me.'

'If you're referring to my beloved relatives, they've all enjoyed my father's funeral, and gone away. Watch yourself there.' He tossed down another handful; as they fell, the fat man stepped agilely out of the way.

'I don't mean your relatives. And it's about your father I'm here.'

Sakis became still.

'My father's dead.'

'I'm aware of that. It's about his death I'm here. Please, stop what you're doing and come down. All I ask is a few minutes of your time. It is important, truly.'

Sakis ran the back of a glove over his eyes as though he might be wiping away tears, and briefly went back to his dismantling; but then he flung what he had just extracted back on to the untidy mass, and descended an old ladder wedged under the guttering. Resentfully, he stood before the fat man, pulling off his gauntlets and his dirty hat.

'You're a customer, so I don't want to be rude,' he said, 'but since you know I'm in mourning, I respectfully ask you to leave me in peace.'

The fat man seemed apologetic.

'If I could, I would,' he said. 'But regretfully, matters are such that it isn't possible to let them lie.'

'Matters, what matters? What are you talking about?'

From behind his back, the fat man produced a bottle of brandy.

'I brought this to toast your father, if you will allow it.

What I have to say will go down better with a drink. Do you have glasses?'

Sakis was reluctant.

'Sit,' he said, at last, and gestured to a table and chairs left out from the summer. He went inside, and quickly returned with two tumblers, which he placed without good grace in the middle of the table. 'I'd be a poor son who'd refuse to drink to his father's memory.'

The label on the bottle was handwritten, copperplate in Indian ink.

The fat man poured out generous measures of brandy.

'From my father's own barrels,' he said. 'I thought it a fitting tribute to your own father.' He held up his glass. 'May his memory be eternal.'

They drank, Sakis downing the spirit in a single draft.

'No offence,' he said, slamming his glass on to the table, 'but why have you made such effort to pay tribute to my father?'

The fat man took a second sip of his drink.

'Two reasons. Firstly, I hold all fathers in esteem if they manage even the basic essentials of bringing up children, that is providing food, clothing, a level of education and instilling a measure of respect for others. The job is difficult, and even a modicum of success deserves credit. Secondly, I think your father was a man of vision. He had an idea that this business – this small farm – could be transformed into something which might thrive in this difficult modern world. I think his vision – his dream, if you like – was to benefit both his own family, and to fly the flag for Greece. He saw your well-being and prosperity as benefitting the nation as a whole. So it is most unfortunate that his desire to do well by you was what over-whelmed him, in the end.'

'Overwhelmed him? In what way was he overwhelmed?'

The fat man poured more brandy – a little for himself, more for Sakis.

'I remember what your father told me about his aims for this business – to provide wholesome oil for Greek families, and stem the tide of imports from Italy and Spain. A heritage oil, an oil for the Hellenes, as he put it. And yet at the wholesalers in Neochori, what do I find? That the whole of your last year's production went for export! And not just your own oil – a considerable amount in itself – but over and above that amount, an amount bought in to fulfil a contract.' Sakis was silent, and drank more brandy. 'That made no sense to me. So perhaps you could explain it to me now. Why did he – why did you – abandon those principles?'

Sakis shrugged.

'What can I say?' he asked. 'We were offered an excellent price. Money is money.'

'Really? That's not what your father said to me. What he said was, some things money can't buy.'

'My father was an old man, and stubborn in his ideals. Blame me. I talked him into it.'

The fat man shook his head.

'Do you know, Sakis, I don't believe that. I don't think you ever talked your father into anything he didn't want to be talked into. Not even getting rid of that old stork's nest. You were a dutiful son in that regard. You respected him and his decisions, or made a pretence of doing so, at least. In some instances, maybe against your better judgement.'

'You'll forgive me,' said Sakis, preparing to rise, 'and I thank you on behalf of my family for paying your respects. But I think it's time you left.'

The fat man bowed his head.

'I understand. But before I go, I think I should explain what is likely to happen next, in case you decide it would be better avoided.'

Sakis scowled.

'What do you mean?'

'If you take no action now, before long the police will come, and they'll bring an exhumation order. It would be both distressing and unpleasant, but it will become necessary for a pathologist to take a closer look at your father's corpse.'

'What!' In a rage, Sakis stood. 'What the hell are you talking about? Mama!'

'Don't call her yet,' warned the fat man. 'Let's you and I talk first. It isn't what you want to hear, Sakis, but I'm afraid there's every likelihood your father was poisoned.'

'Poisoned? Poisoned with what?'

'That would be for the pathologist to confirm, though I have a good idea what he would find.'

'Papa, poisoned?' Sakis seemed bewildered, and sank back into his chair. 'But how?'

'Most obviously, through something he ate. Do you have any idea why someone would deliberately poison him, Sakis?'

Anger rose in Sakis again, spreading a carmine glow over his neck and face.

'Those bastards!' he said, shaking his head. 'Those malicious, murdering bastards! I'll kill every last one of them! I'll wring all their necks with my own bare hands!'

The fat man was watching him.

'You assume a deliberate act,' he said, 'but not all poisoning is deliberate. You have some failing trees in your orchard. Have you noticed them?'

'Yes, of course. We've tried everything to revive them, but so far, nothing's worked. Papa thought there must be some parasite in the roots. Mama thinks it's the evil eye, curses from – wherever curses come from.'

'I think you'll find the cause is more down to earth than curses. Someone has been poisoning your trees with copper nails. Plainly, that can be nothing but intentional, and your assumption of malice on someone's part must be correct. I take it you'd assume the Kapsis's are the guilty parties, but why would you assume that?'

'They resent our success,' said Sakis, bitterly. 'As for Papa, of course it's all about Dmitris Kapsis. They'll never believe it was an accident, and now it sounds like they picked on my father for pay-back. But I'll teach them all about pay-back! Let the police come! I'll be happy to see them.'

His eyes flickered over the brandy bottle. Hesitating for a moment, the fat man poured him more.

'I think you're right, to a degree,' he said. 'This is about revenge, and punishment. But I don't think the Kapsis's are guilty. Not directly. And I suspect the punishment wasn't for any recent offence, not within weeks, or even months. My suspicion is that this is connected to the food-poisoning outbreak in Dendra. The outbreak when your oil caused four deaths.'

Sakis's expression was of astonishment.

'Our oil? Papayiannis oil? Are you mad? Papayiannis oil is a pure and natural vegetable product, containing nothing but olives straight from the tree. The infection which caused that outbreak was of animal origin. That much was proven.'

'I understand that, and I don't say the oil itself was the outbreak's origin. I should be more accurate, and say that whatever was *introduced* into the oil made it deadly. Your oil became the medium which carried the lethal bacteria. It wasn't discovered at the time, because as you say, the bacteria were of animal origin. How could such bacteria be in your oil? But of course the answer to that is simple. Someone put it there. And so now I suspect we come to another act of malice. Do you want to tell me how it was?'

Sakis took a drink, and remained silent. Unhurriedly, the fat man took his cigarettes from his pocket, and offered them to Sakis. When he declined, the fat man found his gold lighter, and lighting one for himself, drew in smoke, and exhaled.

'I want you to appreciate that I'm giving you a choice,' he said. 'If you give me answers to my questions, it may be that I can go away, and no one need ever know that we have spoken. But without answers from you, I shall seek them elsewhere, beginning – and I'm sorry to be brutal – on a mortuary slab. As I've said to you, the police will come, and the crisis you have recently been through with your father's death will be superseded by one far more devastating. The press will return to Dendra to report on your father's exhumation. The coroner will report his findings, and the police will start looking for your father's killer. And their search won't take long, because I shall point them in the right direction. I'm afraid I have little faith in policemen. To be sure, there are exceptions, but generally I find them lacking in imagination and hidebound by rules, which tends to mean they miss the bigger picture, and consequently reach errone-ous conclusions. They look for simple solutions which will bring them the verdicts they want in courts of law, whereas I am interested only in seeing justice done. So often, the two things are not the same. Anyway, if you like, I can save you the wait, and tell you who killed your father, how it was done, and why.'

'Who the hell are you?' asked Sakis, ominously. 'What business have you asking for exhumations? Whatever you think of them, that's a police matter. What authority do you have?'

'I act on behalf of the highest Authorities, who task me, as I have said, in seeing justice done. It is irrelevant to them how that justice is dispensed. Sometimes, the law courts and the prisons are appropriate. Often, however, they are not. And any exhumation would not be performed on my whim, but at the request of a medical professional. I have discussed the case with a senior doctor, and I've managed to persuade him – for the time being, at least, though I think somewhat against his better judgement – to hold off on filing the paperwork, on the grounds that we might get the desired result without any exhumation. The desired result being, of course, suitable justice for your father's killer. Happily for you, the doctor is a humanist, and is prepared to give me a little time so your family might avoid further distress.'

The fat man drew again on his cigarette, and flicked off a length of ash. The wind picked up a downy stork's feather, and carried it to the eaves before releasing it to float capriciously back to the ground.

'But if my father died by anything other than natural causes, how come the doctors didn't know before now?' asked Sakis.

'Very simple,' said the fat man. 'Because the cause of his death was very unusual, and doctors, like everyone else, expect the normal. His symptoms mimicked heart failure, at least in part, and your father told them he suffered from that condition, having done his self-diagnosis. It is regrettable, but after his death, the doctors who had seen him at the hospital were happy to put that cause of death on his death certificate for very good reasons. Unfortunately, their conclusion was wrong.'

'So now they'll come and disturb him in his grave. It'll kill Mama.'

'If you choose that route, you may be right. You would have to spare her as much of the drama as you could. Are there relatives she might stay with?'

'You don't know my mother. She would never leave here, with my father not properly buried. What will happen after the autopsy?'

'Cause of death would be proven, and your father's killer would be arrested. There would be a trial, and the whole story would come out, regardless.' The fat man's cigarette was almost finished; he drew on it one last time, ground it out under his foot, and placed the butt on the table for later disposal. 'The way I see it, you have a chance to spare your mother and the rest of your family significant distress. The truth about the outbreak will come out now, anyway. You must simply decide whether you want your father exhumed in the interim. But if you'll co-operate with me, I have information which will be of interest to you. So tell me your side of the story, and I'll tell you what I know. Do we have a trade? Or shall I go and find the doctor, and tell him to start on the necessary forms?'

Sakis laid his head on the back of his chair and sighed deeply.

'All my fault,' he said. 'All my fault. I never stood up to him. I was raised to respect him, both by tradition and by the strap, and I learned young not to argue, though I grew out of that, in the end.' He wafted a hand towards the debris from the stork's nest. 'We argued over everything, and yet he always seemed to win. But he was my father, and I loved him.' His eyes held tears. 'I loved him, and I couldn't have borne it, to see him disgraced and shamed, to see what it would have done to my mother. He was old, and I couldn't see him brought low in his last years. But he's gone now, and it's right that I should take the consequences for what we did. I should have stood up to him at the right time, and I didn't. And then it was too late. But it wasn't our fault! We were pushed too far by those . . . Those . . .'

He closed his eyes.

'Tell me what happened.'

Sakis sat back up to the table to pour himself more brandy, and the fat man made no move to stop him.

'We'd had an excellent harvest,' said Sakis. 'The season had been good, with plenty of rain over the winter, and the trees cropped well. It was our second year with the machinery. The first had been difficult – we were learning, and there were teething troubles – but this time things had run beautifully, and we weren't on the phone every day to the manufacturer asking advice, adjusting settings. Everything went smoothly, and we had a record yield, almost double what we'd expect from the old stoneground way. We were getting ready to ship to the wholesalers. We'd taken what oil we needed for ourselves, and distributed some around friends and family, sold a few bottles. My father had arranged with the wholesaler a verbal contract with a bottler in Kalamata, a company whose reputation my father admired. You were right about that. He was a patriot, and it was known round about that Papayiannis oil is labelled Greek and sold to Greeks. That had always been our way.

'So a couple of days before shipping, I went to check on the vat. As soon as I took off the lid, I knew something wasn't right. You work around oil for a long time, you develop a sensitive nose. Straight away, I smelled something was wrong, but I couldn't work out what it was. It wasn't the usual bad smell from poor quality oil. And I thought I could see something in there. I fished around, and something was in there, all right! A dead cockerel! And not just any dead cockerel, a well-rotted one – seemed to me it had to be pretty well rotted when it went in there. Now you tell me – how did a dead cockerel get itself into our vat, and close the lid behind itself?

'Well, of course I knew the oil was ruined. I wanted to call the police there and then. But Papa wouldn't have it. How could we? he said. Of course we knew who was guilty.' He spat on the ground. 'But how would we prove it? And how would the business stand the loss of our crop? We had no insurance – the premiums were expensive, and we'd ploughed all our money into the machinery. So Papa said we should just filter the oil again, and trust in its own properties to make it OK. The oil's a natural antiseptic. He said if there were germs in there, the oil itself would kill them. And I let myself be persuaded.' He put his head in his hands. 'I look back now, and I think, why? In my heart I knew it was dangerous. We both did. I offered him a dish of the oil and some bread. I said, if you'll eat this, we'll sell it, and he just walked out on me. There's a difference between knowing and not knowing, he said. No one would ever know. The oil would be diluted when it was blended at the bottlers. But it got worse. When we filtered the oil and cleaned the vat, we found a couple of handfuls of chicken dung thrown in there for good measure. But he still persuaded me. He insisted if the oil was diluted with other oils, there'd be no risk. And I went along with it.'

'When did you find out what the consequences had been?'

'Not straight away. A couple of people were ill, and we thought nothing of it. Then there were a couple more, and those that were ill weren't getting better. Of course, none of us suffered. We poured away what oil we'd got in the house. I bought new in a supermarket and replaced it, and if anyone noticed the rotten quality, they never said. Then someone in Dendra died, and all hell broke loose. There were officials everywhere. And Papa and I could see the pattern no one else could see – that what the households where people were ill had in common, was that they were all buyers of our oil. I said we should speak up, but Papa was desperate. He knew we'd go to jail, and he couldn't face it. I could have faced it for myself, but not for him. I was so worried about him! We did at least get rid of the ruined oil. We gave the wholesaler some story about a foreign contract. He was surprised, but I think he assumed we were seeing ourselves as a fish that had grown too big for his pond. No doubt he wasn't pleased. We'd worked with him for years, and now we were going up in the world, it looked as if we were cutting him out. We fetched the oil back here, and bought some in to cover our domestic needs – walk-in customers like yourself. How could we be an oil mill with no oil?'

'You bought in Kapsis oil – did you know that?'

Sakis gave a bitter laugh.

'How ironic,' he said. 'They poisoned ours, and we bought theirs at a premium. I did wonder. It was a very close match to ours. Perhaps the wholesaler was more annoyed than I thought, and it was a bit of sweet revenge on his part. He knows if we'd known, Kapsis oil would have choked us.'

'That's what put me on the trail of this little mystery,' said the fat man. 'The day I bought a bottle from you, I bought a bottle from Kapsis's, too. I did a blind tasting, and no one – not even I, and I do know my oils – could tell them apart. And I began to wonder, can I not tell them apart because actually, they are one and the same? Which, of course, they were. But you did more than that, didn't you? You deflected any possibility of discovery by foisting suspicion on to some- one else.' Sakis was silent. 'I mean Renzo, the ice-cream maker. That strikes me as very unkind.'

'You're right, it was a mean trick, cowardly. But his name was already being mentioned. Everywhere that sold food was under suspicion.'

'So why did you choose him?'

'Quite simply because we have no family connections with the man. Most others we have some blood ties with – Dendra is a small place, and I have many cousins and second cousins. Renzo as a foreigner has no connection to us. And with him being – how can I put this? – of a dubious sexual persuasion, people's prejudices allowed them to believe the worst of him.'

'You said you had solid information that he was the outbreak's source, and you have almost ruined him. You crippled his business, his livelihood. His life.'

Sakis looked the fat man in the eye.

'I'm not proud of what we did,' he said. 'But they can't touch Papa now, and I'm ready to face the consequences. Though I'm sorry for what'll happen to the mill. We've never missed a season's milling for over a century. Even through the war, the Papayiannis mill was making oil. There's no one else trained to use the equipment. So I suppose it'll all just sit and rust whilst I do my time.'

'You never know,' said the fat man. 'Your vision was inspiring, and it deserves to succeed. What about your wife?'

'Amara? What about her?'

'Does she know anything of what you've done?'

'Nothing. I shielded her from it, the same as Papa never told Mama. How will I tell her?'

'I suggest that you're direct and honest. What kind of woman is she? With help and guidance, might she not be able to run the place for a while?'

Sakis shook his head.

'There's no one to help her.'

'Don't be so sure. And since you have been honest with me, and shown remorse, I may be able to help you, in some small way.'

'How?'

'There's a woman who works for a newspaper, an editor, who's looking to make her name in the business. Maybe your story will appeal to her. I think you would have told the truth at the time, if you hadn't been torn by loyalty to your father. Maybe she would take up your cause, campaign on your behalf and by the power of public opinion help you secure a minimum sentence. And like you, she owes recompense to Renzo for damaging his good name. By telling the real story, she can put that right, and give him some positive press.' He glanced at his watch. 'I must go. There are others I must speak to before I leave.'

The fat man stood. Sakis remained in his chair, his eyes bloodshot from tears and from the brandy, his back bowed as if he already felt the pressure of trials to come.

'What do I do now?' he asked.

'Speak to your wife, and your mother. They must be the first to hear the truth. Then take yourself to the police, and tell them everything.'

Sakis gave a snort of contemptuous laughter.

'Those fools? What will they do?'

'You may not wish to involve yourself with them, but they're where the process must begin. And Sakis, do something for me. The poor storks don't deserve your anger, so leave the nest intact. Many people regard them as bringers of good luck, though that may seem a dubious claim to you at this moment. But they are thought to care for their aged parents, and so doesn't it seem fitting that you should encourage them to stay here, as your father would have wanted you to do? In any case, you've drunk far too much brandy to be clambering on the roof any more today.' He stepped forward, and patted Sakis's shoulder. 'Be brave, son. When your dues are paid, I have a feeling this business will prosper very nicely. And don't underestimate your wife. You may find she rises very well to a challenge.'

He turned to go.

'Just a moment,' said Sakis. 'You haven't kept your side of the bargain. You haven't told me who killed my father.'

'You're right,' said the fat man, retaking his seat. 'I haven't. Pour us a little more brandy, and I'll tell you everything I know.'

Sixteen

'*Kyria!*'
As Marianna Kapsis came out of the oil press, the fat man's call reached her over the creak and grind of machinery and the banter of the working men. She was smiling, the residue of laughter at some joke, and pulling a cardigan around her against the wind, which was gaining strength.

The fat man was seated on a trolley used for wheeling the crop into the mill, his back propped against a full sack, holding up an olive to study its form. He got to his feet, slipped the olive into his pocket and picked up his hold-all.

'They told me at the house I'd find you here. Supervising operations, no doubt.'

'We meet again,' she said. 'What can I do for you this time?'

'It's more what I can do for you. I've come to bring you news about your neighbour, Sakis Papayiannis.'

Her mouth pursed into sourness.

'Why should I want news of him? Nothing that family does is of any interest to me. If you'll excuse me, as you see this is a very busy time.'

'Forgive me. I thought you'd want to know why he's going to be arrested.'

'Arrested?'

'It relates to the death of his father.'

'*Mori!* What on earth is going on?'

'As I say, I came to bring you the news, but as you're too busy to hear it, I'll let it permeate through the usual channels of gossip. *Yassas.*'

He turned to go; she touched his arm to stop him, but withdrew her hand very quickly as if sensing it was something she ought not to have done.

'Of course if my neighbour is in trouble I should like to hear.'

'Naturally.'

'Come and have a seat. Let me get you something.'

She sat him at the table where they had talked before, sheltered from the wind which fluttered the mauve petals of the crocuses below the windows.

'What will you have? There's tea, *glyfoni* or *fraskomilo*. Or would you prefer coffee?'

'*Glyfoni*, thank you. No sugar. I have to watch my weight.'

For a few minutes, she was gone. A man came out of the mill, and wheeled in the trolley where the fat man had sat. The small bicycle he had helped repair lay on its side beside a log pile. The fat man wandered over to it, and pressed its tyres with his thumb. The front tyre was flat.

Marianna brought out a tray of tea and shortcake biscuits, and unloaded it on to the table. The fat man took his seat, and when the plate was offered, took one of the biscuits and placed it in his saucer. He sipped the rapidly cooling mint tea.

'So.' Marianna prompted him with a smile which wasn't warm. She drank, leaving lipstick on the rim of her cup. 'Tell me what's happening with my neighbours. Did Sakis murder the old man? It wouldn't surprise me. I'm sure the old sinner was impossible to live with.'

'You're uncharitable,' he said. 'Do you think you should speak ill of the dead?'

'Should I speak well of a man like him? I'm no hypocrite. I had no love for him in life, and I've none now he's dead, either.'

'You didn't like him. That's common enough. It seems to be human nature to fall out with one's neighbours. But he had his good points, and he might have had several more useful years in him, if he'd lived.'

'What are you suggesting?' She lay down her cup. 'Did Sakis have something to do with his death? Is that why he's been arrested? I didn't really mean . . . I never knew that it had got so bad!'

'In what way, bad?'

'Oh, those two were like dogs at each other's throats! They agreed on nothing! But to have fallen out so badly that Sakis would do away with him . . .'

'Ah, now.' The fat man gave a slow smile. 'You're indulging in a dangerous sport, putting two and two together and coming up with five. Sakis will soon be in custody, that's true. That the old man is dead, is also true. But that the one is a direct result of the other, is not true. Though I grant you that the events are connected, even if the path of their connection is circuitous. And part of the connection, is you.'

'Me? I have nothing to do with that family.'

'Marianna.' He sat back from the table and looked at her, noting her discomfiture in being so familiarly addressed. 'That really is not true, is it?' Beneath her make-up, she blushed. 'You and your clan spend a great deal of time and energy fuelling the fires of your feud – so much time, that literal fires have come into the game, with tragic consequences for Dmitris. I have just come from talking to Sakis, and he told me a very interesting story.'

226

Amongst the chickens scratching across the yard, a cockerel stretched its wings as it prepared to crow.

'That's a fine bird, isn't it?' he said. 'And he has the yard and the flock to himself. Doubtless he has seen off any rivals to win his place as cock of the roost. I find cock fights distressing, but they are nature's way, I suppose, of assuring survival of the fittest. There are regular casualties, no doubt, and this fellow will only be crowing until a stronger, younger bird wins the challenge against him. When that happens, the harem will be unperturbed. They accept new leadership without demur. I wonder if that will be true of the Papayiannis clan, when they find out the natural succession will be disturbed by Sakis's long absence? Who will rule the roost whilst he is gone? Will they put forward a woman, as your family have done? Will Amara be up to the job? You're a strong woman, Marianna, to have taken up the reins and held on to them. But I wonder if your control is all it might be.'

'What do you mean?' Her face, again, became sour.

'I am only wondering if you truly run this household, this clan, or whether things go on over which you have no control, about which you only learn after the fact? We shall come to that. But I was going to tell you Sakis's tale, was I not? When cockerels outlive their usefulness, they tend to end up in the pot. But Sakis's story was of a cockerel which ended up somewhere more unusual. It ended up floating in a vat of his olive oil.'

There was the briefest of silences.

'I expect it fell in,' she said. 'The stupid birds are always getting where they shouldn't be.'

'Maybe. But that would, regardless, make this a very unusual bird. A flightless bird, which levitates to the top of an oil vat, falls in and closes the lid behind itself. All this,

227

whilst in all likelihood having been dead for some time? Please, Marianna, don't take me for a fool. It's something I dislike almost as much as being lied to. The cockerel was put in that vat as an act of pure malice. It was a wicked act, which resulted directly in the deaths of four people, and now, with Donatos, there are five.'

'What do you mean, deaths?'

'That cockerel was the cause of Dendra's poisoning outbreak. The oil was infested with its bacteria, and it was that which killed those people.'

'Don't be absurd. The poisoning was down to the Italian. Everyone knows that.'

'And yet no charges were ever brought against him. His premises were never closed.'

'There was no proof. The proof was eaten, or cleaned away. I don't say it was deliberate, but for certain it was him.'

'Why do you say that?'

Frowning, she hesitated.

'Everyone knows it. It's common knowledge.'

'It's common gossip. That doesn't make it true.'

He took a bite of his biscuit.

'I forgot to ask about Dmitris,' he said. 'How is he?'

She ran her hand through her hair, and hooked a piece of it behind her ear.

'They describe him as comfortable, but he doesn't look comfortable to me. He looks desperately unwell. So I assume by comfortable, they mean he is in no pain. The long-term outcome's uncertain.'

'And how would you feel – how would your family feel – if there could be more certainty?'

'That's a ridiculous question. Certainty's not something that can be manufactured.'

'That isn't true. The right doctor, with the right facilities, might do much for Dmitris. He might be left with very little scarring, and a future as bright as it was before his – let us call it an accident.'

'It was no accident.'

'If the cockerel in the oil was an accident, as you suggest, then Dmitris's misfortune was an accident also. That is how I see it. You are stuck in a cycle of offence and retribution, and I am here to tell you, that is now to stop.'

Her eyebrows rose.

'Forgive me, but what do our family affairs have to do with you?'

'More than you think. For now, that doesn't matter. But I could arrange the best of care for Dmitris, so he could emerge from this episode almost unscathed. Doctors cannot work without finance, so let us call what I would do for him an act of philanthropy. I think he deserves my help. In my opinion, he is less a victim of his contemporaries in the Papayiannis clan than of a legacy inherited from you older generations. He has grown up in a culture of spite and malice. Who put the cockerel in the oil, Marianna? Was it you?'

'Me? Never!'

He shrugged.

'If it wasn't you, you know who it was. And if you won't give a name, then by default as head of the household you're responsible. And as head of the household, please, tell me why.'

'You have no proof it was anything to do with my family, and it's a libel to say it was. And if anyone from that family repeats the claim, we'll see them in court.'

'And perpetuate the feud, and fan the flames. Just remind me, Marianna, what is this feud all about? What is it that's caused all this bitterness and anguish, all this violence and death?'

'They're common thieves,' she said. 'They stole our land. That's how they have money for new equipment. Half the crop going to their mill should be going to ours.'

'Is that why you've poisoned their trees?'

'No one's touched their trees. I've seen some of them are failing, and I assumed some kind of blight. If they'd take advice, I'd give it, but they'd never listen.'

'And what about the *kleftiko*? A mean trick, wasn't it, to put out their fire? Was it the boys, perhaps? Did they think it would be funny?'

'You have my word, that wasn't anyone from this family. The Papayiannis's leaped to their conclusions, and blamed us. They blame us for everything.'

'Of course they do. You've made that rod for your own backs. There's something I want you to look at.' Unzipping his hold-all, he found the envelope sent from the lawyer's office. 'I think what I have here would be most meaningful from a different vantage point. Will you join me in a short walk?'

Vehemently, she shook her head.

'I can't possibly. As I've said, I'm very busy, and you must excuse me.'

'That's your choice,' he said, starting to put away the envelope. 'If you cannot make time for me, then I cannot make time to help Dmitris.'

'Very well,' she said, irritably. 'But I hope we're not going far.'

He walked her back along the road between the olive groves, down the line of the fence dividing the two properties.

'Tell me about this feud,' he said, as they walked. 'Tell me what set you all at each other's throats.'

'It's an old dispute from my husband's grandfather's time. Came one harvest, Papayiannis's encroached on Kapsis land. They stripped the crop from trees which weren't theirs. When they were challenged, punches were thrown. It grew from there. Now they've put up this fence, enclosing our land. They've perpetuated the insult. We've let the fence stand, but the theft isn't forgotten.'

They passed the ailing trees, and the fat man laid his hand on one, as if offering comfort. At the fence's end, he stopped, placed his hold-all on the ground and slid the papers from inside the brown envelope. Away amongst the Kapsis trees were the noises of harvest – the knocking of sticks on the branches, the patter as the olives fell into the nets, the low voices of the workers. Amongst the Papayiannis trees, was silence.

'I want you to look at this,' he said. 'I had my lawyer request this plan from the land registry.' He unfolded a large-scale plan showing both the Kapsis property and the Papayiannis's, and the neighbouring land at their borders. 'Here is the road, and here is your house.' She nodded her agreement. 'And here is the boundary line between you and them. If what you say is correct, there should be a discrepancy between the boundary marked on this map – the legal boundary of ownership – and the line of this fence they set. Do you agree?'

'Yes, I agree,' she said. 'From what I was told, the discrepancy is the best part of an acre.'

The fat man seemed surprised.

'As much as that? Let's take a look, shall we?'

He held up the plan so she could see it, and match it to the features in the landscape.

'Here's the Papayiannis house,' he said. 'And if we look over here, it seems to me as if the boundary line should be directly in front of a chapel.'

'That would be Agios Yiorgos,' she said. 'It's hard to see from here. But there, you can just see the blue dome, above the trees.'

'And the other key feature is this outcrop, here,' said the fat man, 'this change in contours which should be easy to spot, behind us.' He turned, and there it was. 'So the boundary of your properties is an almost direct line from chapel to outcrop. I notice there is a dog-leg here, a small anomaly, about halfway along. So let us see.' He looked towards the chapel, and back towards the outcrop. Marianna looked too, and frowned. 'It seems to me that the fence is exactly in line with the plan, except that the dog-leg juts on to their land, rather than yours. But from here, it would appear the area of land it encloses – it's only a very small area, isn't it? – contains a single tree. Can that be right?'

'It does look that way,' said Marianna, doubtfully. 'But that makes no sense.'

'What makes no sense is that your families have been at war for three generations over one tree. So here is my suggestion. I will buy you a young tree, and you may plant it on your land, anywhere you wish. In fact, I will buy you two trees, as a form of damages for harvests you have lost. Does that seem fair?'

'No. One tree or a hundred, they're thieves.'

'Not intentionally, I don't think. Without these plans to hand, who would know where the dog-leg should go? In disputes like this, where the origins lie in family lore, disagreements are often exaggerated or fabricated. Plant new trees, and let it go. Your family owes a huge debt to this community. You were the root cause of an outbreak which resulted in four deaths. If you wish, I can dig deeper, and find which of your clan was the guilty party, but as matters stand, Sakis will bear the brunt of the disgrace, and his family will have to weather the economic storm his departure will cause them. My offer to you is this. If you will from now on be good neighbours to them, I will extend my help to you, and ensure Dmitris gets the best possible care. In fact I have made up my mind to help him anyway, but if you don't wish to co-operate in healing the rift between you, I shall make your lives difficult in other ways. Look again at the plan. You see the road you share? You'll notice it is, in fact, on Papayiannis property. I suggest that means you have no legal right to drive on it. If they knew that, I don't doubt that they would immediately close access to you. Then you'd be faced with the considerable expense of building yourselves a road, on your own land. But if it isn't drawn to their attention, I don't believe they'll notice. Now, as far as their business is concerned, I think it likely that in Sakis's absence, much of the burden will fall on Amara. She lacks your experience, and would need guidance and help. What do you say?'

Marianna considered.

'If you would do your best for Dmitris, we would all be grateful beyond words,' she said. 'And if you do, I shall ensure there's no further unpleasantness from this family. I cannot guarantee friendly relations, but I can ensure there's no more interference, or nastiness. And I'm sorry, profoundly sorry, if this family's played a part in those deaths. I feel we should do something to make amends.'

'The whole story will soon be out, and there'll be speculation as to the source of the bacteria. Whether you choose to name the guilty party, is up to you. It may be you yourself, and if it is, then you must decide whether to admit it, whether you can take your punishment as Sakis is being man enough to take his. If it isn't you, maybe you can prove your value as the head of the family, and persuade the guilty party to put his name forward, or maybe you'll risk your family's anger, and give that name to the police. It's all up to you, Marianna. It's all a question of balancing your family's honour against doing what is right.'

As they walked back down the road, she said, 'I have a question for you.'

'Ask it.'

'Did Sakis kill his father?'

'Keep your eye on the newspapers,' said the fat man. 'No doubt they'll be printing the whole story, by and by.'

Seventeen

The fat man drove unhurriedly to the vineyard, and pulled off the road before the house came into view. Across the valley was the crag where Meni had pointed out the eagle's nest. There were no eagles flying now, but the trees where they had nested were swaying in the rising wind which portended a change in the weather. Behind the distant hills, the clouds were bloated with rain.

He left the car at the roadside, and walked lightly up the track to the house, catching strains of music as he grew close, a piano prelude similar to the Fauré which the cassette player was broadcasting to the vines.

From the orchard, he heard the clip of secateurs. On a ladder propped against the trunk of a peach tree, Meni was half-hidden amongst the branches, scrutinising for the right places to make her cuts. In his white shoes, the fat man moved silently through the grass. Meni tossed another pruned branch to the ground.

At the foot of the ladder, he called up to her. There was a rustling of branches as she pulled them aside to see who was there, and she peered down myopically, giving a smile of recognition as she brought him into focus. Placing her booted feet carefully, she descended the ladder, and held out her hand, then withdrew it and pulled off her suede-palmed glove before holding it out again. Her hair was untidy from the wind; dead leaves clung to her home-knitted sweater. Over the fresh scents of sap and cut wood was the edge of the perfume he'd noticed before, faint traces of iris and musk.

'*Kyrie* Diaktoros! *Kalos tou, kalos tou!*'

They shook hands; her grip was warm and confident.

'You remembered my name,' he said. 'I'm flattered.'

'You're a memorable personage. I remember your good manners. I told you, you're a rarity in Dendra.'

'You might be surprised to see me back so quickly. I'm here for two things. Firstly – though I hardly dare ask – for more wine. I promised my four bottles to Lefteris, after my brother drank all Lefteris's stock. I'm here partly to see if we might replace it.'

She was doubtful.

'My stocks are very low, as I said to you. Most of it was drunk at this year's feast. But there might be a bottle or two. Let's go and see.'

'I'm sorry to interrupt your work,' he said, as they headed towards the house.

'I was taking care of my babies, but they'll wait. Maybe I mother them too much, but they respond with excellent crops.'

She led him into the kitchen, still in its state of disarray. The pale-blue knitting had grown closer to being a small jacket.

'Shall I get you coffee?' she asked. 'There's some orange and almond cake left, if you'd like a piece. It's one of those that improves with keeping. As I expected, my daughter ate very little. She eats like a sparrow. But then, girls do, don't they?'

'Do they?' asked the fat man, quietly. 'Tell me, Meni, how girls eat. Tell me about your granddaughter.'

236

He crossed to the window sill, and picked up the photograph of the laughing woman and beaming child. The woman was Meni's daughter. The child was not the boy she had been carrying when she came to visit; it was a little girl, dressed in rose-pink frills with a ribbon in her hair.

'I saw her picture at the newspaper offices in Neochori. What was her name?'

Meni gave a smile of sad remembrance.

'Meni, of course. She was named Meni, after her *yiayia*. After me.'

Her eyes were filled with heartbreak.

'Find us some wine and some glasses,' said the fat man, 'and let's you and I sit down and talk.'

She opened the cellar door, and patted her pockets for matches to light the oil lamp, but finding none, began to search amongst the clutter on the dresser and the table.

The fat man reached into the pocket of his raincoat.

'Please, allow me,' he said, and offered her a box of matches.

Under her knitting she found the book of matches she had used on his last visit.

'No need,' she said. 'I have these.'

She used the last match in the book to light the lamp, and brought up two bottles for the fat man, along with a different wine, which she opened and poured. So dark it was almost black in the glass, the flavours of the purple fruit which had made the wine were intense, but it lacked sweetness, and was so dry it was almost bitter. Meni cleared a space amongst the disorder on the table, and they sat down.

'I made this wine for her, purely from the Burgundy vines,' said Meni, as the fat man tasted it. 'It's not the best wine I make, but it suits its purpose. It's my grieving wine. There were a dozen bottles. Now there are six left.'

'You honour me with such a select vintage,' said the fat man. 'Tell me about her.'

'She was only three years old,' says Meni. 'The light of all our lives – mine, her mother's, her father's. They waited a long time for her, and we'd about given up hope. There were medical problems, and it seemed for a long time there'd be no children at all. Then my daughter made a pilgrimage to Kalkos, and said prayers to the miraculous icon of the Virgin, who's blessed a number of barren couples, and only months later, she was pregnant. So little Meni was our miracle child. So pretty, and so sweet-natured, always laughing. She was an absolute delight in every way. Of course I used to spoil her, and she wrapped me round her little finger. I wrote to tell my husband he was a grandfather. I felt sure if he were out there, that above anything would bring him home. I sent him pictures as she grew, but I've heard nothing. It doesn't matter now.'

'What happened, Meni?'

'We became ill.'

'All of you?'

'They were visiting. It was the last day of their stay, and I'd made lunch. I remember exactly what we ate – fish soup, and a sorrel salad, lemon potatoes and roast pork. I helped the child to eat. She had a good appetite, always. She was a good child, who'd eat whatever she was given. That evening, I started to be ill. I was here by myself, and for two days I could hardly move from the bed. Even water made me ill, but I have no phone, and couldn't call the doctor. On the third day, a neighbour came to call. My son-in-law had phoned her to get a message to me to let me know they'd all been struck down too, and little Meni hadn't survived. The neighbour fetched me the doctor, and as soon as I was able, I went to them.

'My daughter was inconsolable. How could I have consoled her anyway, heartbroken as I was myself? We buried the child, and my daughter took to her bed. She had some kind of breakdown. My son-in-law's a good man, but he coped badly too, and took to drinking. That happy household became a mausoleum. They put my daughter on sedatives, and all she did was sleep.

'We weren't alone, of course. Others were dead. I told myself we'd had a lucky escape, but with the depths of our grief for Meni, it felt like the cruellest sentence Fate could have given us, to have her taken and to be still alive ourselves.'

'And at the time, what did you think had caused it?'

'At first, I thought it was the sorrel. Too much of it is poisonous, and I was devastated, thinking I'd made us all ill, even though I knew in my heart none of us could possibly have eaten enough to be harmful. But when we knew others were ill too, we had no idea where to look. The fish was fresh and cleaned, the pork was well cooked, and the rest were vegetables. A doctor came and asked us what we'd eaten, and seemed as baffled as we were. There was talk in the town of ice cream, but I'd eaten none. My daughter and little Meni had, but not that day.'

The fat man sipped his wine, and waited for her to go on, but she seemed lost in thought.

'And then?' he prompted.

She looked down into her glass, and spoke as if reading the story from the dark surface of the wine.

'I went up to the roof one evening, as I often do. I went to console myself as best I could with the view, rather than with wine. The infection had left my stomach very weak, and I was on a diet of dry biscuits and water, a little toasted bread.

That was no hardship to me. In my grief, I had no appetite anyway. But here I was, contemplating the view and the meaning of life, when there down below, near to where the cave entrance had been, I saw movement. So I got out my binoculars, and took a look. And you'll never guess what I saw.'

'Tell me.'

'I saw the Papayiannis men, the two of them, Donatos and Sakis. I know them well enough to recognise them, even from a distance. They must have had a truck nearby – I couldn't see it, but a track to one of the upper farms runs very near here, two hundred metres away at most. They were behaving very strangely. They'd got a number of barrels, moulded plastic, like I used to keep diesel in for the generator – and they were emptying them on to the ground. And when all the barrels were empty, Sakis made a bonfire, and burned them. I watched for a while, wondering what they were up to, until I realised what they were doing. They were pouring away their oil! It made no sense to me. Why would they do that? So I watched, and puzzled, and the truth began to dawn on me. They were destroying the oil because it was the source of the outbreak!'

The fat man nodded.

'Yes, it was. And then you, of course, went straight to the authorities, and told them what you'd seen.'

She looked at him.

'No, I didn't. I watched them until they were done, until after dark when they doused the fire, and went away. And I cried, because those men had done a terrible thing – they had provided me with the poison I gave to my granddaughter! *I* prepared the food that day, *I* fed her, *I* killed her! All night I was awake. I couldn't sleep. I was overtaken by a rage so strong, by anger so intense, it seemed to light its own fire deep in my belly. All I could think of was revenge. They had made me kill my beautiful Meni, and all I wanted was for them to suffer. If I went to the authorities, who knew what might happen? Maybe they have friends and family in the right places, people who would call me a mad old woman, and send me on my way. What evidence was there? All soaked away into the ground, and the containers burned! No, I couldn't go to the authorities. Those people do their jobs if and when it suits them. And I didn't know what was wrong with the oil. I still don't know. If it was something that wasn't their fault, maybe a court would look lightly on them, especially if they had the right connections. So I decided it was up to me. I decided I would act on behalf of my little Meni, and of the other three who were dead. I'd make the Papayiannis's suffer, if it was in my power. And it was.'

'So you began a hate campaign. Those nasty, malicious acts which the Papayiannis's blamed on the Kapsis's, were your work, weren't they? You poisoned their olive trees. I found the copper nails.'

'Copper nails? Where would I get copper nails?'

'They are commonly used in roofing. I saw your matches, and when you took me to see the eagle's nest, I noticed the tools up there.'

'The Papayiannis's love their trees. They're Sakis's pride and joy, as mine are to me, now I've lost Meni.'

'How can you claim to be a lover of trees, when you tried to destroy those beautiful, ancient olives?'

'I love nothing that they own. They're the source of their livelihood. What better way to hit them in the pocket?'

'But what about Sakis's wife, his sons and daughters, all his dependants? You were playing with their livelihood too.'

'They're all of the same blood.'

241

'And what of the bad blood you stirred up between the two clans? You must have been aware that others were being blamed for what you were doing?'

'I needed a smokescreen. The Kapsis's provided one.'

'The *kleftiko* at the feast – were you responsible for their disaster there too?'

'The pits burn overnight. I went up to the church, hauled a couple of buckets of water from the well, found their pit and doused it. And although it wasn't ladylike, I added a little extra of my own, for good measure.'

'But the Papayiannis clan blamed the Kapsis's, and poor Dmitris took the brunt of their anger. He may be scarred for life. Do you have no conscience about him?'

She poured more wine into the fat man's glass, and drank some of her own.

'I can't be blamed for that. Dmitris is an unfortunate victim of the Papayiannis's, as am I. What's your interest in my conscience, anyway? And I'm flattered, of course, but what's your interest in me?'

'You took the administration of justice into your own hands.'

She smiled, and the light of mania was in her face.

'You're right,' she said, and raised her glass in a mock salute, to him, to herself and her actions. 'I've made life unpleasant for them, as unpleasant as I could, and I'm proud of it. Are you going to arrest me for urinating on a barbecue, or hammering nails into a tree?'

The fat man shook his head.

'I'm no policeman, Meni,' he said. 'I'm one who understands the broader picture, and how all the threads of a situation are woven together. Without that broad view, it is impossible to know whether one acts justly, or not.'

He pushed his chair back from the table to cross his legs,

and as he did so, seemed to notice for the first time the muddy splashes his shoes had picked up on his walk to the house. Bending down to his hold-all, he unzipped it and took out a bottle of shoe whitener, and as Meni watched, he shook the bottle, removed the cap, and dabbed whitener first on one shoe, then the other; and when he was satisfied his footwear was at its best, he recapped the bottle, tucked it into his bag and refastened it.

'What were we saying?' he asked, with an almost genial smile. 'You mentioned arrests, I think, so I should probably tell you that by now, Sakis Papayiannis will have handed himself in to the police. I have persuaded him to make a confession of his part in Dendra's five deaths relating to the outbreak.'

'Four deaths,' she corrected him. 'There were only four.'

He shook his head.

'There have been five. Those four who died from the contaminated oil, and Donatos. Maybe you'd like to talk to the police yourself. Go voluntarily, as Sakis is doing.'

She seemed surprised.

'Why should I want to do that? He has blood on his hands, and it's right that he should be dealt with. I've done nothing of that magnitude.'

'Ah, but you have,' said the fat man. 'You poisoned Donatos, over a long period of time, and most unpleasantly.'

'That's absurd! How could I have done that?'

'You fed him cyanide, in the praline you made for him from the old variety of almonds. I had my suspicions after I ate a piece myself. I have a very strong stomach, but something made me ill that day, though I put it down at first to overeating. Then I wondered about the ice cream I had eaten at the *gelateria*. But when I thought about Donatos's symptoms and your orchard here, I began to see there might be a connection. Cyanide poisoning in low doses results in breathlessness and redness in the face – symptoms which might easily be confused, in a man of Donatos's age, with heart failure. I had only a few nuts, and felt how unpleasant the effects are. The risk of poisoning is so great with bitter almonds that in some countries, the trees are now illegal. But there's a difficulty with cyanide poisoning which you and I need to overcome. I myself need to make a small confession.'

Quizzically, she looked at him.

'I took advice from an eminent doctor, who confirmed that my suspicions over Donatos might easily be correct. But how would we prove it? Cyanide leaves the body very quickly, and is undetectable forty-eight hours after death. An exhumation at this stage would be pointless. When I spoke to Sakis, I didn't tell him that. I forced his hand – his confession – with an empty threat, namely the exhumation of Donatos's body. Naturally, Sakis was anxious to spare his family such distress, and so he has gone voluntarily to the police. I am asking you to do the same. Go and admit what you have done – that you took Donatos's life – and take your punishment through the courts, as he is doing.'

'Are you saying there's no proof against me?'

'I am saying that, yes. But I am also saying, it was never up to you to punish Donatos for what he did.'

She drank more wine.

'Don't you think so, *Kyrie* Diaktoros? I disagree. I think his punishment was most fitting for his crime. Bitter almonds, to reflect the bitterness he left here, in my heart.' She lay her palm to her chest, and left it there for a moment, as if making a pledge. 'He poisoned little Meni and those others, so it seemed fitting to me he should poison himself too. He was a greedy man with a very sweet tooth, and the praline was his downfall. The more he ate, the sicker he got. I wanted the same for Sakis, though I never found a medium that worked. But I was careful. I didn't want Donatos to die. If he died, he would be out of pain, and his suffering would be over. It was a balancing act. If I saw him looking too ill, I used more sweet almonds in the mix, until he improved. My aim was to leave him no pleasure in life, to give him a life with no joy in it, a life of ashes like the life he had left me. I wanted him to burn with the same pain I felt, that pain that never abates. That's what's kept me alive, being the instrument of his torture.'

'But you did kill him, Meni.'

'Perhaps. Who knows? He was an old man, and might have gone at any time. You tell me nothing can be proven. And I'm sorry he's gone, but only because I can't reach him now. Though he'll suffer in hell, I've no doubts about that.'

'You made his life a misery, and murdered him. You must see that was wrong. Terribly wrong.'

'I've told you I regret his death. What more should I say? He's been punished on this earth, as Sakis will now be too. When the day comes that I stand before my maker, I shall hold my head high. I'm proud to have made him suffer as I have suffered, as my daughter has suffered!'

'The loss of a little one is always hard. I know that. But with respect, your daughter is coping with her grief in a way you are not. No doubt she thinks of her lost child constantly, yet I have seen her with her son, and she seems happy.'

'The child is not her son. She could have no more children after Meni. The child is adopted.'

'Then all the better for her. She's found a way to give her love to a child who is not her flesh and blood, but who unquestionably needed a home, and a mother. She has not sunk into bitterness and hatred, as you have done. And there's something else we must consider – that once you knew what the poison's source was, you told no one. You allowed contaminated oil to remain on family tables, without regard for who might yet become ill. And people did become ill, for some weeks. How do you know you didn't contribute towards the deaths of other people's loved ones? How do you know what damage your silence did?'

'I had my priorities.'

'You had your priorities, and no empathy or regard for others who might find themselves in your situation. Your intent was on revenge, rather than on sparing others your pain. Do you feel no remorse for that?'

'You didn't know the child. That child was special.'

'All children are special, Meni. But the choice is yours. Either go of your own free will, and admit what you've done to the police, or you may find yourself harshly dealt with.'

She laughed.

'Dealt with by whom? Donatos deserved everything I gave him, and I hope Sakis is as miserable as it's possible to be, wherever they send him. And I shan't hand myself in. If you give them my name, so be it. Let them come. Let them exhume the old man, and find nothing. Besides, it's out of the question for me to leave here. I have my work, my vines and my orchard. Who would take care of them if I were gone?'

'I could find you a caretaker. You have worked hard here, with commendable aims. If you will take your just punishment, let me reassure you that when you return, it will be as flourishing as you would wish. Prepare the house for going away, lock it up, and I'll find you a tenant for the vineyard, who'll care for the vines and the trees.'

'I won't leave them,' she said. 'I shall stay here and take care of them. As I've said to you, they are my legacy now. My legacy and my granddaughter's, since she will have no one to carry her name, either. To leave here would be to abandon both my own memorial and hers. Do we deserve to be forgotten?'

'Forgetting may be a kindness, a blessing and a balm to a troubled mind. Maybe you would be better to forget. Though if you forget those you love and those who love you, the world becomes a cold and unfriendly place. To forget the ones we love is to forget we are ourselves loved, and then forgetting's blessing becomes a curse. But if you refuse to hand yourself in, if that is your final word, our conversation is at an end.'

He rose to go.

'Don't forget your wine.' She held out the two bottles.

'Please, return it to the cellar,' he said. 'I think you'll have more need of it than I.'

Lefteris was updating his guests' accounts, working from a pile of restaurant bills and receipts. The fat man placed three bottles of Lachesis wine on the reception desk.

'This, I'm afraid, is the best offering I can make in recompense for my brother's excesses,' he said. 'It's the last available from the vineyard for a while. Regretfully, I shall be leaving you tomorrow, so maybe you and Tomas would do me the honour of sharing a bottle with me this evening.'

'Gladly,' said Lefteris. 'It'll go well with dinner. No wild boar, I'm afraid, but we got something I think you'll enjoy.'

'I shall look forward to it. Is there any sign of my brother?'

'He's in his room, sleeping it off. He came back around lunchtime, a little the worse for wear. He'd lost his sling somewhere along the way, so the wife made him another. I asked him where he'd been and who with, but he couldn't seem to remember. And speaking of your brother, *kyrie* – I don't wish to disrespect him by talking to you about it, but there's the matter of his bill.'

The fat man sighed.

'You're right to be concerned about it,' he said. 'Dino is never careful with what he calls life's "details", and paying his bills falls within that category. I think it would be best if you prepared one account for both of us, and I'll settle it before I leave tomorrow. Then I'll have the task of persuading him to pay me. And though I told him I wouldn't do it, I shall leave you something for his bills outstanding. No doubt his creditors will be looking for him here, over the next few days.'

'Have you heard the news, by the way?' asked Lefteris.

'I've heard nothing,' said the fat man. 'I've had business to attend to.'

'Sakis Papayiannis has been arrested, charged with manslaughter. The whole town's talking about it. Turns out the source of our outbreak was contaminated oil. And would you believe it, someone's taken advantage of his absence and the family's trouble. All the olives they had ready for processing at the mill have been stolen. Someone's taken the lot. And I know where I'd put my money.'

'So do I,' said the fat man. 'And in this instance, you just might be right.'

On his way across Democracy Square, the fat man met the lottery seller, still hawking tickets in the *kafenions* and bars.

'Lottery, *kyrie*?' he asked. 'Thirty million top prize, this week.'

'Did you have any luck with that ticket I gave you?' asked the fat man.

The lottery seller studied him.

'You,' he said. 'I remember you. No, no luck, *kyrie*, no

248

luck. My wife took my shirt, and washed it with the ticket in the pocket. Didn't I tell you I'm the unluckiest man alive?'

'You did tell me that,' said the fat man, 'and it's hard to argue with a man with such convictions.'

The seller held up his staff.

'Do you want a ticket today, *kyrie*?'

The fat man shook his head.

'No, not today, thank you,' he said, and went on his way.

Looking in the window of the delicatessen next door to the tailor's, the fat man was tempted by the imported delicacies and the attractive display of pâtisserie. Inside, a man in a white apron was serving a customer, slicing a German salami very thin.

The fat man went into the shop, and browsed the shelves whilst the shopkeeper served his customer, who paid and left with several wax paper-wrapped parcels.

The shopkeeper wished the fat man *kali spera*. The fat man returned his greeting, and reviewed the chiller cabinets below the counter, where the cheeses and cold meats, hors d'oeuvres, olives and salads were on display.

'I was here the other day, and you had a sign outside advertising *taramasalata*,' he said. 'But I don't see the sign now.'

'I've just finished making it fresh,' said the shopkeeper, 'so the sign's going back outside any moment. You won't find better.'

'I'll take a quarter,' said the fat man.

He closed the door of the tailor's shop noisily, but the tailor was running his sewing machine, guiding the fast-moving needle along a chalk line marking the seam in a jacket sleeve. When he stopped to turn the cloth, the fat man gave a light cough. Miltiadis jumped round in his chair, and looked at the fat man over his half-moon glasses.

'*Kalos tou*,' said the tailor. 'Your trousers are ready. Would you like to try them on? I managed to get you another three centimetres – I hope that was enough.'

The fat man was doubtful.

'I shall have to hope so, too. More would have been better, but I realise a pair of trousers can only be stretched so far.'

The tailor left his chair, and searched through the clothes hanging on a wheeled rack at the back of the shop.

'You're still with us, then,' he said.

'I'm leaving Dendra tomorrow.'

'If you go now, you'll miss all the excitement. By tomorrow, we'll be full of cameras and newshounds.'

The tailor lifted a hanger from the rack. The fat man's trousers were carefully pressed, and looked like new. He carried them to the bench, and laid them out.

'Such beautiful cloth. It was a pleasure to work with.' He bent down to examine his own workmanship on the waistband seams. 'I let you out a bit in the seat, and in the thighs, too. See, I unpicked all these seams here, and restitched them. I haven't left you much room to manoeuvre, I'm afraid. You'll have to be careful sitting down, if you don't want them to split.'

'No, indeed,' said the fat man, examining the seams for himself. 'That looks an excellent job, thank you. What do you mean about the cameras?'

'The press. They'll be gathering like vultures. They'll be here to make the most of the drama. Haven't you heard? After all this time, they've arrested someone over our poisonings.'

'I'm sorry to hear that. I was intending to visit the *gelateria*, before I left.'

'The *gelateria*?'

'Isn't that where you told me the break-out was?'

'I'll wrap your trousers for you, shall I? As it turns out, it was nothing to do with the *gelateria* after all.'

He reached for string and brown paper, and began to cut a piece of paper of suitable size.

'That's unfortunate,' said the fat man, 'considering poor Renzo's business is already almost ruined.'

'Seems it was something in the olive oil.' The tailor folded the trousers. 'Who would ever have thought that?'

'Renzo must be very relieved, don't you think?'

The tailor tied string around the parcel, creating a loop as a carrying handle.

'I'm sure he is,' he said. 'He's a decent enough fellow, for an Italian.'

Towards dusk, the wind was rising, rattling the shutters and the roof tiles, driving dead leaves in flurries from the branches of the orchard trees. A fall of soot pattered in the empty fire grate. The light Meni was working by flickered, and then failed.

Meni left her knitting on the table and went out into the yard. By the last daylight, she rooted in the outhouse, moving aside the mattocks and hoes and the baskets used at the grape harvest to find diesel for the generator, and carried the container back inside.

The fat man had left his matchbox on the table. She took it to the dresser, and opened it to light the oil lamp. Inside, along with the matches, was a folded strip of paper cut from the top of a sheet, with a single typewritten line: *An eye for an eye would make the whole world blind*. Meni put the paper to one side.

She struck a match, lit the lamp and slipped the box of matches in her pocket, then picked up the container of diesel, and opened the cellar door. The lamp lit her way down the cellar stairs; the doorway behind her was dark in the remnants of dusk. The lamp's flame caught the curves of the only bottles left on the racks: six of the bitter burgundy, and little else. The stair where the lamp had dribbled was greasy, and when she slipped, there was nothing to break her fall.

Outside, the wind was growing fierce. A gust caught the kitchen casement which Meni had pulled to but not fastened, and flung the window open. The wind streamed in, blowing over the photographs on the sill, scattering the brown skins of blanched almonds, intruding behind the cellar door and slamming it shut, snapping the Yale lock into its keep.

Eighteen

When the fat man came down for dinner, Lefteris was laying tables in the dining room. Tomas sat near the bar, sipping a glass of cloudy ouzo.

'I brought a little *meze* for us to share,' said the fat man, handing over the pot of *taramasalata* from the delicatessen. 'Do you know if my brother intends to eat with us?'

'I haven't seen him since he came in,' said Lefteris. 'I'll lay a place for him with us, but I passed his door about half an hour ago, and he was quiet as a mouse.'

They ate the salty *taramasalata* with fresh bread; then Stavroula brought in a tureen of sautéed red cabbage, and a dish of roast potatoes roasted with lemon.

'You should pour the wine,' said Lefteris, handing the uncorked bottle to the fat man, 'since you've donated it to the feast.'

'It will be my pleasure.' The fat man stood to fill the glasses – Tomas's, Lefteris's and his own. 'We should savour this last bottle, and be quietly grateful my brother is still asleep, so we might all get a second glass. *Yammas.*'

'*Yammas.*'

They drank the toast, and the fat man sat down.

'I've been intrigued by the name of the vineyard,' he said, studying the bottle's label. 'Lachesis is an interesting one to choose. In mythology, Lachesis was one of the three Fates, whose role was to determine the length of life to be given to each person. She was said to appear with her sisters within three days of a baby's birth to decide its destiny.'

'I wonder how long she's given me,' said Tomas. He held up his glass to the light, and peered into the liquid as if it might provide him with an answer. 'And if we drink her wine, will it give us shorter lives, or longer? They say red wine is good for the heart, so I should say, the more we drink, the longer Lachesis will give us.'

'Here we are,' said Lefteris, as Stavroula carried in a platter from the kitchen. 'See what you make of these.'

At the centre of the platter were seven woodcock, each served on a slice of fried bread made tasty with a spread of the bird's intestines. The legs had been fried separately in garlic butter, and arranged around the woodcock were a number of tiny quail, oil-basted and baked to a crisp brown.

'I see you did very well,' said the fat man.

'Well enough,' said Lefteris, '*doxa to Theo*. Please, help yourself.'

They ate the birds with their fingers, and nibbled the gamey meat from the thighs and wings, and they talked, as they ate, of the scandal surrounding Sakis Papayiannis, and of the mercy of his father not being alive to share the disgrace. As they were discussing the wildness of the weather, and the chances of the wind blowing itself out, the bell at reception rang. Lefteris went to answer it, and when he returned, his face was serious.

'There's trouble,' he said to the fat man. 'The police are here, looking for your brother.'

The fat man wiped his hands on a napkin.

'Stall them,' he said, and hurried upstairs.

On the second floor, he knocked at Dino's door. There was no reply. He put his ear to the door, but heard nothing. He knocked again, more loudly.

'Who is it?' Dino's voice was blurred by sleep.

'It's me, Hermes. Open up.'

There was a silence, then sounds of movement inside: a key in the lock, and the sound of bed-springs creaking as Dino returned to his bed. The fat man turned the porcelain door handle and entered the room. Dino lay with his back to the door, blankets pulled up to his nose.

'How are you, brother?'

Disregarding Dino's obvious desire to be left alone, the fat man crossed to the window and looked out across the red-tiled rooftops and down to the lane outside. Dino's dirty clothes lay on a chair. There was no sign of any woman, but the air held a lingering perfume.

'Wake up, brother,' said the fat man. 'I think this is where we part company for the time being. There are visitors downstairs.'

Dino's voice was muffled by the blankets.

'I don't want visitors.'

'These visitors are in uniform.'

Dino sat up, and leaned forward with his head in his hands.

'I feel rough,' he said. 'What on earth do they put in that ouzo?'

'It's not what they put in it, it's how much of it you drink,' said the fat man. 'Why are the police here?'

'How should I know? You know my memory's not good. Maybe it's about the barrel. And the broken window.'

'How are you for money?'

'Cleaned out, as usual. Can you lend me something?'

'I lent you something last time, and I've never had it back.'

'Ah, come on, Hermes. You know I'm useless with money.'

The fat man found his wallet, took out several notes and laid them on the dressing-table. He looked again out of the window.

'In your nimbler days, I'd have said go over the rooftops,' he said, 'but these days, I think you'd be better on the back stairs.'

'Are there back stairs?'

'I don't know. If there aren't, you'll have to come up with something more creative.'

Dino swung his legs out of the bed, and standing in his underpants, stretched and yawned.

'I'll go and distract them for a few minutes,' said the fat man. 'But you'd better hurry, brother. They'll soon be here.'

Dino held his arms open and they embraced, both clapping each other affectionately on the back.

'I'll see you soon,' said Dino. 'We had fun, didn't we?'

The fat man smiled.

'Always,' he said, and left him.

The policemen were about to head upstairs, but the fat man blocked the staircase, and offered them an amiable smile.

'Official business?' he asked.

The officers didn't answer, but stood back to allow the fat man out of their way. The fat man stayed where he was.

'This is his brother,' said Lefteris. 'If there'd been any trouble, I'm sure he'd know.'

The fat man's eyebrows lifted.

'Trouble? What sort of trouble?'

'Criminal damage,' said one of the officers. 'If you wouldn't mind stepping out of the way?'

'Ah,' said the fat man. 'But I'm afraid you've missed him. My brother has already checked out.'

Lefteris, though surprised, said nothing. The policemen looked disbelieving.

'You said he was upstairs,' the officer said to Lefteris.

'He used the back stairs,' said the fat man. 'If you like, I can give him a message when I see him.'

'Would you excuse us?' said the officer.

The fat man bowed his head, and let them by. Lefteris had given them a key to Dino's room.

'I'm sorry,' said Lefteris. 'What else could I do? I'm afraid they're going to arrest him.'

The fat man shook his head.

'They won't be doing that,' he said. 'As I said, Dino has already checked out.'

'But there are no back stairs.'

'Nonetheless, have no worries on his part,' said the fat man. 'Now, shall we finish our dinner?'

The policemen knocked only once on Dino's door, and turned the handle. The door opened without the use of a key.

The money on the dressing-table and the clothes on the chair-back were gone. One of the officers crossed to the window, which was latched on the inside.

'Back stairs,' he said to his colleague. 'You lead the way.'

It was growing late. The girl checked the address on the flier, and was bewildered. Stepping back into the street, she looked along it, then again at the upper levels of the buildings. In the upstairs windows of the *souvlaki* shop, the light of candles glowed.

Inside, the place smelled of frying and garlic. The music was a traditional song, turned down low. Behind the counter, lights blazed, but no one was there; there was no one at the tables but a middle-aged couple, one with a beer, one with a lemonade, sitting a respectable distance apart, though their forearms were stretched towards each other across the table top, their fingertips almost touching.

Dora withdrew her hands, and wiped them unnecessarily on her apron. Miltiadis sipped his beer.

'Can I help you?' asked Dora.

The girl was pretty, in a skirt which Dora thought a little short, and a T-shirt which read, *Anarchy is the only option*.

The girl smiled.

'Am I in the right place for the vigil?' she asked.

Dora looked at her.

'I am in the right place?'

'Oh yes,' said Dora, as she got to her feet. 'Please, come through here. The stairs are at the back of the kitchen. Mind yourself on that hot grill. Would you like a drink to take up with you?'

'Thanks,' said the girl. 'An iced tea would be great.'

Dora grabbed a can from the fridge and put it in her hand.

'On the house,' she said. 'Help yourself to a straw. Just go straight up the stairs. You'll find my son up there.'

Xavier was sitting on the floor, changing the cassette in his player to one of Maria Farantouri's songs of protest. The room was ablaze with candles. On the walls were militant posters, and letters from officials and politicians with Xavier's comments scrawled across them. There was a scatter of correspondence and a pile of ironed laundry on his bed, and by his feet, the plate and wrapper from a *gyros*.

When he looked up at her, she smiled.

'*Yassou*,' she said. 'I'm Arethusa. I've come to join your vigil.'

*   *   *

Downstairs, Miltiadis drained his beer.

'You know what?' he said. 'I think we should go out. Shut up shop, and let's go.'

'I can't do that!' said Dora. 'There might be customers.'

'It's a quiet night, and life is short. Close the shop, and come with me. There's somewhere I want to go.'

As they walked through the streets, they kept a respectable distance between themselves. Miltiadis had his hands in his pockets. Dora wore her outdoor coat and a slick of lipstick, and had run a wet comb through her hair.

At the *gelateria*, Renzo had customers. A family of four crowded round a table, the children dipping spoons into confections of ice cream, whipped cream and syrup. They were silent in their pleasure; their parents watched them covetously, their own small dishes already empty.

Miltiadis approached the counter, and risking an uncertain smile, took his hands from his pockets and offered his right to Renzo.

'How's things?' he asked.

Renzo took his hand, and squeezed it hard.

'*Kalos tous, kalos tous!*' he said, in his accented Greek. 'Good, I'm good. How are you, my friend, how are you? Dora, how are you doing?'

'We were just passing,' said Miltiadis, 'and Dora thought she might like some ice cream. So I said, why not?'

Dora's face was impassive at the lie.

'So,' said Renzo, spreading his arms across the freezers, 'what will it be? Dora?'

She considered the subtle rainbow of ice creams, from the creamy vanillas and lemons at one end, through the pinks of berries to the greens of pistachio and mint, the caramels and chocolates at the dark end of the spectrum.

'Take your time,' said Renzo. 'Take your time.'

He settled her with a scoop of chocolate chip, and one of caramel swirl; Miltiadis chose a double scoop of strawberry. They sat, and ate, whilst Renzo hovered over them, wondering how it was.

'Strawberry was always my favourite,' said Miltiadis. 'A real taste of summer, that is.'

'I've been working on some new flavours,' said Renzo. 'Next time you come in, you must try those.'

He was suddenly silent, thinking he had presumed too much.

But Miltiadis nodded agreement.

'There's something I want to ask you,' said Renzo, doubtfully. 'This ice cream will never be what it was until I get back my best suppliers. Would you consider letting me have some eggs?'

Miltiadis filled his spoon with pink ice cream.

'Same as usual?' he asked. 'I'll bring you two dozen in tomorrow.'

Nineteen

During the night, rain replaced the almost gale-force wind, though the rain, too, had passed through, leaving the morning fresh, with the last clouds dissipating on a clear sky.

It mattered to no one what time she arrived at the newspaper's office, but Esmerelda Dimas was on time, carrying an almost empty briefcase in one hand, a paper bag containing a doughnut in the other.

There was a package at the door: a cardboard box, wrapped in a carrier bag to protect it from the weather. She picked it up, and carried it inside.

At her desk, when she had brewed coffee, she opened the box, and found a tissue-wrapped bottle of wine from the Lachesis vineyard. She was puzzled, but grateful for the gift. But as she put the box aside, it rattled with something left inside. A matchbox.

Inside the matchbox was a single ripe olive, and a strip of paper with one typewritten line: *By way of apology, there's a story here if you look.*

A truck loaded with barrels pulled into the Papayiannis yard. Two youths jumped out, rigged a plank ramp off the back, and began to roll the barrels on to the yard.

Amara ran out from the house. Her face was drawn from lack of sleep, her eyes swollen with crying.

'What are you doing?' she asked. 'We haven't ordered these.'

The youths stopped what they were doing, and faced her. She knew them both; they were Kapsis men. One was Dmitris Kapsis's brother.

'Marianna sent us,' he said. 'She calls it a peace offering. We took your olives, and put them through our mill. She didn't want a neighbour's crop to rot in the yard. We didn't take any commission. It's all here, filtered and ready for sale.'

They rolled another barrel off the truck. With tears in her eyes, Amara watched.

'Thank you,' she said, when they were ready to leave. 'Tell Marianna I said thank you. Yiorgo, how's your brother?'

'He's doing better,' said the youth. 'Someone's put the money up to take him to Geneva. My mother's going with him.'

'Tell her I send my best wishes,' said Amara. 'And tell him all the Papayiannis family wish him well.'

At the *gelateria*, several of the tables were taken. Over the counter, the fat man offered Renzo his hand.

'I couldn't leave town without another taste of your ice cream,' he said.

'Are you leaving, then?' asked Renzo. 'I'm sorry to hear it.'

'Business seems much better.'

'It is, much better, yes. What'll you have?'

The fat man considered the display.

'I've introduced a couple of new flavours,' said Renzo. 'There's cherry walnut, here. And a lemon parfait. I think it's a big improvement on the regular lemon. I double whipped it, and used extra cream.'

'You make it difficult to choose between them,' said the fat man. He felt the waistband of his trousers, where he had a little room to breathe. 'Happily, your tailor's given me a few centimetres in my trousers. So – though I absolutely shouldn't – I think I'll have a scoop of both.'

Epilogue

Stavroula returned from the market laden with shopping. At the kitchen table, Lefteris was plucking down from a partridge's breast. Stavroula laid the shopping on the floor, and hung her coat on a hook behind the door.

'I was talking to Sofia at the bakery,' she said.

A pale feather rose up, and caught in Lefteris's moustache. Putting out his bottom lip, he puffed it away.

'Manolis's Sofia?' he asked.

'No, Harris's, the policeman's wife. She says Meni Gavala's in a bad way.'

Lefteris paused in the rhythm of his plucking.

'A bad way how?'

'She had a fall, down in the cellar, and was there alone for days. Her daughter came to the house twice, and never found her. A broken hip, and a nasty bang on the head, according to Sofia. All she had to keep her alive were a few bottles of wine. Cut to pieces, she was, and broken glass everywhere. Imagine it, down there in the dark, with nothing for comfort but a box of matches. Makes me shudder to think how it must have been.'

'Poor woman. You should go and see her.'

'I'll light a candle for her, this afternoon. *Kakomira!* On her own all those years, and now this. Are you nearly finished with those birds? I need to make a start on lunch.'

In bed B14, Meni Gavala was sleeping. Fluorescent lights leeched the colour from her skin, and with the bandages around her head, her face seemed small as a child's. Scabs had formed on the cuts around her mouth and on an ugly graze on her elbow.

Out in the corridor, behind the glass, Meni's daughter's eyes were swollen from crying. Her husband held the little boy on his hip, teasing him with a toy rabbit to stave off his boredom.

'What are you saying?' asked the daughter.

The young doctor's face was grave.

'The scans show damage to the brain tissue,' he said. 'It's hard to say, at this point, what kind of a recovery she'll make. Given the severity of the fall, and the length of time she was left without treatment . . .'

'When she's awake, she doesn't know me,' said the daughter. 'She doesn't know any of us.'

'That's not uncommon,' said the doctor. 'And you may find her memory will improve, with time. The motor functions, too, may well get better.'

'And if they don't?'

For a few long moments, the doctor didn't answer.

'Let's all just hope for the best, shall we?' he said.

In a village far from Dendra, the fat man laid his cigarette down in the ashtray, and took a sip of his coffee. Through the steamed-up *kafenion* windows, there was a view of the sea, and of snow-capped mountains beyond. At the next table, a man redealt cards to his companions. Behind the counter, the patron's wife poured bird seed into a desultory canary's cage.

The fat man opened his copy of *Ta Nea* and browsed the news, picking up his cigarette from time to time, spending no time on the political news or the sport, but taking more of an interest in the items beyond the front pages. On page fifteen, the advertisements began. He stubbed out his cigarette, and folded the paper to review the property for sale.

The entry was insignificant – a small, bordered box in a lower corner – but the heading in the box caught his eye. *Dendra*. He peered closely at the grainy photograph.

The advertisement offered for sale as a going concern a vineyard, a tower house and surrounding land.

The fat man laid down the newspaper. For a few minutes, he was thoughtful.

Across the bay, an incoming ferry blew its foghorn. The fat man paid for his coffee, and wandered down to the quay to catch his boat.

ACKNOWLEDGEMENTS

To all, past and present, at CLLA – your unwavering support is always appreciated.

ALSO AVAILABLE BY ANNE ZOUROUDI

THE MESSENGER OF ATHENS

Shortlisted for the ITV 3 Crime Thriller Awards

When the battered body of a young woman is discovered on a remote Greek island, the local police are quick to dismiss her death as an accident. Then a stranger arrives, uninvited, from Athens, announcing his intention to investigate further. His name is Hermes Diaktoros, his methods are unorthodox, and he brings his own mystery into the web of dark secrets and lies. Who has sent him, on whose authority is he acting, and how does he know of dramas played out decades ago?

'Powerfully atmospheric ... Zouroudi proves a natural at the dark arts of writing Euro-crime'
INDEPENDENT

THE TAINT OF MIDAS

For over half a century the beautiful Temple of Apollo has been in the care of the old beekeeper Gabrilis. But when the value of the land soars he is forced to sign away his interests – and hours later he meets a violent, lonely death. When Hermes Diaktoros finds his friend's battered body by a dusty roadside, the police quickly make him the prime suspect. But with rapacious developers threatening Arcadia's most ancient sites, there are many who stand to gain from Gabrilis's death. Hermes resolves to avenge his old friend and find the true culprit, but his investigative methods are, as ever, unorthodox...

'More transported Agatha Christie here ... Hermes is a delight. Half Poirot, half deus ex machina, but far more earth-bound than his first name suggests ... A cracking plot, colourful local characters and descriptions of the hot, dry countryside so strong that you can almost see the heat haze and hear the cicadas – the perfect read to curl up with'
GUARDIAN

BLOOMSBURY

THE WHISPERS OF NEMESIS

As snow falls on the tiny village of Vrisi, a coffin is unearthed and broken open and, to the astonishment of the mourners at the graveside, the remains inside have been transformed. News of the bizarre discovery spreads through the village and sets tongues wagging and heads shaking. Then, by the shrine of St Fanourios, a body is found, buried under the fallen snow. Rumours of witchcraft and the devil's work abound, and when Hermes Diaktoros arrives in Vrisi he soon finds himself embroiled in the mysteries. But the truth may be far stranger than even he could possibly have imagined...

'Diaktoros is a detective very much in the vein of Miss Marple ... Where Zouroudi scores is in her lovingly detailed descriptions of Greek island landscapes'
IRISH TIMES

THE BULL OF MITHROS

Drawn to the sun-drenched island of Mithros by the myth of its fabled bull, Hermes Diaktoros arrives on the day of a violent and troubling death. The mysterious circumstances surrounding it have echoes in Mithros's past, in a brutal unsolved crime from years ago which, it seems, is neither forgotten, nor forgiven. Hermes sets out to solve a complex puzzle where shadowy secrets and unspoken loyalties are intertwined. And before long it's clear that the fate of the mythical bull may be the least of the island's mysteries...

'Greece has never appeared more beautiful or damaged, and secrets lurk behind every ruin. Fortunately, Zouroudi's masterfully compelling detective Hermes Diaktoros is on hand to sort the facts from the myths surrounding the violent death of a mysterious stranger'
DAILY MIRROR

ORDER BY PHONE: +44 (0)1256 302 699; BY EMAIL: DIRECT@MACMILLAN.CO.UK

DELIVERY IS USUALLY 3–5 WORKING DAYS. FREE POSTAGE AND PACKAGING FOR ORDERS OVER £20.

ONLINE: WWW.BLOOMSBURY.COM/BOOKSHOP

PRICES AND AVAILABILITY SUBJECT TO CHANGE WITHOUT NOTICE.

WWW.BLOOMSBURY.COM/ANNEZOUROUDI

B L O O M S B U R Y

THE DOCTOR OF THESSALY

A jilted bride weeps on an empty beach, a local doctor is attacked in an isolated churchyard – trouble has come at a bad time to Morfi, just as the backwater village is making headlines with a visit from a government minister. Fortunately, where there's trouble there's Hermes Diaktoros, the mysterious fat man whose tennis shoes are always pristine and whose methods are always unorthodox. Hermes must solve a brutal crime, thwart the petty machinations of the town's ex-mayor and pour oil on the troubled waters of a sisters' relationship – but how can he solve a mystery that not even the victim wants to be solved?

'If you don't find yourself in Greece this summer, then Zouroudi's latest mystery brings the Hellenic vibe tantalisingly close ... Once again Hermes Diaktoros – a reassuringly earthbound investigator – finds himself dealing with a chorus of colourful locals'
INDEPENDENT

THE LADY OF SORROWS

A painter is found dead at sea off the coast of a remote Greek island. For our enigmatic detective Hermes Diaktoros, the plot can only thicken: the painter's work, an icon of the Virgin long famed for its miraculous powers, has just been uncovered as a fake. But has the painter died of natural causes or by a wrathful hand? What secret is a dishonest gypsy keeping? And what haunts the ancient catacombs beneath the bishop's house?

'Anne Zouroudi writes beautifully – her books have all the sparkle and light of the island landscapes in which she sets them. *The Lady of Sorrows*, her latest, is a gorgeous treat'
ALEXANDER MCCALL SMITH

BLOOMSBURY